Joss

Joss

A Novel

KATHERINE BACCARO

Archway Publishing books may be ordered through booksellers or by contacting:

Archway Publishing
1663 Liberty Drive
Bloomington, IN 47403
www.archwaypublishing.com
1 (888) 242-5904

Because of the dynamic nature of the Internet, any web addresses or
links contained in this book may have changed since publication and
may no longer be valid. The views expressed in this work are solely those
of the author and do not necessarily reflect the views of the publisher,
and the publisher hereby disclaims any responsibility for them.

Any people depicted in stock imagery provided by Thinkstock are models,
and such images are being used for illustrative purposes only.
Certain stock imagery © Thinkstock.

ISBN: 978-1-4808-3305-0 (sc)
ISBN: 978-1-4808-3306-7 (hc)
ISBN: 978-1-4808-3307-4 (e)

Library of Congress Control Number: 2016913125

Print information available on the last page.

Archway Publishing rev. date: 8/29/2016

For the Angells of Pembroke in Brown.

They sprawled, but decorously, in the coaches of old New York, New Haven, and Hartford, to be preserved in memory one autumn day when the sun had transmuted everything to gold. Beaches of the Long Island Sound, slums, city dumps, Connecticut villages, and Indian grave heaps were all equally gilded to splendor by it. The girls, encapsulated within a train that moved inside that golden autumn day, were not entirely oblivious to its alchemy. They were new or returning from their first autumn weekend, and they were overjoyed to see each other again. They struck gladsome attitudes as they sprawled, not unlike odalisques. They were politely sensuous, latently voluptuous, but mostly untried—so only kidding, really. Their adolescent posturing was vaguely reminiscent of paintings by Matisse, whose work they were a little bit familiar with, since they were now returning to a classical education in the women's college of a major university. Their postures implied leisure, and now lulled by the train, they fell into the delicious stupor of luxury. Semi-sleeping, they indulged romantic imaginings. Not sexual imaginings—sex being frowned upon by the administration, though sex haunted the mind eternally. Anyway, the bravest of them were not very brave at all. They had been carefully reared to appreciate the power of that force when it was allowed to become tangible. How antisocial sex could be; in an instant, it could complicate a girl's whole future. One wrong decision could devastate her. Yet even so, it haunted the idle mind.

She introduced herself on that ride. "I'm Jocelyn Nye. You can call me Joss." She looked so cute in her Naples-yellow jacket. Too cute, she thought, except for her crown of ragged straw hair.

"How old are you?" asked one of the girls.

She was only sixteen. She knew that she looked about twelve. In order to forestall their derision, she answered, "I haven't hatched yet."

"Hey! Sally, don't give that kid a cig. She's still only an egg!" Everyone laughed. That's how quickly they accepted her. She did not threaten anyone. She made them laugh.

"I just hatched," she said as she accepted a proffered cigarette.

"You probably haven't even been laid yet," the girl surmised loudly.

The girls laughed rudely, especially since Joss choked a little on that cigarette.

They were all children but old enough to date, so they knew how to tease. In their time, and as practiced judiciously with their male counterparts, it was called "flirting." But when playing close to a flame, there must be occasional incidents. Sex was a problem. Its power was so explosive. Sometimes vulgar. Everyone knew the perilous consequences. Sordid rooms. Tacky lies. Unwelcome sweaty hands. Déclassé. Simply not gracious.

Even so, the train, with its insidious motion exposing

a continuum of beautiful New England trees in autumnal colors, encouraged a tide of sensuality that simply was not fair. It had to be quelled by bright bursts of chatter, punctuated by the fine shattering sound of young girls giggling. The catharsis of their laughter defined them. It was an audible statement that entitled them to this train, this scenery, to the whole world, including surrounding passengers who might possibly be disturbed by the girlish jabbering. They laughed. They laughed too much. They had plenty of wit and enough erudition filched off their precious education to render anything clever or ridiculous. They could laugh at themselves. They could laugh at their own repressions brought into focus by someone's insightful remark. A tide of laughter would arise. So much to laugh at. They had so much to laugh at then.

How could it all have been linked this way—so contiguous, so unanimous in recognition of a joke, bowled over like dominoes though only proximate in space, when frequently they were dying inside, quite separate from one another? Alone, the enslaved maidens were dying of self-doubt and their slow realization of pain for the joy and the terrible vastness ahead of them. They were afraid of the beauty of life as experienced for the very first time.

Cascades. Garlands. Chains of laughter. Laughing was like a part of their expensive clothes. They wore tartans or tweed skirts that fell exactly to the middle of the calf. The length was imperative. A centimeter off measured out to unacceptable gaucherie. They wore matched sweater sets in muted shades. Oatmeal and wheat were popular. Only a girl absolutely sure of her physical perfection dared the recently fashionable spinach shade. "Rotten green" the girls called it. Though natural brown was conceded to be smart, very few browns were visible. One of their numbers, Susan Dash, had conducted a psychological study and proved to their satisfaction that brown clothes repelled boys. The Dash Report gained fame. It concluded that males responded to girls in light blue. They liked red, too, but it inflamed the animal. None of the girls wore red. Too blatant.

Some brave types wore Bermuda shorts. Susie Dash, the intrepid psych major, was one of these. But Susie had such flawless legs. When in skirts, the seams of her stockings were always straight.

Many sported headbands to frame their pageboy hairstyles neatly. Neatness reigned. It was conventional.

Amid the compatible band sat this wild little Jocelyn Nye. She wore scandalous purple Bermuda shorts of fine cloth but of a loony pattern—a plaid never dreamed of in the highlands—and an expensive jacket in her favorite shade of Naples yellow. She had cut her own indomitable yellow hair haphazardly because she was always mad at it. Like her hair, she could not follow the patterns. Having just finished her first cigarette, she looked to be a baby in that company of young women.

"How old *are* you, little girl?" that girl had asked.

Crazy Joss Nye—quick, glib, and little. For once she sat quiet as if against the sidewise glance of her own reflection in the window she spun a fantasy. Another vehicle, a box for her own ego.

Long ago.

Chuckle along, feel fine, rain and chill blur in the dark. In homely clothes, so good, one cuff drooped in back, wicked up the damp, so good.

—From the *Codex* by Jocelyn Nye

The sophomore class at the women's college had arranged a welcoming dance for the incoming freshmen at both the college and the university. They called it the Dream Dance, and it truly was dreamy. Beauty glided all around the floor of the huge conference room at the college. Under speckled lights rushing around them like the waters of a magical flume, girls and boys danced over waves. The myriad colors ended up flinging themselves athwart the decorated walls in a final splash.

Under the twinkling lights, everyone shone. The girls were so pretty. No one was ugly. They wore their long fairy-tale dresses in pastel shades. Many had tied a ribbon around their necks. It was the style that season to have a live flower pinned at the throat, or at the wrist, or attached to the long, white gloves that were a fashion statement that year. The boys were all straight, groomed with care. This was important. Their faces shone. Their hair was short, combed straight back or in the military brush cut many of them had arrived in.

Joss had not been at school long enough to meet boys, but just that very morning at the university, she had met one. It was a comical meeting, like in a slapstick movie. The guy had such long legs he didn't really fit in the classroom desk-chair provided. When his pencil rolled to the floor, he was trapped in a tangle of legs trying to pick it up. Joss reached over to help.

"I'm such a klutz," he moaned.

She laughed. The word was new to her, but she caught the meaning. She put it with her store of new words and thought she'd like to use it later with her new friends in the dorm. "Hello, Klutz. I'm Joss."

"No! No. Not my name. My name is Frank. Frank Graham."

"Well, good, Frank Graham. If you can get untangled, I'm pretty sure you'd like to go to the Dream Dance with me tonight."

In spite of short notice, Frank Graham grabbed the invitation.

But that evening it seemed both funny and uncomfortable to be dancing with him. He was well over six feet tall. Joss barely cleared five. Couples dancing by made silly remarks. "Hey, little girl. Why'd you bring your father?" Frank was delighted. He grinned. Joss studied him. She could see he really *was* a hopeless klutz. Every individual bite of the comb was visible in his shiny, dark hair. He smiled toothily to all and sundry.

He said, "I love that, Joss. I could put you in my pocket." That only annoyed her. She would rather he did not start making any declarations of love right now, certainly not for the size of her. The dance was fun enough for the moment. Some of her new dormitory friends sailed by, chiming in with their funny remarks.

Everyone looked so wonderful. Then the most beautiful couple in the room swirled right past them. He was handsome Harry Hannigan, the most perfect man on campus according to Jeannie Irslinger. Jeannie had already pointed him out to Joss in front of University Hall. Harry, as befits the king of masculine beauty, was pushing along the most beautiful girl in the world. Joss had never seen her before. She, too, was extremely tall, with dark hair pulled back like a ballerina. Her air of serenity was unmistakable. This girl *knew* she was beautiful.

The band played a Lindy Hop. The tall girl swung into it like a professional dancer, but both handsome Harry and klutzy Frank were lost at sea. So Joss just danced all around Frank as if he were a ship's mast. Marvelous. Such fun.

At the break, handsome Harry approached Frank. They were both of a matched height. It was such a coincidence that Joss supposed they knew each other from some team. Probably basketball. Harry wanted to talk, but she could see Frank didn't. He kept trying to move away and come back to her.

The two girls, unattended by their dates, stood there and examined each other. After a long silence, the tall girl exclaimed, "My goodness. But you're little!"

Joss, at a loss in this land of giants, cried out, "I am not! You're too big!" She felt her face grow hot. She knew she must have been blushing. Her voice had squawked out of her control at this intimidating stranger.

The incoming freshmen girls were all domiciled at Harmon House. It was an old frame house that had been donated to the university by the Harmon family in memory of their daughter, Hortense. The minute the girls got wind of that name, a wave of mirth passed through them. They thought it the funniest name they had ever heard, even though Hortense herself had been far from funny. She was one of the abused female pioneers in the higher education of women in the early years of the twentieth century. Nevertheless, her name now passed into the realm of the ridiculous. It became part of the local vocabulary, guaranteed to bring up a laugh.

Not long after the Dream Dance, a new phenomenon arose in the corridors of Harmon House where the freshmen women had recently been admitted. There were those who compared it to the mating presentations of some primitive hominid species. Roommates, originally sorted together by the incomprehensible whim of the dean's office, were already beginning to fall apart. As the dean well knew, wherever the arrangements were precarious, there was a real possibility of explosion. After all, these were very young girls, many of them away from home for the first time.

Since the term was just beginning and the pressures of acquiring an education were still new, the young ladies affected were encouraged to find themselves new roommates within the week. It was this dean's decree that started what Jeannie Irslinger called "The Roommate Ramble." Solitary girls began wandering mournfully up and down the halls, peering into dorm rooms. "Watch it," Jeannie said to Joss. "You're fair game. A prize catch for anyone on the prowl."

Jeannie lived with Mary Ellen Rigg in the room adjacent to Joss's. They were all set. They had been friends since high school. "Copacetic," Jeannie pronounced their relationship. Since they indulged in frequent disputes, they already knew how to fight with each other, or thought they did. But Joss, next door and assigned to a roommate who, on the very first night, had already distinguished herself by earning a scandalous dismissal from the women's college, was now occupying a room alone.

In the very first moments in Harmon House, Joss had met her assigned roommate, Gloria Demaris. She was prepared to like her. It was not very difficult, as Gloria was chatty and just as silly as all the rest of them. But she stared so hard at Joss. At first that was scary. Then Gloria explained that she was wearing those pioneer prototypes of contact lenses. That explained her owly look. The girls weren't sure if those contraptions were safe or lethal. "Against nature," someone said.

They were all so green, they weren't even sure if tampons were safe. Was there danger of untimely deflowering? Jeannie laughed hard at that idea. "Sure. Be careful. Maybe a Tampon can get you pregnant, too." She sniggered at that notion. "You'd have to marry your sanitary device!" she added, slapping her knees with hilarity.

As for actual slugs of glass in your God-given eyeballs ... what if your eyes were to jam open like headlights just when they needed to be lowered demurely? But Gloria Demaris was vain and hopelessly nearsighted. Those rigids of target glass made her seem lamped like a robot, though she was really a handsome girl, horsey and sexy. A large girl with a tiny voice, a voice like ice tinkling in a glass.

Then came the scandal. Gloria Demaris already had a boyfriend at the university, and he talked her into spending a night in his room at the Quad. The very first night! Caught with no story ready. Scandal! Dumb as a doorpost. Just stood there in her size-nine saddle shoes blinking her lamps and declaring that they hadn't *done* anything. Hadn't even *tried* to do anything. Her tiny voice stirring the ice frantically as she avowed that they hadn't even *considered* doing anything. But the dean found out. Gloria got suspended. All of Harmon House thought it to be right and proper. Gloria's parents, of course, had to be told. They, in turn, told the boy's parents. The combined wrath of the elders came down upon them, and they got married by Christmas. And that was that. Good-bye, Demaris.

Jeannie and Mary Ellen were the first people Joss had met at Harmon House. Joss liked them. Though she liked everyone, these two she liked especially. They were silly and fun. They accepted Joss as quickly. Joss was cute and so quick to laugh, a big favorite throughout the whole house. Yet, because of the indiscretions of Gloria Demaris, her appointed roommate, she remained solitary in one of the nicest double rooms in the front hall.

"Anyone could get you, kiddo," Mary Ellen warned, puffing out one perfect smoke ring, as if in emphasis of her warning.

"Well, I need a roommate, don't I?" Joss said.

"Yeah, but you could get some horror," Mary Ellen clarified.

"You could get Madge Perle," added Jeannie.

"I like her," Joss assured them.

"Madge looks like Raggedy Ann," Jeannie continued.

"I do too," Joss assured. "I don't care about that."

"You could get Ella Klutz!" Jeannie insisted, and the three of them began laughing so hard they almost choked on their cigarettes. The new word had taken fire. They were all smoking. Joss had, in fact, gone into their room for a study break and a smoke. Ella Klutz was a name they had just invented to describe some impossibly gauche imagined character. It was as good as Hortense, guaranteed to crack them up whenever mentioned. "Come on, Joss. We live next door. We want you to have a nice roommate, because she'll practically be our roommate too," Jeannie insisted.

"Some monster is likely to come creeping up and grab you like a serving of roast lamb, kid," chimed in Mary Ellen.

Joss laughed. "Roast lamb, sweetie? More like smoked pig. Besides, I can always say no, can't I?" At that moment, Joss begun to notice that someone was hovering outside the next door—her door. She stepped into the hall to confront the stranger.

It was the beautiful girl, the one she had seen at the Dream Dance. Joss stared at her and took a long puff on her cigarette. "Hello," she said as she stepped out into the corridor.

"Hello," echoed the tall girl. "You're Joss Nye, aren't you?"

Joss waved her cigarette gracefully in the air and watched the smoke billow toward the ceiling. "I am Jocelyn Nye. Joss. Yes."

"I saw you at the dance the other night."

"I remember. You said I was little," Joss said petulantly. At the dance, Joss had not been thrilled by that description. Now she saw the girl looking slightly uncomfortable.

"Was that bad? I didn't mean it to be," said the beautiful girl quietly. "It was just the contrast. You were dancing with that towering boy."

"Oh, yes. Towering. That would be Frank. He's like the Empire State Building," Joss agreed. "I'm really short in *that* context. But I am really Joss. Who you are is what I'm wondering right now."

"I'm Montrose," the girl replied. "Montrose Arbejean."

"Oye!" Joss yelped. "What a moniker!"

Montrose gave a crooked smile. "How well I know. I'm the one that's had to bear it. I think someone went crazy when I was born."

"Montrose I can handle. But Arme-something—what is that? Is it some foreign language?"

"Arbejean. It's French. At least I think it may be French."

"Well, nice meeting you, Monty." Joss saw Montrose begin to cringe. She didn't need to be polite, but she didn't want to be too flippant either. She sensed she was on the winning side of an exchange of some kind. Did she want to win anything? She wasn't sure, so she amended her words. "I mean *Montrose*. I guess I can say that all right, but I don't think I can handle the French part." In the corner of her eye, Joss could see Mary Ellen Rigg and Jeannie Irslinger lurking in their doorway, taking in everything they could of the conversation.

"Why would you need to handle the French part anyway?"

"Well, I would need to if someone came to my room and asked me for the full name of my roommate," Joss explained.

Montrose began to laugh. "You are very perceptive," she said. "That *is* the reason I came by today."

There was a definite bustle, a disturbance of the smoke

filling the doorway of the neighboring room. Joss couldn't tell if that meant approval or reproach.

"Is it okay?"

"Welcome to my home and heart, Montrose Arbezzhh," consented Jocelyn Nye.

Joss looked forward eagerly to her first writing classes. She assumed she would excel as she had in high school. Words always poured through her mind. She expected they would continue to do so, pour onto the pages just as easily. A few days after the Roommate Ramble, actual classes began at the university.

She arrived at Dwight Hall prompt and polished, with pencils sharpened and notebook ready to receive.

Montrose and she walked over to class together. Montrose thought she might be a writer too, but she was assigned to a different section. Montrose shared the aspiration to write, but she was aiming toward children's literature. Not Joss. Joss intended to write adult narratives that would illuminate the dark corners of the human soul.

In other words, Joss meant to create literature. And perhaps a few best sellers as well.

She looked at the teacher. "Alan Resnick," said a card on the door. He was a short man, perhaps topping Joss by a mere few centimeters. A skinny string of a man, not very imposing, wearing tweedy clothes that didn't quite fit. Patches on his elbows sewn on badly, trying to look collegiate. He wore thick spectacles with tinted glass. People compared that kind of glasses to "the bottom of beer bottles." They tended to obliterate any suggestion of eyes. Behind she could see a watery confusion around two drilling points. These points he now directed her.

"Miss Nye," he said. He extended his hand, and Joss

grabbed it though it proved to be as clammy and limp as she suspected it would.

"Good morning, Professor," she chirped. But he interrupted her.

"Not yet, I'm sorry to say. I'm just an instructor. Mr. Resnick will do."

She continued to stare. His round head was almost bald but topped by a corona of light brown fuzz, baby hair. He looked to be of an indefinite age, but Joss guessed he was probably young, possibly on his first teaching assignment to judge by the self-conscious way he kept fingering a new-looking knobbed watch. It was a very large, old-fashioned watch with numbers so big she could still read them even after she had taken a seat in the far side of the room. She expected he'd have a silly, piping voice. She was surprised, however, at the mellow tone that came out of his mouth when he pronounced her name. He made "Miss Nye" sound like a line from a song. "Come in and find a comfortable seat for yourself, Miss Nye. There are no permanent places in this class. It's like King Arthur's round table. We sit ourselves around wherever it suits us," sang Mr. Resnick.

Joss sat. The class was under the conspectus of the university English Department. That meant there would be boys enrolled as well as the usual gaggle of girls from the women's college. This class was called Beginning Exposition. She didn't like the title much. It implied rules and restrictions. Because it was a requirement, it would have to be suffered through, but "exposition" sounded so dull. Even "composition" might afford more leeway than that. Since she had tested as exceptional in writing, she was encouraged to undertake this as one of the advanced freshman sections. Whatever it might turn out to be, she was keen to start on her bright path.

She looked around. It was a small class, three boys and four girls. She knew the girls, Sally Petrucci, Maddy Traywick, Emily Fortray, Angie Sing. Three of them lived in Harmon House. Angie was a townie. Mr. Resnick was still standing at the door, waiting to greet newcomers. Joss smiled brightly at the room. "I'm Joss," she announced.

Mr. Resnick swung around. For a minute he looked startled. Then he chimed in, "Great!" he declared. "Introduce yourselves with your familiar names." He spoke as he walked toward the front of the classroom. "You're going to get to know one another in this class. We're all in together on this project. Creating and critiquing, if you will. It's going to be great. Oh, we are going to have so much fun!" With his enthusiastic words, Joss felt a chill of disagreement. Starting with the very title, it did not sound so inviting to her. Expository definition—explaining by defining. To Joss it sounded blooming restrictive. And now with this little elflike man declaring it was going to be such a garden of delight, she knew she'd landed up in the wrong place.

The first assignment was even more disappointing. It didn't offer Joss the kind of challenge she liked. Mr. Resnick asked them to produce an expository definition. The explanation of a process, he clarified. The explanation of what?

"A process—how something comes to be," he said.

She hunkered over the paper for an hour or two, wrote her fingers blue, and handed in her study the next day. "How to Make Soup." She described a cumulative process like in the children's tale of stone soup but full of calculated errors.

Mr. Resnick loved it. At least he said he loved it. He also pronounced that she had flown away on a flight of fancy and missed the purpose of the assignment, and so it must now be rewritten, of course. "A process, Miss Nye. A process—how something comes to be."

"Yeah," she said. "How your lunch got to be late today."

The class laughed heartily at that as they did at her silly tale of misadventures with the soup, but that gained her little. She still had to redo it. A subject that had bored her once now came to bore her again, and in a more serious mien. The soup thing had been funny. She thought. At least the class laughed. Even Resnick laughed.

She spent one unhappy semester in that class, writing expository definitions and what she called "articles for *Popular Mechanic*." She stuck it out because her major depended on a favorable conclusion.

Writing meant so much to Joss Nye. She'd written ever since she'd learned to spell. Even before. She could remember her first story. It was called *Blood on the Munny*. The title sounded arousing to her childish mind. She had known there was something wrong with *munny*, but it was the best she could do at the time. She'd begun writing *Letters to My Notebook* when she could just hold a pencil. It was so important and magical to trace out squiggles on a page and know they meant something. When she compared herself to others, she knew she was the lucky one. Perhaps they all felt that way, like chosen people. Mary Ellen argued, "Math is not magic unless you are really terrifically *good* at it. Then it is more magical than anything." And Jeannie Irslinger, planning to be a psychology major, was already fancying herself an expert on Freud, ready to psychoanalyze everyone, with annoying insights on what had gone wrong in each person's private id, ego, and superego.

Joss had an endless series of conferences with Mr. Resnick. An easy camaraderie gradually grew between them. Mr. R. followed the rigid, old rules of the establishment. When Joss suggested that he call her Joss, he said, "I'd be honored to, but here in the office, not in class. There we will observe the decorum of the classroom." He continued to call all the girls Miss together with their last names, and all the boys by their last names only. At the end of this particular conversation, he said, "My given name is Alan." Joss hoped he would not invite her to use it. As far as she was concerned, to do so would probably give decorum too much of a kick on its behind.

"Joss, you'll be taking the Short Story section soon. I hope you will keep me informed about that. You can indulge your love of words there. You can let your imagination and humor take wing and fly. And I will always be glad to hear of your successes."

So she liked Mr. Resnick that term. She had trouble understanding the assignments. She did not like subjecting herself to the discipline they required. More than liked, she needed Resnick. While criticizing her lack of discipline, he complimented her writing lavishly. She was shamelessly hungry for appreciation. It would grow, she expected, into adoration, exaltation. Maybe a Nobel Prize.

Art D1. In producing a picture, your hand learns art from your eye, and your eye has learned its lesson from organs just slightly superior. You must experience, above sight, how the interior contour of the model may impose a super validity on its outline, and how the outline may break as if some essence of the object has attempted to escape the cage of space. You must physically acknowledge how small a detail, an eye, or something even smaller, can dictate the relationships and the proportions of all the model furniture, all the tables, chairs, and cabinets stored up there. The furnishings of a face are different, lumps and bumps that represent the differences from one person to another. I stared at Peggy Matthew's ear in art class yesterday, wondering how this complex, impossible-yet it's the only possible-shape could come to be."

Joss' Codex

On a Saturday in September, Mary Ellen's parents came for a visit. Her father, Alfred Rigg, was an alumnus of the university. He came for homecoming weekend, but Mrs. Rigg, a true mama, came to scope Harmon House and their only child, Mary Ellen, who reverted to babyhood in their presence. She did everything but talk baby talk while her cohorts expressed enchantment. They were thrilled to have the presence of an actual mama and papa. Mrs. Rigg had brought a great red pot that she put on the little portable stove in Mary Ellen's room. A complex and wonderful smell of unfamiliar cookery wafted through the house. Ravenous girls came sniffing by the door. All the growing girls were half-famished by the miserable food the dorm system provided. Mrs. Rigg explained that the pot was full of something called "gawumpkie," stuffed cabbage rolls in a delicious tomato sauce. In a few seconds, the pot was empty. "You girls really like hunkie food?" Mrs. Rigg laughed. Jeannie made loud, wet smacking sounds of appreciation.

"What is hunkie?" Montrose asked.

"Polish," explained Mary Ellen. "It's a not-so-polite word for Polacks or Hungarians. I'm a hunkie," she said. "Well, half a hunkie anyhow," Mary Ellen added. "Because Poppa's English—a bloody limey." She spoke as though disparagingly, but all the while she leaned against her father and sheltered in his protecting arm. It was too much—like a scene from a really cornball movie they'd all have laughed at but, here and now, in the reality of the moment, they envied. These parents enchanted them.

Mrs. Rigg told them about her own Polish parents. Her mama, a pioneer, came over from the old country alone. "Mirka Barczak. She was alone, only fourteen years old," explained Mrs. Rigg.

"What a beautiful name," Montrose declared.

"Rather a hard one to spell out for Americans." said Mrs. Rigg. "I ought to know. My name is Alenka."

"But so pretty," insisted Montrose. "Do you speak Polish, Mrs. Rigg?"

"Oh, Mirka saw to it that we all came up Catholic, proud and respectful, and with as many Polish words as the environment would allow. I know I had a terrible time in school with writing out Alenka Kowalski and trying to explain it. I was born in Connecticut, you know, and I grew up there."

Montrose drew in a long breath. She sighed. "Alenka," she sounded out slowly, "So lovely. So singular. Such a special name."

"Look who's talking," Joss laughed.

Montrose grunted.

They listened as to a strange tale of the remote past, an unimaginable time when their own parents had been young. Real days of yore.

"Yes, in this land I'm thoroughly a Yankee," said Alenka.

They were enchanted. Inside their soft, gray cocoon (they were all smoking), they felt safe and homey together in that room.

"You'd think Alenka Kowalski was a new toy for us," Joss commented later to Montrose.

"Maybe we did act like stupid idiots," Montrose agreed. "But she was wonderful. Mary Ellen is lucky to have such a sweet mama," she added.

"Isn't your mama sweet?"

"I don't remember her, Joss. My mother died when I was four years old. My father panicked and thought to send me to the nuns in Quebec. I grew up in a convent. Sister Marie Therese there was almost a mama to me. My high school was St. Etienne Boarding Academy. When I try to think of a mother, all those sweet French nuns float into my mind. Sister Marie Therese, now *she* was so special. She loved me so much I could feel it. I could taste the love. What about your mother?"

"Joe says I'm the spittin' image of her."

"Well, then she must be very cute, like you."

When Montrose said that, Joss's reaction was immediate. She slammed her notebook against the wall. She was annoyed. "Don't call me cute!" she demanded.

"Why?" Montrose wondered. "You *are* cute. It's a *good* thing. Everyone says that about you. Darn it, you're not beautiful. You're not classical looking in any way. You don't look like a candidate for the movies. But you have that thing. You are just plain *cute*. Hells bells! You have a cookie-face. It's meant as a compliment. Now you're getting mad at me. All I did was tell the truth."

Joss had been standing by her desk. Now she plunked down on the bed to give the matter some thought. Well, it was true. She knew it. She *was* cute. She looked like her mother, Kitty McCorkle Nye, who was the epitome of cuteness, the queen of cutie pies. Couldn't be much sillier than that, could it? "I'm sorry," Joss admitted. "I just don't like any adjectives that translate as small or little."

"Being as big as a giraffe, I don't get it. How wonderful it must be not to have legs that hang two feet off the edge of the bed."

"Well, you're exaggerating," Joss asserted. "You are tall and lofty and graceful, slender as a reed. And every inch of you is beautiful. It just vexes me to be called cute because I think words like cute, little, pert, pixyish— even the supposed compliment 'petite'—diminish me. I think they are all words to make you small. And keep you small!"

"For heaven's sake!" Montrose exclaimed. "I had no idea. I'm really sorry. I would not like to say anything to minimize you. Have I been dwelling on your size or using words that hurt you, Joss? I hope you know I really love you. I wouldn't hurt you just for the sake of some stupid adjectives."

Perched on Joss's perfectly oval face was a small nose, not a pug nose but just slightly upturned. Pert. That was another word that bothered her. Often she suffered from a sprinkling of damn freckles, like icing on her cake.

A cute decoration, her enemies decried. Her eyes were good, large and greener than the sea. The spoiler of this adorable picture was a head of yellow hair that would not lie down. It was not hair but despair, she often complained. It made her crazy. Mary Ellen, the doyenne of beauty, well actually a student of beauty products and devices, frequently and futilely worked on Joss's hair. Joss kept it very short, but still it insisted on looking like something scratched over by a chicken. In part it looked like a chicken's crest. "You must check every morning," she told Montrose, "to see if I have finally laid my famous egg."

They paused in pensive cigarette smoke. Joss watched her fume rise upward to disperse in the upper latitudes of the room. Then she spoke.

"I have to say that Kitty did what she could, but sweetness was never her long suit. She loved the movies and dragged me to the films all the time. Then she liked to hang around the soda shops where all the teenagers gathered. Her friends then were all giddy girls and pimply boys. She was hardly more than a teenager herself," Joss answered. Then she gravely added, "They used to mock me there. She loved to tell people I was her little moment of inattention. That made those kids laugh in a way that was definite mocking. I liked people to laugh but not *at* me. Even as the smallest baby, I could tell one kind of laughter from another. I thought they were laughing because I was so little. Far too little, I thought. That always amused them. When I was about ten years old, I finally figured out why I was called her little moment of inattention."

"Did she mean what I think she meant?"

"You bet she did," Joss averred. "You know Kitty McCorkle was barely sixteen when she married my father, Joe Nye. He was twenty years older. There must have been a compelling reason to merge, wouldn't you think?"

"Indeed," agreed Montrose Arbejean.

Most nights at about nine, a male voice could be heard calling through the corridors of Harmon House. He had to shout from the open door as, except on special occasions—graduations, medical emergencies, plumbers, or parents—males were not permitted in the hallowed halls of Harmon House. "Sandwich man! Sandwich man!" came the rallying call. Famished girls tumbled out of their rooms eagerly.

Many men now scrabbling for an education at the university were veterans. Some of them had entertained little hope of a getting a college degree until the blessed GI Bill came along. Smart guys grabbed at the boon. If they were married, the good wives struggled along to support their men in the pursuit of a higher education, usually without getting one themselves. They did what they could. While the husbands worked toward the building of bridges, the curing of diseases, and the planning of cities, the wives slapped bread on ham or cheese or salami. That usually built something good—a degree, a future, and a sandwich.

After dormitory dinner hours, the vets would canvass the dorms for the famished. Sandwiches, made in mass, cost the customers twenty cents apiece, which gave a pretty big profit margin. The GI Bill was enabling the guys, but it didn't make things easy. They were relegated to off-campus housing, sometimes at some distance from the university. Of course, whatever sacrifice they made, the wives made with them.

One night while Joss suffered the agonies of creating her stories, the sandwich cry came. Montrose leaped eagerly out of the room at the first call. Montrose was always restless.

Joss was staring into space. She often did this when writing. She was stuck. She had decided to try meditation, which, as far as she knew, meant staring into space. Without success, she plumbed her own depths seeking something more meaningful than mere narrative.

Nothing came.

Joss loved living at Harmon House. Until late in the evening, it buzzed like a hive. There was always something going on. Even when the bell was rung for quiet hours, girls would be whispering, gossiping, arguing, and muttering. No bell could still their exuberance.

For Joss, it was all fun. The contrast to her earlier life was clear. She had gone to special boarding schools for brainy kids. She was always much younger than the others. Brainy kids are just as cruel as any others. Joss was mocked at school.

At Harmon House, she loved everyone. She got all the companionship that her sociable nature craved. Now, since apparently her brain was not producing anything literary, she turned out looking for company. Montrose had fled at the sandwich man's first cry, so Joss wandered next door where Mary Ellen seemed to be intent on her studies.

"All work and no play makes Hortense a dull girl," Joss said to Mary Ellen. She would inveigle her if she could, but she wondered whether it was possible. Mary Ellen seemed so occupied. "What are you reading, kiddo? You look like a kinked rope. Have you got exams or something?"

Mary Ellen raised a smiling face. "You'd be surprised," she said. She waved her copy, not a textbook, only a trendy publication. Mary Ellen was addicted to fashion. She bought the most expensive ladies' magazines and kept up with all the latest styles. She knew the names of all the top models, their salaries, and as much as she could find out about their personal lives. Makeup was her latest passion. "Look at this girl," she demanded as she waved the magazine toward Joss.

On the cover, Joss saw a pretty face, heavily ornamented with paint. "It's the new makeup," Mary Ellen chortled. She was clearly excited. "This is Georgianna Fritz. She's the top model in New York today. That could change tomorrow, of course."

"Very pretty," Joss agreed. "But maybe if she'd wipe about an inch of gunk off her face, she would look like everybody else."

"Well, why should she? She's gorgeous, kiddo. Why shouldn't she perk up her good features? She's a model, you know. A *top* model. She earns seventy-five dollars an hour just for sitting in a chair or walking down a runway. The competition for a job like that is cruel. Those girls need to use all the improvements they can get." Mary Ellen was flipping through her magazine as she spoke, pointing out one beautiful babe after another. "Look at the eyes. Look at their eyes, Joss. They all do this big makeup job on their eyes now. They call it 'doe eyes.'"

"Hmmm," Joss hummed. "It definitely enhances."

"Wanna try?" suggested Mary Ellen, giggling.

Both girls became enamored of their reflections after just a little application of Mary Ellen's magical potions. So glamorous did the touch of a grease pencil make them that they applied even more. Both were enraptured, crouching together in front of Mary Ellen's mirror.

"We're dreamboats, kid," Mary Ellen commented.

"We're unbelievable," Joss agreed.

"We could be a couple of the pharaoh's daughters sashaying down the border of an ancient Egyptian frieze," Mary Ellen marveled.

"Hmmm," Joss hummed. "Or we could be a couple of tarts advertising our goods down the length of Benefit Street on a Saturday night."

"Oooh, ladies of the night," Mary Ellen said. "Scarlet women!" She giggled. She seemed thrilled by the idea. "Jeannie would like that too, I betcha."

"Where is Jeannie?" Joss asked. "Did she go for sandwiches?"

"No, she's never hungry. I don't know where the heck she is," Mary Ellen replied. "She's always like this—in and out of the room as if something's biting her behind. She's always coming out of her skin over something or other. Nowadays she says she's measuring the building. Crazy. But I'll bet she would go for the doe eye thing in a big way."

"Well, she'd look great, but you know, neither one of you really needs it. Nor does Montrose."

"Not Montrose, of course. Montrose is our established beauty."

"And *you* are the *prettiest* girl in Harmon House, Mary Ellen," said Joss, who truly thought so.

"No, I am not. You are the *cutest*, Joss, but I'm nothing. But I have to admit I'm a lot better looking with the doe eyes. I've tried it," she admitted. "Every girl in Harmon House would be improved by a long shot with just a walloping dose of eye makeup."

Mary Ellen had picked up a box. It was her precious makeup box. Stirring carefully in the contents of the box, she sought something special. She held up to the light a little pot of gold theater paste. "Look at this, Joss. I've been collecting this stuff for a long time. Would you believe this tiny jar cost me four dollars? I've never dared to use it. Now maybe we can get to try it."

"Well, let's do it! Let's *get them all* to do it. Everybody! We can have a Doe Eye Party. Everyone comes—embellished to the maximum," Joss agreed.

"Uh-uh. What about Montrose?" wondered Mary Ellen. "Do you think Montrose'd go for it?"

They had reason to wonder. The concept of makeup was still very connected with the ancient profession—prostitution, and the girls at Harmon House were all bona fide good girls. Of course they were. And of good girls the best and most worthy of the standard, the very goodest of good girls anywhere was Montrose Arbejean.

But before sandwich call on the next Friday night, nineteen scarlet women of the Harmon House gathered together in their decorated best for the never-to-be-forgotten Doe Eye Party.

Montrose, with golden eyelids, edged in deepest black, appeared to wow all of them as much as they wowed themselves.

In the evenings, as a quiet reward for those good girls who had dutifully returned from evening dates, studied their books, prepared the requisite themes, glosses, and trots, brushed their hair a mandatory hundred strokes, and performed all ablutions and required beautifications, they talked. The residents of Harmon House usually gathered for the evening in the lounge. Joss had just come in from a coffee house meeting with the so-called literary crowd. Abbot Parish was there. He had a thing for Joss. If she allowed him to come near, he sprouted arms and tentacles like an octopus, attempting to board her.

"It's embarrassing," she declared. "He's so scruffy. He doesn't smell too nice, either. I believe he thinks soap is an offense to intelligent thought. With him, cleanliness is a political thing. He insisted on walking me home tonight, and then I had to keep hopping all over the sidewalk to stay out of his range. Tonight I maneuvered all the length of Douglas Street, hopping from side to side like a kangaroo."

They laughed. Some girls were nodding. The octopus experience was a common one. "Boys are all hands nowadays. It's because of that book," Jeannie said angrily.

"What book?"

"There's an awful book out that tells all about the nasty things men like to do," she explained. "And the worst part is, it implies that they have every right to do them!"

"What book?" shouted one of the girls, "Gimme that book! I want to read that book!"

"It's new," Jeannie said. "My uncle has it. He's a doctor. He showed it to my father, and the two of them were whispering about it. They guarded it as if it were the atomic bomb. No way he would let me or my brother see it."

"Not even your brother?"

"No, but Rusty knows about it for sure. He threw a million hints at me when I was home. I think it has been going around to all the boys in the United States."

"Betcha those guys at the university are reading it ragged too. Seems to me that there has been an awful lot of grabbing and wrestling of late," said Weezy Danton.

"Lucky you, Weezy," Mary Ellen remarked as she emitted one of her trademark smoke rings.

Everyone laughed.

"It's not even funny," Jeannie insisted. "Boys used to want me to like them. They tried really hard to *make* me like them, being polite and all. They thought they had to be gentlemen to score points with girls. Now they don't care. They have this whole line now about their *needs*."

There was a murmur of general consent "Yes. I haven't met a gentleman in a long time," someone asserted.

"I'm telling you, it's that disgusting book," Jeannie insisted. "It's changing everything."

"Got along without you before I met you; gonna get along without you now," her voice climbed. She made the end words tumble, rush together, pulling each other out on hooks. Spiky. Spiky voice. Spiky eyelashes. Spiky humor, too. That crazy Irslinger. Joss just loved her.

She was coming down the corridor making the ukulele wail to her comic song of love gone sour. If she came into the room, Joss couldn't possibly finish writing the story she was working on because Jeannie pulled in all the attention. She simply had to have her stage. Not a restful person. She was definitely not one to sit companionably in silence. And she was forever getting thrown out of places for her shenanigans. They wouldn't even let her enter the Breslau library anymore since it had been noticed that all the silent scholars presented her with an irresistible opportunity to put on a show. On Halloween, she walked in there with her front teeth covered with Black Jack chewing gum. Then she pretended to faint in the middle of the main reading room right in front of big Erik Anders, who manfully caught her as she flapped her spiky eyelashes and declared, "Forgive me, sir! I haven't had anything to eat for three days!" That broke everybody up. Those critical three days. Such an echoing evocation of a dozen movies of the troubled and hungry times they lived in.

After being regaled with a couple of her shows, they no longer would let her in the Breslau. Her uncontrollable seizures of giggles, for example, muffled so comically that everyone in the room soon began to catch the irrepressible disease. Or hiccoughs! You should have caught her hiccough act. It could hold your attention for an hour. Her timing was so professional. The way she held her book at arm's length. Deliberately intense, pretending to study, making her eyes bug out after each loud hic. Even Mary Ellen, her good-natured little roommate, had to throw her out from time to time in order to get any studying done. She was such a bad, bad girl. How could anyone help but like her?

Somewhat grudgingly, even Montrose Arbejean liked her. Not officially, however. Jeannie had different priorities and ethics altogether. She lied. Not for evil but for fun. She was a romancer. A perpetual performer. She could be vulgar. She walked naked from the shower down the corridor. She said she had absentmindedly done this during visiting hours on a Sunday when Val Kolodny's father suddenly stepped out into the hall, so she calmly took her towel, covered her face with it, and continued walking. That probably wasn't even true. Just one of Jeannie's funny stories. But it was exactly the kind of story that made Montrose's eyebrows wing up like startled birds. Montrose was officially loyal to another kind of girl, controlled, unobtrusive like Nevada Gertz, Dorcas Tannenberg, or Daisy Way. They were like her— the rich ladies, endowed. And, of course, Joss. She loved Joss. Everyone did.

Most of them admitted to admiring crazy Jeannie Irslinger exactly for her style of broad irreverence. She broke the glass and let the air in. Big blonde with congenitally open mouth.

She made them laugh.

But she cried. She was tragic. That was the other side of her coin. Since the beginning, her heart had been in some stage of self-imposed fracture. They loved big Irslinger anyhow. Joss did. She was going to start a fan club.

Come on, Jeannie, she thought. *Sing. Make the ukulele weep.*

"Gonna

Get along

Withoutcha

Now."

"Did I tell you that she destroys boys?" wrote Joss as Irslinger began to develop in the material she was writing. "She decimates them. She has a boy for dinner, and she picks her teeth with the bones of the boy she had for lunch. She spikes them, I think, with her voice, her eyelashes. She really doesn't care a toot. They are a necessary agglomeration of interchangeable parts to her. She flirts with all of them, locking her eyes into theirs over the rim of the coffee cup. It's a ritual. She showed Mary Ellen how to do it, but Mary Ellen got shy when it actually came time to put the action into effect. Then Jean will turn around and flirt with the waiter right in front of the guy she came in with. That infuriates the poor fish. Hooks him. Boys can't seem to get enough of her abuse though.

"Oh, she's a wicked one," Joss continued writing. "She came in our room earlier. Had I been alone, she would surely have cried about the condition of her heart. Real tears appear when she does that. But Montrose was in the room, and that constituted enough audience to put on a divertissement. It's very clear she loves to shock Montrose. She cried, 'I'm so fed up with men! They are such a collection of opinionated fatheads. Boring. Boring! And then you have to pretend to agree that they know everything. It's such an outrage. I've even written a poem about it.' Then she produced a spurl of paper on which, over Montrose's shoulder, I read her amazing, scrawled composition:

'Every man thinks he's a genius

Just because he has a penius.'

"Only one of Montrose's eyebrows jumped. Otherwise her expression did not change. A very dangerous sign. That's the ultimate of her disapproval. I thought it was brilliant though. Well, I think Jeannie is brilliant—volatile, precipitous, gifted with both laughter and tears. She is going to be a great actress someday, and I will write a great book about her.

"She was in here weeping some time back. She bit her lip hard enough to leave a mark on it. Her face was blotched with anguish. 'Joss,' she pleaded. 'What's the matter with me? It's Saturday night, and here I am. The only girl in the dorm. It's awful. Alone!'

"'Jeannie, I'm here,' I said.

"She shook her head, refusing to be consoled. 'You don't count. You would be out with Frank if he didn't have a basketball game. And you could have gone. I heard him ask you. But *nobody* asked me *anywhere!*' her voice broke pathetically. She believed it, too, her own nonsense. I know at least three boys who went into decline, became seriously depressed when subjected to her tactics of rejection.

"'I look in the mirror, Joss,' she lamented. 'What do I see? A big, dumb blonde. An overgrown oaf. Clumsy and stupid. Oh, I'll never find anyone. I'll *always* be alone.'

"I'm going to write a story," Joss wrote on, "about an actress who acts all the time until she cannot remember what she feels anymore and can only make a joke, a farce out of it. For example," wrote Joss, "Art Brashear is one notorious lady-killer. Everyone had heard of him. Handsome, spoiled, and loaded with dough. He used to brag that there were so many girls in the world that he would never date any one girl more than three times. Veterans—girls who went the full three dates—mooned over Art in vain. To get another date would be triumphant. But Art pursued variety. Then he met Jeannie Irslinger. When he tried for a fourth date with her, she was shocked, refused him, reminded him of his well-published rule and very sweetly, flirtatiously even, told him that knowledge of his three-date policy was the *only* reason she had consented to go with him in the first place. In other words, she could not stand the idea of going out with him *more* than three times.

"He was crushed, completely chastened, though in the long run it did him a power of good. He certainly seems to have become nicer, a little less full of himself. He long since gave up trying to corner Jeannie, but he continues to admire her, smiles at her with genuine pleasure when he meets her on campus.

"Art will be in the fan club. I am going to be the president of Jeannie Irslinger's fan club," Joss wrote.

"When we took the required speech class, Tanice Wincote was the instructor. She's an assistant, the fair-haired female of the Drama Department. Rumors abound about how she got to be the darling of all those pompous Shakespeare profs, a pack of Poloniuses trying to act like Hamlets. Some say the rallying cry is, 'Anyone for Tanice?' Well, let that go by. Winky and Irslinger have known each other for ages. I wouldn't exactly call them friends.

"Winky has a round face, fat cheeks about which Jeannie, with usual irreverence, says, 'She's got the cheeks, all right. Upstairs and downstairs.'

"Winky is one of those that cries, 'Darling!' and falls all over people, brushing them with lateral kisses that never quite hit their mark while wearing an expression of slight disgust. Jeannie, enthusiastically showbiz, does it right back.

"Everybody knows Winky has a predilection for young men. They don't have to be virginal, but it's all right if they are. She usually picks out the beefiest boy in her class and exerts wiles on him. It's a game. But she is ridiculously serious about it. And she's old. I bet she's thirty, at least. She singled out David Vickery in our speech class. He is neither overly beautiful nor overly bright, but he is huge. And he has got this basso profundo voice that is a positive gift from the heavens. Every girl is aware of it. He can make vibrations that enter you through the soles of your shoes. You can actually experience all sorts of reactions to the man on the visceral level. A nice guy, too. Winky fronted right up to him.

"I liked his friend, Pleshion, who is slender and shy. At conniving Jean's instigation, I tried to vamp him, running one more check on the attracting power of colors as laid out by Sally Dash in her famous psychological study. Swaddled in light blue, I engulfed Frank's friendship pin under voluminous sweaters and addressed my celebrated if eggy charms at the thin, sensitive face of Oliver Pleshion. But it did not work at all. I could almost hear the thud. Pleshion hardly noticed me. Pleshion liked Vickery. You didn't have to be a psych major to piece out the story. Vickery tried really hard to be pleasant to Winky—poor guy, there was always the specter of his grade depending on his pleasing the teacher—but he perspired a lot, because he really preferred Pleshion, and that must not show. Winky was causing a situation that made it show. That embarrassed everyone.

"I found it slightly confusing, though I was only playing around. I don't know if Winky was just playing, however. Does one play at that age? I did mention that she's at least thirty, didn't I?

"Jeannie signed up for the Restoration Workshop this semester. It's Peletier's pet project. He knows everything there is to know about Restoration comedy. But unfortunately he had to spend a month in Boston working with the publisher of one of his last treatises. So Winky was sent in. She lost no time casing the local talent. Dave Vickery is in that class, but by now Winky and, sad to say, everyone else in the Drama Department is familiar with his idiosyncrasy, basso voice or no. Her appraising eyes then fell on Hal Merriam. Not a basso profundo, it's true, but a quite respectable baritone. On occasions like this, in advance of her pounce, Winky indulges herself in the slightest subtle smile. Immediately, the spikes of Irslinger's eyelashes sharpened. She turned upon Hal a glance that bathed him in radiance and glory.

"But as Peletier lingered on in Boston, the situation began to simmer. Jeannie said, 'If Prof Pelly doesn't get back soon, Winky will do the grading for the course, and she will have my scalp. I will fail! In a major course, too! She hates me because Hal likes me, and she is not too noble to not play her position and hand me a big, fat F!'

"'How does Hal handle this?'

"'Like the louse he is. He's a perfect player if you admire that sort of thing. He's so good at being discreet. That's what he calls it. Being sneaky is what I call it. When he takes me out, we have to walk out far from campus. And we never go anywhere where there is the remotest chance of seeing faculty. He *says* he doesn't want to endanger my grade. Ha ha. He *says* he doesn't want to hurt Winky's feelings. He *says* a lot of baloney, Joss. If you ask me, I think she's putting out for him. That's my suspicion. You know, that old bag has actually trotted him along to a few faculty parties. You'd think she'd be ashamed. If Pelletier would just get back, I'd tell Miss Wincote what I think of her. I think she's some kind of fat-bottomed old ... *pederast*, that's what!'

"It was her new word, and she had taken the trouble to look it up. Professor Pelletier returned, just like the US Calvary in an old western. Jeannie did not accuse Miss Wincote of galloping pederasty. She found a different spike. Apparently Hal had jokingly been inviting her to marry him now and then, a few times, on and off, in whatever predatory spirit Hal did such things. In her own style, Jeannie had consistently ignored the offer. The day Pelletier returned, Winky once again became a mere assistant. Jeannie was standing very close to Hal on the stage. Everybody was watching the scene. She leaped back, upstaging Hal, made a full histrionic turn to the audience, and declaimed, 'Hal! You darling! I won't make you beg any longer. Of course, I'll marry you!'

"Since it was at least a month since the humorous offer had last crossed his lips, Hal was surprised. Winky flinched. Only slightly though. After all, she was not an assistant in the Drama Department for nothing. Everyone else laughed. Irslinger does know how to be funny. Well, maybe it was an unfair play on Winky, her being over the hill and all. Jeannie's like that sometimes.

"So now she's engaged," Joss wrote in her diary.

And here she still came wailing her ukulele, trailing a little aura of tragedy, singing her parody of love. "You ran aroun' with every girl in town, never knew how it got me down ..."

Leaning in doorways, trying to spike accomplices to cut up with.

Joss hoped she would stop at her room this time. She hoped for Jean to make some silly mischief and stir the air that clumped so stultifyingly around their student lamps.

From deep within arise all ills, springing from
a source of pure mischief expressed in manifestations of devilry: orneriness, indigestion, excessive solemnity, or contagious woes. What have
we done with days and days but wish for different
ones?

-From Joss Nye's *Codex*

Words swirled constantly in Joss's mind. When she paused to seize them, they sometimes evaporated, and that bothered her. Perhaps they contained the germ of an important idea or the basis for a short story. Because the words were so important, the loss of them was serious, so she began early to carry around a small notebook in which, even as she walked, she jotted down these gems only to find that sometimes the brightest gems were base pebbles of no particular merit. Writing had been a habit since childhood. Then when asked by observers why she scribbled all the time, she had replied that she was writing a letter to herself. "To yourself?"

"To my future self," she maintained. "Because I think adults lose the best part of childhood. I want to remember what it was like to be a child." At that time, she had addressed the many things she wondered about. She wondered what it would be like to be someone else. Famously, she asked her friends, "What does it feel like to be you?" but no one could answer. It seemed a simple question, but asked with such serious intent, it only disquieted the others. Yet something made them "others," and it seemed that "something" could never be defined.

She also wondered about the borders of things. Where did the edge of sleep lie? It was another thing you *fell* into. The transition was so abrupt. One minute you were here, and the next you were on a different plane. Even when no dreams appeared, one entered into sleep as a stranger going into a strange land. It was another case of falling. *Falling* asleep might be a condition akin to *falling* in love. All of her observations of this phenomenon were made in the movies where her mother, Kitty, frequently took her. Kitty was addicted to the cinema.

Joss observed that when people fell in love in movies, there was a whole preamble, a whole codification of what must go on. Even with all the clues, people did not seem to realize that they were about to fall into something. It must be a precipitation so sudden and unexpected that it frightened Joss. Joss wondered about love. There had to be an entrance to it. Joss had observed that falling in love led to a case of immediate insanity. They could speak, but nothing they said made sense. One couldn't just tumble over such a radical change as if from reality to complete madness.

"How can people realistically deal with romance when it so unrealistically arises?" Joss wrote. "Everything about their life becomes different." Joss did not want that. She did not seek it. Her life suited her. Change was just scary. "Before the idea of romance came up, how did people deal with such a difference?"

Kitty had taken her to see movies no little girls should see. Action evolved above a child's understanding, and Joss worried about it. Like any child, she needed to absorb the incomprehensible. Joss watched as if seeing a documentary. She strove to understand. After watching a silly movie, as if a student at an ongoing visual, she wrote: "The man approaches to kiss. He frames in his hands the too-white blossom of her face. Actresses always look whiter than actors.

"He's staring at her lips. They look different from before. Bigger than before. Darker on the screen. Maybe more lipstick. Her eyes look fixed but soft in a way, looking both intently and softly at him. That means she is awakened to it. In the language of the movies, that means yes! They will kiss. She has fallen in love."

Joss immensely enjoyed being at college. She liked all the girls at Harmon House. Sharing her room with Montrose Arbejean pleased her immensely. It was a sort of triumph. She was, as she told her cronies, three-quarters in love with Montrose. She loved to look at her, was in awe of her beauty. She thought Montrose's face was a perfect oval, and the almond eyes, eyes of darkest brown with startling pupils, glinting like black beads of jet. Her skin was pale and smooth as the petals of a flower. In contemplation or serious study, it seemed to Joss the face of a saint at her orations. And that analogy was very strange, coming from Joss. Perhaps it arose because Montrose was indeed religious. She attended Mass every Sunday, never missed her "days of obligation," days that Joss, in the heathen ignorance of her agnosticism, could not identify at all. For Joss, all the orations and oblations and obligations were just part of the mystery that was Montrose Arbejean.

Montrose, in turn, was tolerant of Joss's religious ambiguity. In the quiet of their shared room, she remained lenient. She was the most considerate of roommates. Unlike the cuckoo girls next door, Montrose was quiet, composed, and so polite it threw Joss's friends for a loop. Her grace of manners was noted, often lampooned by Jeannie. Even though the neighbor girls frequently crashed into the room like gangbusters, she maintained her polite equilibrium. Jeannie Irslinger mocked it. Mary Ellen Rigg marveled at the lack of objection when she came crashing in upon them. Montrose cared about her studies, yet not one reprimand crossed her lips. Jeannie was always amazed. She herself would have indulged in some elaborate cuss words. Montrose, instead, was unfailingly polite.

Joss felt that by admitting Montrose to the room, she had adorned it. A proprietary acquisition, like buying a painting. A triumph of interior decoration over the usual dormitory grey. She even told the girls one evening, "Guess what we've got in our room? An original Montrose Arbejean." The real Montrose Arbejean laughed at that. Perhaps she was amused, perhaps offended. Joss wasn't sure. There was always an aura of mystery to the girl. It tantalized Joss and her unholy cronies. All the girls at Harmon House were a little bit entranced by Montrose.

For a while, Joss and Montrose had another interest in common. They were both going to become writers. Montrose said she wanted to write stories that would elevate the young minds and illuminate for children the beauty of existence. What Joss wanted was to write books that would clarify the dark recesses of the human soul and sell a million copies to eager adults.

When late at night they talked, compared writings, shared secrets, Joss could not help probing a little. "How did you get such a peculiar name?"

"It's geographical," Montrose replied. "I think it's a place name. I've no idea where or why they gave it to me.

My mother wasn't around to tell me, and my father did not always seem to know my name anyway. How did you get yours?"

"My father's called Joe. He wanted me called Josephine, but my mother and all her cronies threw a fit, demanding something less old-fashioned. Somebody came up with Jocelyn. My mother liked that because it had a Y in it. Isn't that crazy? Typical though. She's a very vacuous woman. Anyhow, it went from Joe to Jocelyn, then reduced itself to Joss. And there you have it. Joss. That's me!"

In these quiet moments, Joss was pleased to share her life with Montrose.

"Montrose," Joss whispered across the room one late night. "Frank Graham wants me to wear his frat pin. I tried to give it back to him, but he wouldn't let me."

"Do you love him?"

"Not even remotely," Joss answered. "He's a really boring guy. But I like having him for a boyfriend. He's nice to go out with. He's kind to me. He is patient about being physical. Doesn't demand too much in that department. I think I should keep him."

Montrose knew Frank. She liked him. They were in the glee club together. "Is that fair?"

"Well, is it fair of him to want to pin me to something?" objected Joss.

"You realize that wearing his pin implies a promise?"

Joss didn't care for that question. She decided to divert

the subject. "How about you and handsome Harry?" she asked.

"We're good friends."

"Doesn't he ever want more?" Joss probed. "Don't you?"

"Harry is always the perfect gentleman," Montrose declared, which told Joss not much about anything. There followed a long pause in the conversation. Then, in a very small voice, hardly above a whisper, Montrose added, "Harry is kind, he's sensitive, and he is honest with his friends. I just want to be with him."

"How do people fall in love?" Joss asked.

"What?"

"How do people fall in love? Because it isn't a natural state, is it? In the same way that I've always wondered how people manage to fall asleep. I've always wondered about how it could involve such a change of circumstances. There has to be a relaxed area, like a moat between wakefulness and the alteration into a mind when all sense falls away. The mind has to cross over space into the realm of madness that is the dream state of falling in love."

"Don't you want to get married some day?"

"No!" Joss emphatically declared. "I'd be scared to death. Besides, when marriage comes, the movie ends."

"Go to sleep now, Joss," Montrose mumbled.

"Every time I go down this corridor, I pass your room, and I usually see you scribbling in that ratty notebook," the girl said. She was Sarah Petrucci, called Sally, an occupant of Harmon House and a member of Joss's writing class. Joss, visible from the doorway, was writing in a common black-and-white speckled school notebook. "Are you working on a dissertation? Must be a long one. I see you writing all the time."

Joss laughed. "Just words," she replied.

"Like a few thousand," Sally said. She was hanging in the frame of the door as if looking for conversation.

"It's not a dissertation, but it is a compendium. Come on in, Sal. I'll tell you all about it."

Sally slouched in and flopped into Montrose's desk chair. "'Compendium?'" she parroted. "Oh, Joss, you and your ten-dollar words. What the hell is a compendium?"

"Well, if I've got it right, and, as you know, I frequently don't, it's a collection. In this case, a collection of words. I collect words," Joss explained. She motioned toward the high shelf above the desk. It was full of black-and-white speckled notebooks.

"Holy Hortense!" Sally looked up. "All full of words?"

"Yeah, all full. They're all part of the *Codex*. Probably a few hundred thousand words," Joss acknowledged.

"No wonder you can bring those wonderful *baroque* compositions into class."

Joss jerked back visibly. "Sarah Petrucci, you write in

short, aimed sentences. Your writing is like bullet shots at a target range. You are measured and spare in your direction. I really admire your style. It's up to date and contemporary. It's terrific. Very modern. But my approach is different. I try to capture a certain reality or set of circumstances by encircling the truth with the tools I know, and that, girl, is words ... And my writing is *not baroque!*" Joss concluded. She tapped out a cigarette from a pack and lit up.

Sally lowered her gaze.

Joss passed the pack over. Sally took a cig. "Joss," she said, "I love your stuff. It wasn't me that hung that baroque label on it. I don't even know what baroque means. It was Abbot. He's the one that called it 'arty farty.' Abbot Parish started that word and kept it going because everyone laughed. Even Mr. Resnick smiled."

"Abbot Parish," Joss scoffed. "He's a worm."

"Detestable worm," agreed Sally, now puffing hard. A little nicotine halo formed itself above her nodding head. "He wants to write pornography but realizes he just doesn't *know* enough yet." Both girls laughed.

"He's not going to pick up any significant paragraphs from me!" Joss declared.

"Nor from me," agreed Sally. "Tell me more about this word collection approach, Joss. I've always admired the terrific vocabulary you bring into your stories."

"Perhaps it was misleading to say the notebooks are full of words. Of course, I do collect words, but the books are full of phrases that may or may not contain special words. I try to get together just the right units of language to capture a feeling, a situation, or even a mood. I've been doing it for years," Joss explained. "There's a lot of personal satisfaction in getting something right. It's a catharsis. A well-spaced sentence or paragraph can even *look* like a work of art. And there is surely musical cadence in words. They may ripple like songs. They can even rise and fall symphonically, rise in crescendo, then crash into a dramatic conclusion."

"Voila! Poetry!" exclaimed Sally.

"Exactly." Joss laughed.

"Wow! How great!" Sally said. "Maybe it's a habit I should develop too. I like it when you tell me my writing reminds you of firing bullets, but surely there are times when one needs to be more subtle.

"All those books," she added, waving toward the shelves above Joss's head, "all filed with words."

"Yes," Joss asserted. "Every one of them. It's the *Codex.*"

"Do you let people read your stuff? May I read some?" Sally added.

"It's not modesty, Sal, I swear it, but the handwriting on some of this stuff is so atrocious you would never be able to decipher most of them. My professors all objected. You know I'm just now learning to type. They're all scrawled. I write them on the go, sometimes while walking, or eating, or talking. I write them in bed. I have to scrawl fast because they're so evanescent."

"Joss!" Sally exclaimed.

Joss laughed. "Okay," she said, "I mean they are so slight they may vanish in an instant if not caught on the fly. Sometimes I'll wake in the night and scrawl something, and later in the morning I have no idea of what is on the page. But really, I am not at all shy about these gems. Some are great. Others stink. I would not mind you reading them, but they can be more illegible than the hieroglyphics. If you like, I would happily read you some."

"Shoot!" Sally exclaimed. She leaned back in the chair and puffed away contentedly.

"Mine won't be bullets!" Joss warned with a smile.

"Whatever they be ... let's hear some," Sally said cheerfully.

"Okay. But be warned. Some are just fragments of an idea or a capricious thought. I'm always searching to make things better, to sharpen a concept. Here's one." Joss began:

"One night, not once upon a time but recently, you had a load of sorrow to unburden. You had to get drunk to do it. I kept very quiet. I hardly understood a word you said, but I made sounds that seemed sympathetic. 'Uh huh,' I said, and, 'Mmmm. Yeah.'"

Sally laughed. "Oh, that's great!" she exclaimed. "Is that true? Did that really happen?"

"Everything *sort of* really happened and yet didn't. Listen. I'm going to fill your ear.

"People have died to whom I hadn't finished speaking. The last word had not yet been spoken."

"That's good, but I didn't hear any especially big words."

"Oh, come on, Sal. Big words are not the complete object of these exercises. The *right* words are. The right words are liberating."

"Okay," Sally agreed. "I get it. Read me some more."

"If Jonathan, when he was young, could have seen an image of what he looks like now, he'd stagger in consternation. But since he grew up inside that face, I'll bet he thinks he's handsome."

Sally giggled. "I think I've met him," she said.

"Here's another, maybe more to your taste:

"Mrs. Neodakis raised her misty blue eyes to behold her image in the mirror. 'Why you've made me disappear!' she cried to Henri, who stood observing his handiwork smugly. He had created a casque of golden curls that overtopped her little cranium and framed her face in a frenzied sea of agitated waves. Mrs. Neodakis felt she was small enough without this coif to diminish her so aggressively. She was tempted to shout out at him, 'Hank, you stinking fairy. Stop looking so goddamned smug!'"

Sally laughed long and hard. "Oh, write that one up, Joss. That will make a terrific story!"

"I'd rather not," Joss said. "Sounds too much like autobiography. Except for the cascade of golden curls, that is."

"Read me some more," said Sally.

"Gladly," Joss agreed. "Here goes.

"She's still up there playing the coquette, and her old face hurts so much from smiling, smiling, and smiling. She is smiling so hard that rage is beginning to seep into the interstices of her mind. And the features of her face kept reassembling themselves.

"Here are some shorties," Joss said. "'A bottle,' I kept muttering. 'A bottle.' Because I knew he'd popped his cork and let the genie out.

"Here are some one-line jabs," Joss continued.

"Trees like amputees ...

"An unforgiving, everlasting itch ...

"Eyes, shiny green like a beetle's back ...

"The inimical yard ..."

"What does that mean? The inimical yard? Explain that one," Sally demanded.

"I can't," Joss admitted. "They are just germs. Gems or germs of ideas. I've used a few of them for writing class, fit them into short stories."

"Well, I love your short stories, whether I understand them or not," Sally declared. "I want to hear more of your paragraphs and germs. But I have a class. I'll be back when we can have more time for it," Sally said as she rose and moved toward the door.

"You'll be welcome, Sal, whenever you come by. And you'll usually find me right here searching for the felicitous word."

Day gone walk close night on, night over, and sky. The sky like surf and swept in tides. Churn and foam over. Each figure fought the wind, but over, the sky excelled in battle, and beauty was carved into the remembrance of all those aged walkers.

"Faces, then, one must capture, in the instant, the angle of the planes. Oh, life, what a blasphemy, and all the faces keep returning.

"In light that buzzed like an injured bee, wounded, rendered to menace while yet with an absence of threat, I gazed on something green, something black-striped like the skin of a watermelon. What crazy thing is this that keeps imposing its superiority on reality?

"Oh, crud, down I cast my sword. What sparkled with brilliance seemed so adamantine, now lay like curdled milk. You. Yield. You're neither with your sword nor on it. Oh, crud. The pinnacle of manifold adventure is no higher than the rump of a fallen runner, and /whoopeeing down on it/ the valleys get deeper and deeper. You are reduced to human concourse."

—From the *Codex* by Joss Nye

As Joss read aloud, Mr. Alan Resnick sat with his elbows planted on his desk, resting his chin on one hand.

"Eyes that grasp at city vision: they go bad. One sees nothing while one sees. That girl (it was easy to miss her) stared through lenses as confused as swirling water. She was Emily Cappo. Her eyes too much exaggerated in her head's mild firmament."

Joss paused to look at him. Resnick was not her teacher in the new writing courses she was taking, but he had agreed to listen to her most recent work. Now he angled his head to return her gaze. She saw him scribble something and stopped reading.

"Go on, fire away," he said impatiently.

Joss smiled and rustled the sheaf of papers. "But her head hurt," she read. "Another headache besieged her. She bore it down into the subway while it shot out a new root that found, unfairly, its foothold in a brain still vague with the last night's dreams. It was early. Cappo had not yet begun to think, so thought could set up no barrier against the pain.

"To awaken this way, coming conscious with the motion of the train, each jar rolling her into contact with the common humanity, was a shock. She jumped into wakefulness only to recognize pain as pain. Oh, it hurt. Another headache.

"Every day another. She had blamed them on the queer, blaring lights of the under-passages she had to tread.

Then she had her glasses tinted. Nothing helped. Nothing mattered. Headache followed headache, carrying, each, a sharp little message of fallibility so they seemed to kill her mind off piecemeal. Subdivisions of this daily death opened a space where fear might enter and make itself a part of her. Or was it the fear that generated the headache?

"Such a question winds in upon itself like the mathematical symbol for infinity."

"Math, Joss?" asked Mr. Resnick. "You're into math now?"

"Just listen, Mr. R," she demanded. "Patience," she said, and pulled the manuscript higher to her face.

"Too early in the day to play with limitless possibilities, so Cappo, instead, allowed herself to stare at things that quickly sharpened her discomfort.

"Hanging on straps beside her swayed a man. His lips splattered out raw as butchered meat while he peered down his great horn nose, his head back tilted to scan the headlines of his screaming daily. Cruel, hyper sensuous lips, their corners bleeding down, hinting at animal evil. Cappo found danger in the mere sight of him. Yet he flowed with the same motion of the train as she did. That proximity of their flesh depressed her.

"She half-turned to afford her eyes new vistas. Humanoids there. Passengers. Nearby stood a beast without his tail—bull-made-man whose fresh-scraped jaw seemed about to bristle out before her very eyes. A stud he was, domesticated, only enrage him not. Look only with what superiority he snorted. He had a seat and fancied that she coveted it. In a spasm of her imagination, she saw a great gold ring pinned through his thick nose, and thus she regained her own ascendancy. He too bent with the motion of the train just as she did."

Alan Resnick chose that moment to shift his eyes downward. Joss sat upright and glared, fearful that he had stopped listening.

"And there was a woman seated beside him," Joss resumed. "The woman tottered senselessly as she indulged the pseudo-sleep of subway trains. Unguarded muscles, nerves gone slack, displayed the flaccid swell of her dark skin where her eyes pulsed behind small, swarthy marshmallows of flesh. Oh, a beauty. She had doctored her slack lips with fuchsia paint. A paint, too opaque, betrayed the line of the actual lip. She had painted this lurid line over the skin to create her masterpiece—an idiotic expression of disdain. Nodding in her almost-dream, she became the inspiration of a new throb in Emily's head. Those lips. They cloyed to nausea. Wet as the memory of an unwelcome kiss. Emily forced away her pained attention."

"Ugh," declared Mr. Resnick.

"The next stop admitted to their community a woman without a chin. Her face, foreshortened, appeared fat. Cheeks bloated with resentment. Where chin should be she sported a cavity depressing her face to the throat.

What super punch of fate had rammed the jawbone back into the skull? There she stood with her upper teeth exposed as they tripped, each one over its neighbor, long and misshapen off the edge of her lip. A shade of yellow ivory, rare, or of some less rare morsel of a bad breakfast."

Resnick sat up straight. "Joss, for Pete's sake. What's the matter with you today? This doesn't sound like your writing. Or rather, it does sound like your writing, but it sounds like your prose with indigestion."

"You could be more specific," Joss complained. She felt wounded. She hated to be criticized even though she did recognize the need for it.

"So could you," he commented.

Annoyed, Joss returned to reading her pages. "Casting her eyes anew, fishing for relief, she found, directly across, a face of complete reason. Dim and composed, it was a face impervious to its mean surroundings. A wonderful countenance, a girl whose high and smooth forehead, whose features, perfectly aligned, belonged entirely to herself ... an entity drawn apart, all contained in a black coat. They, this paragon and Emily, awarded each other a nod of cool admiration. Yet something was wrong. The girl swam in a fog too dreamlike for the subway. She seemed unreal. Emily smiled. She smiled back. In an instant, the joke was comprehended. Haha. Emily had seen her reflection. Just herself spied on the window that protected them all from the dark tunnel outside.

"Only herself. Emily admired Emily."

"Is Emily nuts?" Resnick asked.

"Isn't everybody?" Joss commented. "Last time I was in the city, Mr. R., a woman who was crossing the street got so mad at the traffic she started beating up on a passing car. I mean, *actually* beating up. Punching. She was attacking the chassis just as if it were a person. Another flaming case of Manhattan madness.

"Now, if you will just stop interrupting with mingy remarks, I will get to the sense of my tale."

"Will you, Joss?" Alan Resnick stood up to say this. "I mean, is there a tale? Have you got a *real* story?

"No," Mr. R. insisted. "Joss, everybody here already knows you have a killer vocabulary. Now I want you to soft pedal it for a while and concentrate on telling a walloping good *story*."

Miffed beyond replying, Joss left the hall and went to the dorm for lunch. Jeannie Irslinger was already there, occupying their usual table. Joss fell upon her with all the anger of her recent rejection. "Well, Resnick *said* he'd help, but he just drags on about the story line of things."

"That's important, isn't it?" Jeannie asked. "Can't you just start a story and *tell* it?"

"Not me. I can't," Joss answered.

"Story is important," Jeannie insisted.

"Sure. Sure, but it's not the *only* thing that's important."

"I know your writing, Joss. Kiddo, you can make a banquet out of a peanut shell."

"Words matter, Jeannie."

"But you writing types think *every* word you pop out is as wonderful as a golden turd just dropping, still warm, from the asshole of the great god Lily."

The slope, the swagger, the arrogance of me, the insolence. I won't admit it. A young man jogs by as if to bump me, and reading *insolence*, I respond insolently, keep walking straight, staring at the level of his head but through it, nothing very pretty in my mind, perhaps changing his mood, which may have been one of innocent flirtation /an insult then!/ into that moment of hostility I really wanted from him.

Joss Nye THE CODEX

In a span of dreary days, a glorious day dawned. It was one of those days when breathing is sweet. One puts aside the ordinary travails of life to admire the air. Even some of the professors were influenced by the suggestion of joy. A few older profs dismissed their classes early. Joss and Montrose, struggling in their separate classes, were among the students benefitted by this largesse. They immediately headed for nature, the Greensward.

The Greensward was the big park between the women's college and the university. It was regarded as a treasure by both student bodies that were, as was well known, the same student body divided by ancient bias. Boys belonged to the university. Girls only attended classes there.

Joss and Montrose went to the Greensward. They brought their unfinished manuscripts with the idea of completing them on the lawns of the park, but for Joss, nothing came. She grew restless. Montrose, sitting firmly on a pillow she had brought, scrawled away at her pad. Montrose sat neat, always prepared for school. Joss mocked her. "You look like little Miss Muffet, sitting on your tuffet," Joss teased. They both laughed. Montrose was the last person in the world to look like little Miss Muffet. She was always so long and composed. Even sitting on a Greensward lawn she looked elegant.

Montrose smiled. "Stop procrastinating, Joss. Sit down and write your heart out," she said.

"I think I'll just take a walk around to see if I can get inspired."

The park looked so wonderful. Students with smiling faces were walking or sitting with their friends. It was a moment of precious illumination. If you couldn't get inspired there, you never would, Joss thought. And, as she thought this, she became aware of a sound. A small but repetitive noise. It was a peeping, as of a bird, but it also was a ragged, liquid sound, like the palpitation of a frightened heart. Joss was drawn, as if pulled on a string, to near the origin of this circumstance.

There was a tiny bird, maybe a fledgling though out of season, and it rested on the palm of a guy's hand. She neared. She looked up. She found herself looking at a quizzical, mocking face that she had never noticed before. He raised his eyebrow. Sunlight glanced off his lips. It was a perfect face. Before she had time to place its identity or think any more about the man, he circled his free arm around her. Then he planted a hard kiss right on Joss's lips.

She stood perfectly still. She couldn't believe it. Her insides were in turmoil. He did not seem the least perturbed. She watched him quickly toss the bird in a nearby bush. "Thanks," he said. "Who are you?"

"J—Joss," she managed to whisper.

"Jazz," he repeated. "I like that. I'm Bobby Ochs." Then he turned around and was gone.

Her insides were in such a snarl she could barely think.

"The nerve!" she finally croaked. "The pure unadulterated nerve!"

As she approached, Montrose started to rise. "Did I just see you kiss that boy?"

"The nerve of that bum!" Joss exclaimed. "I never even saw him before in my life. I don't know who he is. He just grabbed me. Out of a clear blue sky, he grabbed me. He just smacked one on me. I should have slapped his face!"

"You should have," Montrose agreed cheerfully.

"He deserved more. He deserved a hard sock in the jaw!"

"Too late now," Montrose said.

But Joss was not to be placated. She was furious. Other friends were coming up. They too had probably seen the display. She was soon surrounded by a ring of girls. She didn't know all of them, but Mary Ellen Rigg was one. "Joss Nye!" said Mary Ellen in a tone of reprimand. "What were you doing with the Ox?"

"What ox?"

"Bobby Ochs," Mary Ellen explained. "The guys call him the Ox. He's notorious. They say he can drink like an ox and fuck like a rabbit." She was giggling madly, probably proud of having used that forbidden word.

"Oh, noooo!" Joss wailed. She felt abused and humiliated. "That's repulsive! I'd like to kill him! Where is he?"

"He ran for it," Mary Ellen said happily. "Just like in the nursery rhyme, kiddo. Kiss the girls and run away."

What mystery is resolved by loving?

At night, safe from men in the Harmon House, they brought their romantic riddles to one another. Their neighbors had dropped by the room for a smoking break. "How does one start to fall in love?" asked Joss.

"It's just nature," Jeannie pontificated. "We're just built to let it happen." She was sitting at the dresser, waiting for Mary Ellen to put her hair up in giant pink rollers. Mary Ellen was the dorm beauty expert. She had even tried to tame Joss's blonde dishabille but usually had to pronounce it a hopeless undertaking.

"I don't think so," Joss contended. "There must be a weakness, like a moat around your feelings," she insisted. "That's the bridge. And you've got to be receptive to it; only that will make it possible to cross the moat."

"Well, holy Hortense, I'm as receptive as a body can be," said Mary Ellen. "You know that on this campus it is reported that there are three university men to every girl at the college. And here sit I, Mary Ellen Rigg, ready to receive love on all fronts. Yet nothing ever happens to me."

"You're not a bit receptive, Mary Ellen," argued Jeannie. "Take Charlie Linkus. He's always hanging around here with his tongue hanging out, but you don't even want to look at him."

"Oh, Chooky Linkus! He's a fool. You know that idiot likes to tells me really stupid jokes, and then he says, 'Did you *get* it? Did you get it?' The stupidest jokes ever. I heard them all in kindergarten.

"Oh, and he likes to make a voice like Donald Duck when he tells them. He thinks he's hilarious when he does that." With a few rings of smoke, Mary Ellen dismissed Charles. The others laughed. Chooky's obsession for Mary Ellen had been well advertised. He followed her like a sick puppy, and he had the secret of always finding her. The funny thing was that Chooky spotted her, on campus or in the Portal where they gathered for coffee, by following the smoke rings. Mary Ellen was the only girl who could do that, and she unfailingly did it when smoking. Chooky just turned his eyes upward. He knew that under the rings, somewhere sat Mary Ellen Rigg.

"Isn't it true that Charles Linkus has American Indian blood?" Montrose commented, and the three of them laughed, but Mary Ellen only looked confused. She still did not get it.

"What about this guy who grabbed you on the Greensward Saturday, Joss? Are you interested?" asked Jeannie.

Montrose's head came up sharply at the same time as Joss's. "Who the heck was he?" Joss asked.

"You should know, kid. It was Bobby Ochs. He's famous," Mary Ellen replied.

"What for?" Joss wondered.

"The guys call him the Ox," said Mary Ellen. "They say he can drink like an ox and fuck like a bunny."

"You told us that before," Jeannie said, giggling merrily away. Joss could see she was still delighted by the forbidden word.

"That's disgusting," Montrose said.

Mary Ellen was blushing while laughing uproariously. Joss thought she must be especially pleased with herself for having uttered a taboo word. "But who is he? I mean ... who is this Bobby Ochs? How come I've never seen him before? Where does he come from? What does he *do*?" Joss demanded. "How come I've never seen him around the campus?" In her mind's eye, Joss could see him now. At the time of the incident, she had not really looked at him, but now, in retrospect, he appeared very plainly before her. He was a rather short blond boy. His face was broad at the temples, handsome in a tough kind of way. He had a snub nose. There was a lot of power in his face. Actually she thought he looked a little like her father, Joe Nye, but of course in a much younger version.

"Well, he's everywhere," Mary Ellen said. "I don't know why you haven't bumped into him before. He's one of the only guys on campus with a car. He calls it the Joy Jumper or something like that."

"I can imagine why," Montrose interjected.

"Oh, I remember now. It's called the Jitney Jalopp," Mary Ellen explained. "They all say he's a big man on campus."

"A big baloney on campus, I think," Joss said raggedly. She was warm. She was beginning to feel the fluster and embarrassment she had felt at that explosive moment Saturday on the Greensward. "The Ox indeed. Bobby Ochs. I should have slapped him across the face. Hard. Bobby Ochs just took me by surprise. Who was Bobby Ochs to dare to do a thing like that, without permission, in front of God and everybody?"

"I dunno," Jeannie Interrupted. "Grab a kiss, like that? I think I might have liked it."

"Liked it!" shouted Joss. She was indignant, irate both with Bobby Ochs and with Mary Ellen and Jeannie. With everyone, as a matter of fact. "Bobby Ochs had the colossal nerve ... the unmitigated gall ... Ask me what it feels like to be manhandled in the park in front of God and the whole student body of both the college and the university."

"Probably God was watching," Mary Ellen teased, "but there simply wasn't room enough for the whole student body."

"Damn Bobby Ochs!" That was about as strong language as Joss ever used. "Bobby Ochs drinks like an ox and ... and looks like a jackass."

"No," said Jeannie "He's short, but actually kind of good-looking."

"No, he is not! Bobby Ochs is just a sorry-looking example of the most conceited, full-of-baloney, obnoxious boy in the world." She felt her argument growing weaker, but she continued to argue for some time further. "He's even cruel—holding the bird that way.

"What did he do with that bird?" she asked.

"He threw it into the bush near you when he walked away."

"He just left it? See that? Bobby Ochs should not have just dropped the bird. I think he's is cruel and unkind as well as stupid."

"I don't think he hurt it," defended Mary Ellen.

"It was a damn stupid thing to do in every way," insisted Joss Nye, and the argument between herself and her friends raged on for quite a while. At the end of the controversy, when Jeannie and Mary Ellen had returned to their own room, Montrose commented, "That was a long disagreement."

"I was too upset to argue," Joss said.

"Well it didn't seem to stop you. Are you aware of how many times you pronounced that name?"

"What name?"

"Bobby Ochs," Montrose replied.

"His hair was white," Joss began. She was reading to Alan Resnick from a messy sheaf of crumpled papers. As she read, she attempted to iron them out against the table with her fingers. Mr. Resnick held the stub of a pencil Joss had discarded on the tabletop.

"Beautifully, flourishingly, white haired," she read, "like an amiable grandpa in a family story. He was rising to leave when Hope jumped in front to block him. One could see by her silly grin that she found him very attractive.

"He was moving to leave, so he turned. It was at that moment that she first saw his face. He saw her too, now slumped in that strange, destroyed posture she sometimes affected, as if swooning against the doorframe. He stiffened. He remained very still. Then Hope, funny, cat-faced Hope, ignorant of everything, backed off and chirped, 'Why, see, here she is now!'

"For the first time, Emily really saw him."

"Emily again!" complained Mr. Resnick. "I hope you're at least going to keep a leash on her. Maybe even a muzzle. Don't let her run out of control."

Joss gave a little snort but returned to the reading. "Emily saw him," she read. "She could not pretend otherwise, nor would she. For the first time, she'd truly seen *him*, not just a spirit or his doppelganger.

"She noted well his handsome, healthy face. It was almost a rosy face. He sported a trim, white moustache.

He was fine. He groomed himself. He had a straight and noble nose, a mouth surprisingly pink and sensuous, and a small chin. It was a face all telescoped onto its upper stories. The vast forehead of a thinking man.

"He stood no taller than Emily herself, but he carried himself with hauteur. He had charm and an obviously considered bearing. And his eyes! If she came closer, she knew they would be startlingly blue, electric blue and astonishingly hypnotic. Reflecting Amelia and Amelia. The apple of his two bright blue eyes.

"Though she had never seen him before, she knew immediately who he was."

Joss glanced up inquiringly. She wondered at Mr. Resnick's pained expression. He was tapping her stubby pencil on the table. Not a good sign. Joss thought. They were sitting at a table in Dwight Hall, both hunched over whatever sheet of paper Joss managed to extract from the jumble she was holding. "Well? What's wrong?" she demanded.

"Nothing's wrong," he replied. "But you're flirting with a lot of possible disasters. Look at these words ..." With the pencil stub, Resnick pointed to *doppelganger, hauteur!*

"I'm not even sure how to pronounce those, Joss. Why do you insist on putting such a strain on your reader? Most normal readers would be looking at the trash basket about now. Surely you of all people have enough words to say whatever you mean in plain American English!"

Joss reached across and tugged the little pencil out of Mr. Resnick's hands. "Okay. Okay," she said. "I have the wand now. I'm in command. Of course, I can rewrite and tone down the words ad infinitum—"

"There you go again," he interrupted. "You have no shame about dragging out Latin, Greek, even Esperanto if the whim should strike you. What are you trying to do, kill your reader on the sword of your erudition?"

Joss glared at Alan Resnick. He was just a stunted little guy with those beer-bottle glasses he had to wear. Gnomic. There was a good word for him—gnomic. Perhaps he needed to be told that. Take the wind out of his sails. He was just a weed, a little guy with his hair starting to go thin right over his pate. Yet he took this special time over his former students. Why? People had wondered about possible ulterior motives. There were times Joss just hated him, like right now, when she uneasily suspected he might be right.

"Mr. Resnick, do you know Jeannie Irslinger?" Joss asked him, suddenly overwhelmed by her own contrary nature.

"Who doesn't?" Resnick responded.

"Last time I showed her one of my stories, she said my words were golden," Joss said.

"You don't say?" remarked Mr. R.

"Well," Joss muttered sheepishly, "what she actually said was that my words were like golden turds."

Alan Resnick tipped so far back in his rickety school chair that Joss feared he might crash down on his poor balding crown. He began laughing and so long, so hard that, as he straightened up again, he had trouble finding his voice. "Great!" he gasped. "Keep that girl! You need friends like that, Joss. Friends that will keep your ego from floating you up above the chimney pots. Jeannie tells it like someone who might someday read your books."

Sufficiently mollified, Joss settled down and put down the stub. She really valued what Mr. Resnick had to tell her. He had been advising her since her very first writing classes at the university. She knew he thought she was worth working with. She crumpled all the papers she was holding and tossed the balled lump into the far wastebasket. "Do you really think it's hopeless?"

"Good shot," said Alan Resnick. "No, Joss. Not hopeless. It's just that I don't see what you're getting at, and I don't think you know either. Why has Emily Cappo turned into Amelia all of a sudden? You've introduced two new characters, a white-haired man and Hope. Who are they?"

"The white-haired man may be Emily's father, whom she has never actually met before. Hope is some kind of cousin or something. I haven't quite figured that out yet. I didn't want to really get her into the scene when Emily and the man begin talking because I am not sure how to write dialogue when there are more than two characters conversing. I get fouled up."

"With good reason, I assure you.

"Here is what I want you to do, Joss. Write up a statement of what you expect to achieve with this piece of writing—whether it's to be a short story or a novel. You know, like the idea behind it, the theme if you please. Then you write an outline of what *happens* in the story. A plot outline is what you should be trying to pull together. It will make it much easier to proceed that way. This shotgun method that you usually want to work with has got to stop. Nothing is more devastating than you shooting random golden ... ahem ... *words* all over the place."

The Varsity Players were going to do musical selections from *Carousel*. Joss was excited. She had seen the Broadway production with Kitty a few seasons before. After the tryouts, Montrose was selected to play the lead role of Julie Jordan. It was posted in University Hall. To Joss's astonishment, Alan Resnick was listed for the part of Billy Bigelow. Joss was astonished. *My Mr. Resnick?* she wondered.

"Alan has a beautiful voice," Montrose answered. "He's the mainstay of the Glee Club. You should have heard him at the auditions. He's a good actor, too."

"Well, I'll be my uncle's donkey," Joss remarked.

"That's not all," Montrose asserted. "There are more of your friends in this pastiche. Frank Graham's playing Mr. Snow, and we have Weezy Danton to play Carrie. She's from Harmon House too."

"Maybe we ought to call it Harmony House," Joss said.

"Some people do."

Joss was simply astonished. It brought to mind her story of *what goes on behind walls*, tales both near and yet unknown. She could only see Mr. Resnick as her teacher, though he had been an especially interested one, almost a friend. She had formed the habit of stopping by his office to show him her work. He was always thoughtful in his critique. He thought she was a good writer and told her so often enough to please her ego. He told her that before becoming an instructor at the university, he had a job as a reader for the prestigious publishing company of Goldschneider & Moran. It was he who told her about the G&M program for encouraging new writers. Each year they offered an award for a new novel by the most talented young writer, he said. It was established in honor of one of their most venerated editors, now defunct. The Smithson M. Walker Memorial Trust paid a small stipend. The important thing was that at the completion of the novel there was the possibility that publication might be picked up under the very esteemed aegis of G&M.

"Oh, yes," Montrose assured her again. "Alan has a beautiful voice. And he's a good actor too. I am privileged to play with him. Even though he is faculty, he's the pillar of our Glee Club. He can do any male parts."

"I never dreamed that he could play the hero in a musical!" Joss exclaimed.

"You know what else may surprise you? Frank Graham tried out and got the part of Mr. Snow. Weezy Danton is in it too. She's in Harmon House like us."

"I know," Joss said.

Now that three and a half friends-of-hers were rehearsing, Joss spent an afternoon or two at University House watching them practice. Weezy Danton counted for the half friend. Joss barely knew her.

She was amazed at the virility of Mr. Resnick's rendition of "My Boy Bill," and Montrose singing "If I Loved

You" actually brought tears to Joss's eyes. But, of course, she already knew that, among her many attributes, Montrose had the voice of an angel. Frank acquitted himself with honor. He had a staccato style of singing as if speaking. It wasn't really lyrical, but it was rhythmical, and it worked.

Weezy Danton was another thing. Joss once watched her through the window of the exercise room. She walked with crooked arms and fists forward, a muscular Germanic walk like Nazi maidens in the movies. She had a chiseled profile, stern glasses, short, dark blonde hair, and a no-nonsense air like one of those Nazi *uber-madchens* in the old wartime propaganda films. She strode around the gym as if looking for men to castrate or young women to violate. And the way she sang distressed Joss. Of course, she must have had a voice. She had passed the auditions. But she had a way of starting in the upper reaches without words, intoning something, like religious chants. Then she would begin flinging notes higher and higher. Like ghostly images, they'd hang up there for a moment after she threw them. It was terrible to Joss. That beautiful voice squeezed out and up so mercilessly, like the cry of someone hurt or just on the verge of killing, or on a cliff about to jump, or fame, or life.

Jeannie Irslinger had tried out for that role, and Jeannie was not a good loser. She started calling Weezy Danton "Weasel Wanton," though her actual name was Louise.

Joss scolded Jean. "It's so childish, Jeannie. Like what little kids do, distorting one another's name just to discredit them."

Jeannie returned a strange look. "I hate her. I'll tell you there's something weird about her. She's a stinking dyke bitch." Jeannie shuddered. "I think she's tried to put the make on me," she whispered.

"What do you mean?

It had to be explained, and Joss was shocked at both the language and the explanation. It was something completely outside her range of experience. Bad language was not the norm at Harmon House. Girls avoided it with the knowledge that bad words often became habitual: this was clearly happening in Jeannie Irslinger's case. She was becoming a fountain of prohibited vocabulary. The taboo words could pop out the most solemn moments. Shocked as Joss was at the language, she was even more distressed by the rest of the answer.

"You should just stay away from Jeannie," Montrose advised when consulted. Joss, however, was part of the production now. Though she had not tried out at all, she just yearned to be a part of it. She secured a job as part of the crew. She would be listed in the program as "Joss Nye, Costumes." That meant that she wore a long necklace of safety pins and was called "Pins!" whenever there was a hanging hem or a split seam. It also meant long hours of attendance. She was happy to be a part of it.

Backstage at the old theater brought other disturbing thoughts. Late in the night, after an afternoon of watching, Joss wrote:

"You forget some things, details about the ambience. That too-human smell in the backstage of the little theater, for example. The actors go there every afternoon and many a night, and they have to wear the same tired costumes provided by the Drama Department. There is no time to clean them. No telling who wore them before. There might be pediculi, lice, impetigo, scabies still lurking in the gussets. In the half light of backstage, there is little chance for examination, but grease paint has a smell, and there probably still is some smeared into the collars and seams of the clothing provided. The actors have to smell each other. Perhaps the smell is clear enough to differentiate one person from another. As dogs do. Even sadder to smell oneself while waiting out there for one's next cue. Some of the young extras, with their usual boyish impatience, cannot wait, and they'll be swatting each other with the sleeves of their stinking costumes. Well, they have to do something. They are just kids with an eternity to wait before their moment to go out and hold a candle or hum a bar."

They gave three performances. The night of the final performance, the players were all in a state of exhilaration, except for Montrose. They were celebrating what they thought had been an excellent repertory. "A dry party," Frank complained, but he saved the occasion. He had secretly brought in hooch for the group. The guys always managed to find some firewater. Hal Merriam, Jeannie's on-and-off fiancé, brought some too. Irslinger elbowed up for a share even though she was neither a member of the cast nor welcome there.

Montrose remained gloomy throughout the whole bash. She remained, as always, a mysterious person.

Later on in the room, Joss asked, "Why aren't you ecstatic like the others?"

"I was bad. I don't know enough about music. I think I need to change to a music major. The play was so tacky," Montrose replied. "It was so amateurish."

"No," argued Joss. "It was wonderful. The social reporter from the *Eagle* was there. She applauded her head off." But Montrose, unfathomable as usual, wasn't to be comforted.

Later Joss wrote in her book: "It was as if, in attempting the play, M. had exposed inadequacies in herself that compromised her future."

Jeannie had been behaving terribly since rehearsals for the Varsity Show began. Mary Ellen told Joss that she was actually worried. She knew that Jeannie fancied herself as an almost professional actress and had set her heart on participating in the Varsity Show. Since the cast for the *Carousel* parts had been posted, Jeannie had gone wild. If she was unpleasant to Montrose, she was even more wicked to Weezy Danton, who had nailed the coveted role of Carrie Pipperidge. "She's just damn jealous!" Mary Ellen said. "What the heck, Joss. She just was not at her best at those auditions, that's all. Kiddo, she hasn't got the range to sing that role."

In a new, shaky voice, Mary Ellen continued, "Somebody has been going into Weezy's room." Joss saw that Mary Ellen was sincerely concerned. She and Jeannie had been friends since childhood. "Stuff's been disturbed. Cosmetics moved around. Clothes in the closet tossed on the floor. Assignments have disappeared. Weezy even called the housemother on it. Nothing was taken. That action had *spite* written all over it. Mrs. Emry thought it must be the maid. They fired the maid and still ..." She slanted her eyes at Joss as a sign of collusion even though Montrose, in the room, could hear every hushed word anyway. "Do you think she could be doing it, Joss?"

"That would be too crazy," Joss said by way of reply. It was an answer that did not answer anything. Clearly

Mary Ellen was not satisfied with it. "There's more," she added ominously.

Joss nodded.

"She's drinking like a sailor."

"Weezy?"

"No. Jeannie."

"I keep telling you to watch it, Joss," Montrose interrupted sharply. "I know you and Frank Graham join her in drinking her smuggled alcohol."

Mary Ellen started. She had forgotten Montrose was in the room.

Alcohol in any form was strictly forbidden in all the women's dorms, but everywhere else it was plentiful. All the girls went to parties at the fraternity houses, and there liquor ran like the Narragansett River in flood. Frank Graham was very dependent on his firewater. He always invited Joss to join him. Frank often drank until his speech was thick and he found himself stumbling. Everyone thought it was funny. Joss laughed with everybody else at the whole sorry spectacle.

Mary Ellen left. After about ten minutes, she returned. "Joss, can you come to my room a minute? I have something I want to show you."

Puzzled, Joss followed. Montrose stayed at her desk.

"I could say more, and there is more, kid, and it's worse than alcohol," Mary Ellen said in the quietest voice she'd ever used. "She's been cutting."

"What do you mean? Cutting? Cutting what? Classes?"

"No. Not classes, Silly. *Cutting*," Mary Ellen said with unmistakable emphasis on the one word.

Joss was baffled.

Mary Ellen pulled up Jeannie's laundry bag and extracted a T-shirt. "Notice all the turtlenecks she's using lately?" Mary Ellen spread out the fabric of the collar with her fingers. Joss looked aghast at the dark splashes of dried blood blooming over it.

"*Cutting*," Mary Ellen repeated gravely.

Joss was feeling grumpy. After staying up half the night to complete her latest short story, *Everybody Has to Eat*, it had disappointed the class. "All words and no story," Abbott Parish announced. Abbott was quick with his critique of her, probably because she shunned his amorous advances, but Maddy Traywick, with no such reason, had the temerity to pronounce the story, "Stupid." Just plain mean, Joss thought. And Miss Alwyn, the instructor, had done nothing to restore civility to the class. Because, Joss knew, she agreed with the general opinion. Joss even agreed with it a little bit herself.

She was already mad when the inevitable happened.

She turned a corner in dusty old Dwight Hall and came face to face with him.

Bobby Ochs!

She was already boiling. Now she felt new anger rise up red inside her.

"Jazz!" he said. "I've been looking everywhere for you."

It was just too much. When she tried to speak, only spurts of her anger came forth. No words. God knows she was full of words, some of them very bad. But ladies didn't used to talk that way. For more than a week, she had been practicing what to say should this meeting ever occur. Muttering to herself in the bathroom, she had unearthed some old and powerful imprecations. He deserved a rounded reprimand for making a fool of her. And now he was doing it again.

"I think I need to apologize, Jazz," he said.

She was not even seeing straight. Was that smile one of apology or derision?

Apology? Apology!

"Yeah. I know it was really bad of me. But I need to explain to you. Hal Merriam and Danny Flax, they're always needling me. They said I was chicken, and they dared me to walk right out and kiss a girl. It was a real challenge. I spotted you over by the bush where the girls were. You were the prettiest girl around, so I went over to get rid of the bird, and I grabbed you. It was really a bad thing to do. I'm sorry."

"The bird?" she gasped.

"It was a toy bird," Bobby said. "One of those Tweetie things. Danny shoved it at me, handed it to me just as I was going. I've really needed to tell you how sorry I am." He smiled again, and now she could see it was a real smile. It was even a nice smile. "I'm really sorry, Jazz."

"It's Joss," she managed to say. Well, what could she say as the fires of indignation mounted within her, transmuting themselves to something totally unexpected? Her heart was pounding like an overcharged engine. Maybe this wild pulse was a heart attack. Floods of heat were permeating the chambers of her heart, and then she knew, then she realized that without the need of any margin, without crossing a moat of any kind, she was there.

Joss was in love.

Secret ... sweet jewels ...
Stones ...
Pains of a quiet cache,
In the place where jewels are stashed
Against piracy;
Against the eye of day
That comes to polish
Treasures not its own.
Night´s wealth,
a clutch of rubies
swathed in dark velvet."

—From the *Codex* by Joss

With Bobby in time suspended, they watched a furred bumblebee, which had found the honeysuckle and stumbled there—maddened with joy, staggering and tumbling its jolly, unlikely body from bloom to intoxicating bloom. The sin of gluttony filled the gaudy little bee and drove it to mania.

As if the air rang, the silence shouted, joy so encompassing it could not endure beyond the next to last echo of its penultimate cry.

—The *Codex* by Joss Nye

In summer when the spring storms were over, rain had inspired the rose bushes into profusions of scarlet, salmon, white. Outside the window were riches in the Greensward gardens. Joss wanted to collect armfuls of lush blossoms, even if gashing herself on the hidden thorns that lurked amidst such loveliness.

Then she considered the pansies, less violent, valuing each precious face, hooded in dark, moist velvet-mauve, grape, or the velvet brown of Montrose's eyes.

She jumped over the puddles. With each jump, her heart leaped. She was celebrating a part of her soul that was intoxicated by love. She jumped too high. Her words gushed out too fast. They probably made no sense. She laughed erratically and too often. Love was a form of insanity. Love was the chatter of catching up and the noise of words, scuffling, exaggerating things, and laughing. And then it was quiet, watching. Love poured into her eyes and filled her. Watching him, his perpetual forward surge, interpreting his actions. Seeing him merely glance at a beggar, she thought she saw a part of him that could go soft with compassion, and she swelled with love for his humanity.

—Joss Nye's *Codex*

Studying together. Watching him across the broad tables at the Breslau, his face so intent on his book as if he might devour it. She knew he must have been grasping ideas, concepts beyond her comprehension. He was so smart, much more clever than she.

Whenever his face came close, she was watching him watching her. She saw her raggedy blonde image twice reflected in the black core of his blue eyes. She saw love there. She had somehow bridged the gap into love.

There was no longer room for disputing within her. She felt herself to be totally committed. And this all happened in a moment of inattention. That old joke of her mother's took on new meaning. She herself was the result of a moment of inattention, and he happened to her the same way. This coincidence, like so many others these days, like the way their fingers fit together, or the laughter that escaped from their lips at the exact same second, struck her as a sort of miracle. But she was not being rational. She knew that. Love was a pathological variation that imposed itself upon the mind.

It was in his eyes. They inspired her to love. A power flowed between them by rays of his eyes. But she could not touch him tenderly as she longed to. He hated to be touched unless he himself initiated the touching. So she waited.

The concentration of his eyes on her eyes. His look gliding boldly to her lips. This brought forth passions from so deep within that she became a different person, a stranger, someone of whom she had reason to be frightened. She was afraid, again, when she saw the love in his eyes deepening into desire, though, eventually, it did. And only then, when he was completely engrossed in desiring her, did she feel the full force of his attention.

—From the *Codex* by Joss

She searched the edges of things. In the meadow, apart, cresting a ridge, a stand of trees stood like a troop of old men, like clerics in an ecclesiastical conversation. Serious old codgers. The suggestion of a breeze swayed them. Before her, in full front face, Bobby sat on his crossed legs, as usual poised to leap. He joyfully gnawed a joint, dripping. Green hedgerows before the green bushes before a majestic line of trees framed the landscape.

Bobby in the plainest view, yet in the periphery of an eye filled to overflowing with distant things—horizons beyond reach—far vistas and details of strange vines with waxy blue-green leaves that sidled out of the woods to thrust out clumps of bulbous berries filled to bursting with tiny scarlet seeds, so pretty they must be poisonous. If she turned to examine the vines, her eye's edge picked up the previous combinations of things but in another position.

Codex +

It must be a picnic, for there upon the feathery green of the field a swatch of paled woven straw was Montrose's favorite Hong Kong hamper, borrowed for the day. And, dipping down into it for plunder, Bobby swam into the center of vision. Grease anointed his chin. He shone with ventral lust. Big square teeth cracked the bones for their marrow. She caught her breath with a thrill of delight. *He's not kidding,* she thought. So serious was his gusto. So beautiful that her eye had to return to center him. Frame him forever in this set of skies, bushes, vistas, and scarlet berries. Her eye, having taken a measure of everything for this purpose: to hold him there, like the excellent subject of a lusty painting.

"Bobby devoured the meat. Stripped the bone. He laughed."

—*Codex* by Jocelyn Nye

In a shanty filled with the sour smell of mice, a gypsy in a housedress told their fortunes. Amalia Eugenie, she said her name was, after some royal beauty in the days of empire, though this one was slovenly, her eyes were encrusted, her fingers swollen. She refused to tell their fortunes jointly, as though their fortunes weren't linked. Joss felt slightly annoyed even though she knew such things as fortune-telling were no more than superstitious sops for the weak of mind. It didn't matter.

Uncomfortably fat, the woman looked like a giant bolster. She couldn't properly bring her knees together. She sat obscenely agape. She called Joss "dearie" in a kind of nasal drone. Her face slipped off on either side into wattles of thick, superfluous flesh. In her mottled paw, she cupped Joss's palm and out of these layered hands purported to pluck a star of fame. "Looka that, dearie. People are gonna hear about you. People you never even heard of. See the way those lines cross? We call that the X of success. You're gonna be a star or something. I see paper. Like newspaper. Maybe you're gonna be in the newspapers."

Books? she wondered and was ashamed of herself for wondering anything over this pile of unadulterated crap. But could it be books? People someday reading books she had written? Reaching out to other minds with her thoughts? Joss wiggled uneasily in her chair.

There was no invisible way of truth. Of course, she

knew that. This was just a fat slattern in a lean-to hitched to the side of a broken-down trailer where mice lurched across the floor and soiled the corners with their pellets.

The woman misinterpreted her discomfort. "Oh, don't worry, dearie. No bad stuff. Y'unnerstan'? You're gonna get in the papers for somethin' good. You're gonna be famous. Maybe not rich. I don't see much here about money."

It made Joss nervous. She suppressed a giggle.

Eye of newt. Horn of unicorn. In the corner of the mousey den, a corpse of petrified basilisk: you could only get one of those by showing a basilisk its own image in a mirror. Or trash. The gypsy swooped down into her palm again. Her wattles hung. She frowned and squinted. "Love ... mmm. All mixed up."

The mention of love caused Joss to throw at Bobby a look of phony amusement, a sort of smirk.

Amalia Eugenie snapped her head up abruptly. "You don't believe me? I know you college kids. You think you know God-all. What I'm doing here is a science, see? Not just anybody can do this. Look. See this line?" She stabbed out a fat little finger and tapped it angrily on Joss's palm. Intimidated, Joss nodded quickly. "That's your line of fortune. You got a strong one too, dearie. See? This other line over here, that's the line of life and crosses over, one over the other. Makes the X. You see it?" She did. "You don't hardly get many with that. That's special. You're marked. You're marked from before you are born, even. But it don't do no good just to say that. You gotta know how to read it. A science, that's what it is." Her crafty eyes, lively amid all the pendulous flesh, fixed Joss. "Of course, you gotta be psychic, too," she said with a dark air of confidence. "I am. I'm psychic. I got the gift."

Once more she plunged. For a while she studied Joss's hand, making little glottal sounds to herself. "Now, take this top line, dearie," she suddenly announced. "Well, it's supposed to be a line. Yours isn't. The heart line, that one is. Yours is kind of all broken up. Like bird tracks. It's like you're gonna keep changing. Never love one person for long. But still, it keeps coming in and out on two lines that keep coming in together. A mess. Here, look at mine." Proudly she extracted her left hand from under Joss's. It was like a small, pink rubber glove pumped to the full with fluids, but sure enough, a splendid line of love was cleft across it like the scar of an old knife wound. "See that, dearie? It means I'm a one-man woman. Hot and strong for the same man forever. And him a low-down no-good, too." If the last was meant for a joke, the woman certainly did not smile but offered all this intelligence in the same proud tone before she went on with the reading.

Joss didn't like it at all. Silly. Nonsense. One of those shaky pseudo-sciences based on superstition and a tradition of stupidity.

Glumly, she listened to Bobby's reading. All about an

orgy of gold. Money, the fat woman declared. Bobby was going to run through rivers of it. He'd be picking it out of the trees, carrying it home in pails. There he sat, hunched forward, leaning over his own outstretched hands. It was just what he wanted to hear. His head almost touched the fat lady's. He wasn't very big but so incredibly intense. Joss could see plainly that he was having a wonderful time, drinking in tales of future wallows, high financial excesses. He grinned. He swung his lower jaw, just barely, from side to side as if chewing on hard millions. His little-boy look said, "Gimme more! Gimme more! I love it."

So what about her hashed up heart line? Not going to love anyone for long? Hell's bells! That hippo had almost made her feel dirty with all the mumbo jumbo ignorant superstition. Nevertheless, she'd felt a pang. Frank. Steady old Frank Graham was still trying to offer her his pin. He was a junior now, a year ahead of them, and he wanted to get serious. She was sorry, but there was nothing for it but to tell him. Just tell him. That's all. The truth.

As they came out of the lean-to and into the garish carnival lights, Bobby said, "How's your line of hunger, Jazz?" He still always called her Jazz. "Mine runs clear up my arm, right through my heart and boing! Right into my stomach!" He grabbed her hand to pull her to a hot dog stand.

On their way out, they passed an amateur contest.

Anyone who wanted to could perform. An old man was on, singing "Danny Boy" in a sad version of an Irish tenor—quavery, too tremulous. He flailed his arms in spasmodic gestures, futile, nothing to do with the song. Everyone was laughing at him but clapping very hard to egg him on. There was cruelty in it, and Joss felt sorry for him. Yet he was happy. He obviously thought he was a big hit.

They held hands. Their fingers played. His thumb caressed her broken-up heart line. He dragged her out of the lights and hugged her in that too-enthusiastic way of his. "Bobby!" she squeaked. "You'll break me."

"I'd like to, Jazz. I'd really like to," he groaned. He began to kiss her exploringly. His lips nibbled at hers. His tongue began to work at a sensitive spot in the middle of her upper lip. It triggered a reflex to open to him, but she fought it. All the while he was trying to pull her farther from the lights, and she was trying to pull him back under them. It was an exhausting battle for her because Bobby had only to struggle with her, but she had to fight herself as well as him. She was surprised to find herself afraid of her own response when he pressed close. Nothing in her life had prepared her for that response. "I can't. Bobby. I can't," she groaned.

He sighed. "I know," he said, and he released her.

They walked hand in hand. They passed a tier of crank-up movies. *Nothing to Wear. Naughty Girls. For Men*

Only. A grubby man in shirtsleeves was cranking vigorously away at *After the Bath.* Bobby gave Joss a knowing wink. She laughed.

The stars clinked on.

She was happy, too, but in a bittersweet way. Sad about Frank. And worried whether she could give to Bobby Ochs whatever it was that he might need from her.

Joss had an arrangement with Mr. Resnick. She had come through his essay class with a reasonable, not great, mark. Resnick was apologetic about the B grade. "You were undoubtedly the most promising writer out of that whole bunch," he told her. "But, you know, you never did meet the required level for the class. You balked. You could have done it. It was more a question of attitude than ability." From the inside, she could feel the surface of her face souring. It must have curdled just enough to make a sourpuss. Resnick became apologetic. He offered atonement. He told her that he would be available for help and critique as she passed through the various required phases of her major. For a time, Joss took advantage of his offer.

After classes, she would seek out his office in Dwight Hall to read him her latest masterpieces. Resnick was extremely cordial. He always had a little package of peppermints to share with her. He listened with attention. Joss was in a short story class now, much happier with the work. No more expository definitions for her. Not always pleased with Resnick's responses to the writings. He had the usual criticism—too many words, too exceptional. She pulled out her usual response, "I believe in words. They are our language's gift to us. And I'll write the way I *want* to write."

His usual response came right up again too. "Okay. Unless you're eager for someone to *buy* it."

But Resnick's office was in Dwight Hall, and the classes

Joss attended for creative writing were in Mason, a different venue and not next door. It wasn't convenient for her. An occasion came when she simply dropped her pages into his mailbox in office of the English Department. These were exceptionally good pages, she thought. She had labored over them long and hard the previous night. She couldn't wait for his admiration. She expected their return either at her college box, which she checked every day, or at her mailbox in Harmon House, but they were never returned at all. Never. She wondered about them. Had he read them? Had she transgressed by leaving them the way she had?

Joss knew they could not be lost. She thought of theft, indulging a paranoia attack about someone stealing her stories to plagiarize, to copy, and publish, and grow unbelievably wealthy withal. That's how good she believed her pages to be. But would Mr. Resnick stoop so low? Do that to her?

The pages, of course, were not totally lost. Though she had initially written everything out in long hand, she only had recently learned to type. All the professors expected typed papers. Now her production was facilitated in a new way. At the cost of perpetually blackened hands, Joss knew how to make carbon copies of everything.

But what had happened to her pages? As time went by, she became even more anxious. Her friends said she harped on the subject. "Why do you think he is taking so long?" she griped.

She consulted with Jeannie, who always had an opinion. "Do you want to do something about it, or would you rather just mouth off?" Jeannie asked her

"What? What could I do?"

"I think he wants you to go to his office," Jeannie said. "I think he has his eye on you. He's got a case on you, baby. He wants you."

"That's idiotic. It's nonsensical," Joss retorted.

"You go to his office, Joss. Confront him. You'll find out."

After classes on Monday, Joss returned to Harmon House searching for Jeannie Irslinger. She came home full of new information about Mr. Resnick. She had at last had the courage to confront him. "Jeannie, the man was so *glad* to see me," Joss recounted. "He was just bursting peppermints and grinning all over the place. I just couldn't stay mad at him."

"Hmmm. I told you so. So why did he throw your stuff in the garbage then?"

"Hold your horses! He didn't. When I accused him of just chucking the pages, he said, 'Joss, I'd rather not make too much of my woes, but what would you say is the first thing you notice about my physiognomy?'"

"Huh?" Jeannie snapped.

"'Your giant eyeglasses,'" Joss completed her reply. "And that was exactly it, Jeannie. His terrible beer bottle-bottom lamps. His eyes are awful. And he has to correct those miserable expository definitions every night. There are still some idiots who hand in longhand assignments. It's cruel to those poor eyes.

"So he requests I come to the office and read my entries to him from now on. He says he is eager to hear them. And it is really helpful to read your work aloud to someone. You pick up a lot of crazy mistakes and typos that way. Especially someone who knows something about writing."

From out of her vaporous nicotine cloud, Jeannie insisted, "All I hear is him worming his way to getting you closer."

"Don't be such a cynic, Jeannie. I told him, 'Resnick, with those pieces of target glass on your face, I actually thought you didn't *have* any eyes.' He moaned when I said that. It was a pretty sad scene. So next I heard myself saying, 'Let me see your eyes, Mr. R.'"

"Pretty nervy," said Jeannie.

"You betcha! I don't know where I ever got the nerve, but I even lifted up the awful spectacles and let myself get a good gander at his naked face. The eyes were very red and rheumy, but they were there. Actually there. And looking hard at me were two sorrowful eyes the color of blue candy."

"Blue candy?"

"Yes, chips of blue candy. You know, Vicks cough drops."

"Oh." Jeannie gave a great sigh.

Joss flipped open her notebook and began to read aloud. "It is woven through the fabric of her indifference, along with all strong feelings. There's no yes or no to it. The writer gives up the pen at that point, says, let me chronicle numbers, let me render recipes; give me back reason even if it's just a platitude.

"She, like anyone, is mostly concerned with the idea that she wants to be different from everyone else, apart and controlling, while still appearing just like the rest of them."

"*That's* what you read him?"

"Yeah."

"What did he say?

"He said it was brilliant. He promised that I am a blooming genius," laughed Joss. "What do you say?"

"I say you'd do well to shut up while you're still young, Joss."

"But, Jeannie," Joss laughed, "it was *you* I was writing about."

Of course she'd have to tell Bobby. In effect, she couldn't wait to tell him. With Kitty, she had seen enough movies to anticipate the celluloid reaction to the situation. First he might faint. Well, no, being Bobby Ochs, he would never faint. Some guys did. But he would at least stagger. He might even blink for a few moments. Then he would think about it, seriously, becoming overly concerned. Then he must start to hug her—too enthusiastically at first. Then—stop! Wait. She's fragile. Then—soften. Then—focusing her face in the screen of his beautiful eyes, she would appear in duplicate in the two cerulean pools, cast as the goddess of affection, the object of his fondest desires. When they made love, she'd always see herself there, doubled as his beloved.

Whereupon, suddenly aware of the portent of this cinematic moment, he might next speak loving words—that is, if he still could speak. In tender concern, he'd gently try to direct her to a chair, or pillow, or divan, or whatever soft surface his pleasure projected. She would laugh. He'd begin laughing too. They would hug and laugh for a while. And then the moment came when they'd speak of plans. They'd speak of June. June was coming. Soon with blooms and moons. And they would face the long future ahead for both of them.

But Bobby Ochs did none of that. Instead he exploded. He shouted some unintelligible words. Joss was not accustomed to rough language. Except for Jeannie, who was a rebel, nobody used those words in her circle. He flushed bright red, almost purple. It scared her. She thought he was having an apoplexy.

"What the hell is wrong with you, Jazz! Jesus Christ! How the hell stupid can you get? How could you do this to me?" he roared.

And the veils began falling from Joss's eyes.

She was shaken. "I couldn't help ... What should I have done?" she managed to say.

"Surely you could have gotten yourself some inside information from that pack of broody hens you live with!"

She tried to interrupt. "None of my friends know—"

"Oh, they know. They certainly do know. That Irslinger bitch, for one. She must know every trick in the book."

So much for a life as informed by the movies. She was aware that something bad had happened, but whatever it was, it had happened outside of her own volition.

Riding in the Jitney Jalopp, the little long-ago fun machine.

He said he had an address in Cranston. It wasn't raining exactly, but it seemed like it wanted to. He looked furious. He was angry with her. He said little, and when he spoke, something inside her, something like a swarm of fireflies hovered in her field of vision then burst, burst like fireworks, shattered and spurted—so many little points of light. Perhaps she could chase them, fix them in her sight, stare them back into her brain, but they just slithered away when she tried to grab them. Besides, how must she look anyway, rolling her eyeballs at him?

What was he saying? She had forgotten to listen.

But she was good. A good girl. Biddable. She did what she was told. He said, "Get in," and she got in. The door stuck. He had to jump back around to slam it from outside, and she so regretted that. She was so sorry about the sticky door. Of course, he didn't know how sorry she was though she did everything he told her to do. He said, "It's all set. This guy I know made the appointment. We'll be in and out in half an hour. All you have to do is cooperate. Understand?" She thought he barked. His jaw was set so tight it surely hurt him. Of course she would cooperate. She intended to do everything she was told to do. He'd see that. Maybe that would ease him, ease the tension in him.

He had a flask. He offered it to her. She pretended to drink. The cheap liquor barely touched her lips. Some spilled onto her jacket. He took a long pull before initiating the ritual that brought the Jitney Jalopp chattering to life. His face so concentrated on the task. His finger jabbing buttons, turning knobs. It was freezing in the car. She dared not say so. He was so far away from her. Whenever he came back, he was angry. She wanted so much to avoid that.

She stared. In the failing light from outside, she could see his profile now. Hard. Like the head of a stone idol. Eyes hooded. Snub nose. Pugnacious. A little fighter. She could feel him fighting. Fighting the battle that was this night. If only he wouldn't be so angry with her. He must know she was on his side.

He turned a corner. In her mind, she tried to turn a corner too. She thought about those fireflies. She tried to enlarge them into suns, stars, solar systems, galaxies, universes. Within her consciousness, she tried to work up some pyrotechnics. But she could kindle no heat. It was freezing.

Though early in the evening, it was already dark. Better than yesterday. Weren't the days getting longer? The city streets looked wet. It wasn't raining though. There was a kind of oily slick on the street.

"... borrowed the money." Abruptly, he was speaking. She had missed the beginning. "Hell to find the place. They make you park your car about three blocks away. At least they request that you do." Stressing each word as if this was something important. Maybe it was, but it didn't make a lot of sense to her. Though she concentrated very hard, it still didn't make any sense. Nothing he said made sense. Her teeth were chattering. Without looking, he shot his arm back, plucked up the tattered car robe, and pushed it at her. "Here," he said gruffly.

"Thank you," she said. It was the first time she had spoken since they started.

In the moment, she had a revelation in which she realized art and literature as the progress of destroying raw materials in pursuit of an elusive truth. She was trying to make a story out of it. The title would be *Love Is* _____, and that last word would have to be something superbly clever, very meaningful. It would have to turn the idea into a thrillingly modern concept, but she could not grab anything. She was in the middle of a negative confusion, like night thoughts—where things go on so many different levels you are afraid your brain will pop. And then the title shot out at her: *Love Is a Misplaced Modifier*. Good. She liked it. Now, what did it mean? Somehow related to the grammatical structure of the story, a verbal riddle, a conundrum. Too arch. Maybe better to say *Love Is a Transitive Verb*. Yes, transitive—takes an object, whether the object likes it or not.

She sniffed.

He glared at her.

She didn't want him to be angry, but she was so scared.

And it was so primitive, this fear. You didn't need a college education to be scared this way. Why did Joe spend all that money and she the time getting her educated if only for her to find herself in a moment of primal fear from which she might never emerge?

"*All hinged with pain*," the words in her head were now saying as if she couldn't allow herself to take seriously this terrible fear. They were driving toward something terrible and irrevocable. They were driving toward a drastic moment. Words scribbled themselves in her mind. Part of a message to her future self. Suddenly she glimpsed his tight profile and changed the phrase. "*Fringed with inconvenience.*" Ugly. The drama of her life. This moment, which she now knew, was a terminus, an end station in her personal history. And it was an ugly station, dirty, and inconvenient, as she herself was.

The car skidded. The JJ faltered sometimes on the slick. It had ancient, skinny, balding tires. He wasn't speeding though. Often he did. He was an excellent driver. He'd raced cars one summer; he told her that once, maybe showboating. But now he was methodical, precise. Perhaps they'd crash. She wouldn't mind. The idea didn't bother her at all. It even beckoned. A possible escape.

"Why don't you say something?"

She couldn't. Her tongue was stuck.

"You're blaming me for this, aren't you?"

It would cost her too much to say, "No." But she did

realize he was handling the situation in the only way he could.

The strange thing was how opposite they turned out to be. For a time, they had been so united on everything. The remarkable thing was how much she had wanted the conventional solution, how much she had wanted everything to proceed in lock-step, it but it was no good wanting it alone. Alone she was without power. What a come down. Her confidence was diminished to a speck. She wondered where she would find those shrunken elements again—her pride, her ego.

The ride seemed interminable. Eternal.

He offered her a cigarette. She shook her head dumbly. Under the old car robe, her fingers were locked painfully over her belly. They were passing some farmland, then the outskirts of Cranston. He asked directions at a gas station. He was not to give the name of the street but of a street some blocks away. Cloak and dagger. It could be fun. Sort of a game they'd play, like in a movie. Except, of course, it was no fun at all. It was a leaden blanket laid over the workings of her mind, giving no warmth. A stratum of earth. A grave for her to lie in while she lived.

He parked the car as instructed. Rain drizzled now. They had to walk the three blocks. Instinctively she reached for his hand, but he slid her hand up and hooked it to the crook of his arm. He made some foolish chitter-chatter. He was trying to look like no one, no one at all, but to her he looked furtive. To her he suddenly looked like a thief. Perhaps they both did—a pair of rats scuttling through the rain.

He checked the address on a slip of paper. She saw that his hand was shaking. That galvanized all her fear, and she clutched wildly at his arm with both hands. She could tell he didn't like that, but she couldn't help it.

At least the neighborhood was not too dirty.

A woman answered the door. She was wearing a white smock. It didn't look like a nurse's uniform—more like an artist's smock. She said, "Oh! Mr. Jackson! You're too early! Come back in an hour!" in such a false tone, such a pitch of evasive urgency that it was terrifying. Suppose something was wrong. Suppose they were hiding something awful. She didn't want to go in there. A tide of hysteria rose within her. It was arrested by the look on his face.

They walked in the direction away from the car. There was a diner reflecting neon lights onto the street.

They sat in a back booth. He looked at his pocket watch. His father's watch, as he'd once told her. "Want a BLT?" he said dully. She shook her head.

"I can't be like those people, Jazz," he finally said. "I've seen them. They live in little compartments. They get tickets to the radio broadcasts, and when somebody holds up a sign that says Applause, they clap like crazy fools. And when somebody holds up a sign that says Laughter, they laugh till they pee their pants. That's how it would be. And I can't be like that.

"And neither can you," he said.

Joss looked at her fingers' ends.

"Look, we both made a mistake," he continued. "I know I made one. But you're in it, too."

She nodded. "Okay," she wanted to say, but it was hard to speak because, periodically, she had to swallow back an unpleasant metallic taste that welled up at the base of her throat.

Their table was a dingy white slab of ersatz marble. It had been swiped too many times with dirty washcloths. The jukebox poured out a song:

"Heartaches, heartaches. What does it matter how my heart breaks?"

The crooner reveled in a moan of assumed sadness. Putting the song over. It was a song they'd heard on a dozen bright evenings when that phony sadness had seemed exactly right, had set up just enough contrast to stress her happiness. Now it swirled around in the air, purposeless, meant nothing more than a singer's exercise in self-pity.

He ordered coffee and doughnuts. She tried to drink the coffee, smoked the cigarette he gave her. She stared at the long glass window and read the words UHL'S Diner backwards. Right under the E, reflected in flyspecks and given sensuous motion by continuous seepage of the rain, she saw reflected something yellow. Her scraggy yellow hair.

Poor little cowardly egg.

Scrambled this time.

Satan is a smooth guy.

He'd have to be clever to be the devil. An inverse god had given her an evil potion that suspended her in the gummy billows of a foul sleep. Inside the illusion of space, the torn girl dreamt of innocence, a quality of her past, like wonder. Confronted with that innocence, in the dream she watched her own hand, beyond her volition, unexpectedly jab out an obscene gesture. With an effort, she turned away, feeling thick and ugly and ashamed. Feeling more culpable than Satan.

She probably had lain in stupor for a few hours, entertaining her conflicts.

Her body reacted hard. She had to fight to keep from slamming into the wall.

Then it quieted, and the dark grew softer, less cruel. Joss felt her guts torn into little shreds. She felt swollen out of any semblance of herself, weeping like some gross penitent that she had never meant to be.

On the Greensward walking toward her. Dynamite. Locked into her memory of emotion. His arms jabbed at the air when he walked. He made fists of his hands, and he punched. Going somewhere. Going to do something. Always with an objective. Urgency. He caught her heart. It was in the palm of his hand. He surprised her. Then her young body, healthy in spite of tampering, began to escape from under the oppression of the filthy dregs that some malevolent drug had imposed on her.

At two in the morning, she awoke. She was stinking from the whiskey Bobby Ocks had tried to give her. It had spilled all over her jacket. She heard the ticking of her Little Ben. That hurt. Everything hurt. Her eyes and her fingertips. The clock's ticking hurt them. And then the various pains joined. She began to heave. Racking. But nothing came up. She thrashed, slamming her body against the wall with a fat thud. She couldn't even cry but kept emitting sounds like a sick animal.

What makes one person love another?

Something to do. "Jazz, the wind's blowing … Let's go fly kites. Let's sail on the river. Jazz, come on. Go punting with me. Let's rent bikes. I know where. Don't you want to ski? Jazz, meet me at the Golf Club. We'll hit balls. I'll show you how. Haven't you been to the dog races? I'll take you Saturday. Let's go. Jazz. Jazz, make love with me."

All his sports were singular. He never joined a team. It might affect his tempo, which was fast. He wouldn't play the game, made no polite excuses for lust. He had only to let her be aware of it to bring her into his desire. Hers was informed by love.

Dynamo. Dynamo man.

His intensity. Those fists balling up. His jaw always tensed. He smiled that way. Clenched teeth, as if he would bite you. Impatient. Rolling up onto the balls of his feet. Precipitating things. Always in a hurry to go on to the next thing. Tired of this. Hurry to the next. He rushed a springtime meeting into a kiss before ever a word was spoken. The kiss he precipitated into passion with remarkable speed considering the girl and the times. Then he parlayed the passion into a problem.

He solved it by smashing everything. Did it matter? It was only a fake bird after all.

In late afternoon, a couple crossed the terrace. Two figures. The slanting light elongated their shadows. As Joss watched, they paused to hug each other.

Everyone was relaxing in Nevada Gerdts's room. Nevada had the only radio in the dorm. On Saturday afternoons, they convened there regularly to listen to Milton Cross and the opera.

"I felt pity for the lady in the portrait, born sophisticated, therefore deprived of the pleasure of learning evil," Mary Ellen said portentously. She was still going on about the downtown museum she had visited with Joss that morning. Joss stayed silent, lost in her thoughts. As they came back up the hill that morning, Joss had seen everything—pavements, doorsteps, and garbage pails—as intersecting planes and spatial relationships. An alley cat that slinked across her view moved by pushing forward the front edge of its mass, flowing, as if conceptualized by a dynamist. Seeing everything anew. It was incredible. Pure intellect, her emotions unaffected. Now she said, "Oh, Mary Ellen, the lady in the portrait was *you!*" It was a meaningless remark, made because she really wanted to slap Mary Ellen across the face and admonish her, tell her to stop being so pretentious. Instead, she said this dumb thing in a snooty voice, very superciliously, to make them all laugh, even Mary Ellen. But with that idiotic remark, hadn't Joss found herself just as phony?

Montrose looked up from her opera book and gave

Joss a reproachful glance. Joss regretted what she had said at once. It was a curse. This being too glib. Even if she herself was numb, she did not really want to reflect any of her hurt on others. Montrose had said to her, "All that laughing has begun to depress me. Have you noticed, Joss? Our friends laugh at almost anything. That laughter must mean a lot of peculiarly different things. Some of them are bound to be less than amusing."

Nevada was taking about Charles Laughton. She had heard him do a reading at the Quad. She said he looked around at his audience and then based the reading style and content on the people he saw in front of him. "For instance," she explained, "he'd take one look at my roommate, and he'd start reading *Winnie the Pooh*." They laughed. Anna Destri, the roommate, laughed the loudest.

Joss knew that people constantly made mistakes. Then, perhaps, they were sorry about them. Glad, sometimes. Maybe, at times, they didn't even care. But she had experienced all three. Her mistakes had at first made her delirious with joy. Ridiculously proud. Then they had plunged her into despair. And now she felt indifferent, detached.

No big snowfalls came. From the dormitory window, Joss could see the evening. Light rain had begun to fall on the all-American boys and girls. It darkened the pale stones of the terrace. Rain fell reluctantly, peevishly, out of the dull sky. The all-American boys turned up their collars. From Joss's vantage, the all-American girls looked like bright little dolls as they emerged from Harmon House in red and yellow slickers, sou'wester hats. Campus bells rang five.

The afternoon deepened to dusk. The couples walking outside seemed secure in their happiness, but their happiness could have been illusory like their other assumptions about life.

"... wouldn't wear that to a barn dance," someone asserted.

"Tell Hortense!" cried Sally Dart, and she was rewarded by the immediate crackle that was their laughter. It was a private joke, a hallmark joke for their crowd. No one could remember its origin, but it tickled them all, every time.

The opera had ended. Nevada Gertz was telling about her classy friends in Springfield. "Any time anyone tells a joke or something funny, they all say, 'Verrry funny,' but nobody laughs," Nevada explained. "And, you know, it really comes out hysterically funny."

Across the room, Mary Ellen, with a wonderful nasal intonation, said, "Verrry funny, Nevada." A pause while it took, and then they all laughed.

Nevada wore a fraternity pin at her left breast. Her demure explanation was, "Engaged to be engaged."

Back in her own room, Joss returned to her writing.

She tried to bypass these things. Such a lot of tradition involved—pins, rings, newspaper notices, engraved plates, china lists, and silver patterns. Society undoubtedly required these artifacts, Joss reflected. It was trivial but somehow fundamental to the perpetuation of the species.

Except for her brain that went right on ticking, everything else inside her had been busted up, or misplaced, or maybe killed, and it didn't even hurt anymore.

An unconvincing sun shone. The air smelled like snow might be coming. Joss longed for snow. She needed it.

"With the sloped and infinitesimally pea-brained look of a Modigliani portrait, she slanted along the avenue leading her defanged jaguar kitten," Joss wrote. It was the closing strophe of her much rewritten love story, *Love Is a Transitive Verb*.

Montrose looked at her. "That's almost beautiful," she said. "It is beautiful but just beautiful words."

"Just words. Nothing but sonorous words. It's not at all what I had in mind when I started the story. I wanted to tell the truth."

"Which truth?" Montrose asked.

"Well, about pain ... about little betrayals. About youth slipping away into callousness."

"Hmmm. The elusive truth," Montrose said quietly. "But you can't tell the truth unless you know what the truth is."

"About the part of things that are there though you can't see them," Joss added. "I think of all the spaces behind the things we look at every day. The houses on Webster Street, for instance. Have you ever really looked at them?"

"The ones that are falling apart?"

"Yes, but if you really look, you'll see a kind of past splendor about them, bourgeois as they may be. They may have fallen into slums now, but they were designed by some architect with a classical education. The windows alternate arches and have pediments, and they are braced with ionic columns in low relief. Montrose, that builder had pretentions. Where now the rodents range and the bugs proliferate an old keystone is engraved with Peregrine Estates in neo-Roman letters.

"After a hot night of rot gut and wife-beating, some hung-over bum can look out at the morning through renaissance arched window recesses even though his bloodshot eyes probably never see much."

"Wow," said Montrose. "And what is your point?"

"That we can't see it either. We can't really see what's around us. I've stopped in the Portal after classes almost every day. After all the times I've lingered there over coffee or a malt, I thought I knew that place almost as well as I know this room. Well, you remember that Gabe Couzatt boy who is so crazy about Sally Dart? He's been working there as a busboy. This afternoon he beckoned me into his inner sanctum to ask some pertinent questions."

"Impertinent, you mean," Montrose interrupted.

"Well, you know the poor boy begged to hear who Sally's been dating, who she talks about, how serious she is with the pinning business, what a feller needs to do to capture her attention, and all that stuff. Gabe is desperate.

"But that's not what I was getting at. He led me through the door that's at the end of the counter. I've passed it a million times. Well, he might as well have led me to the end of the other side of the moon. There was an unfamiliar world in there—great big mysterious cauldrons, packing cases, huge windows that face right on to South Quad. I thought about how often I've walked past those windows, every day for the whole term, and never once wondered what's behind them.

"That's the true story, Montrose. There are always things behind things—secret alcoves, cupboards, abattoirs, and hanging rooms, dressing closets. If you're in back of the wall, you forget the other side or you imagine it as something like the set for a movie while you, behind the scenery, always assume you inhabit the *real* space.

"All the while Gabe was cross-examining me I was watching this crazy woman who works back there. She was washing dishes and screaming. Maybe she thought it was singing, but it came out like screaming. I can swear she was another thing I had never seen before. If I had, I would have noticed her. She was the most startling element of the reality behind the wall.

"She kept lifting her arms out of the soapy water and flirting her skinny fingers at us as if to hex us. Then she'd scream a little. Maybe she thought it was a song we knew. Gabe took no notice at all. But you should have seen her—nostrils like black jellybeans, hair like couched rats, crumpled lips, dank with steeped grease. She screamed and clamored for your eyes to see her, but I don't think Gabe Couzatt ever once noticed because, even though he's standing right there, he's left all his perceptions, and imagination, and concept of reality on the other side of the wall where—"

"Where Sally Dart is."

"Exactly."

"Poor Gabriel."

"Tell Hortense."

Now that she was gutted, Joss sought to see the whole truth with the eyes of her dispassion. She wanted to look full on at situations but use words to relate what was happening in the corner of her sight as well. Even if a lateral glance might better serve for capturing elusive truth. She was writing her book now. In her book, she wanted to explain that all their civilized studies, all their seasons of museum going, concerts, operas, poetry readings, films, both domestic and foreign, did not alter the fact that life was not especially civilized. Men and women, connected in an intimacy that they called love, did not speak in revelations of rhyme but often just in grunts and obscenities.

Joss had come to realize that people did not seek each other out for the mutual enlargement of their souls. They wanted each other for reasons of ego or for exploitation—financial, physical, or psychological. Clearly there was not much civility to it. The question that bothered her most was whether there ever had been. If not, she and her friends were wasting their years on the worship of nothing.

No. Bobby Ochs had cost her far too much. There had to be broken things inside her. Self-doubt, distrust, and cynicism took their place. How unfair was the new knowledge that civilization was a mockery, as false as Bobby Och's feelings. Her heart and his were not instruments for love but uncivilized organs, possibly remnants of Paleolithic savagery.

She had spent the short examination break in the city. She had gone to meet her mother, who was staying at an uptown hotel. Whatever was Kitty doing in the city without Joe? Another problem. Not good. It couldn't be good. Joss would avoid casting a glance, either sidewise or full, at Kitty Nye. She couldn't afford to know too much about Kitty right now. So she delayed by walking. She walked, and words flooded her mind. She counted on those sonorous words to be her last remaining solace.

She stopped for a coffee at a long, gleaming counter, and she could feel her own solitude on her like clothes, something that enclosed and protected her. She could pull misery over her head like a cowl. It was familiar, something from a movie she had seen. Bette Davis jerking around her cigarette. It was satisfyingly benevolent while emotive enough to suit the griege of the day. Eventually she turned back.

She walked on Sixth Avenue, past the Ziegfeld, past the automat, the outdoor tables of the St. Moritz. No one there. Too cold probably. She walked to the beginning of the park.

She eventually walked to Fourth Avenue. This was familiar territory to her. She liked the stalls of the used-book stores. She watched a huge, black-bearded man, magnificent looking in spite of ragged clothes, browsing with hungry intensity. Joss invested him with glorious qualities of nobility and art. He might be a giant of the bohemians, writing a book to be banned like Henry Miller's. Writing a book as she was. Creating a great work, fixing his pen into the heart of the truth. Too raw to publish. She, Joss, knew she would recognize truth if it appeared.

Inside the yellowing cover of a slim volume, she found an inscription. "To our beloved Mary Matilda on the occasion of her graduation. Mother and Father. June 1908." What story was here? The elaborate, attenuated letters crawling under the penciled price, five cents, became the focus for all her pain. It hit her aberrant emotions like a slap. She felt tears welling into her eyes. But Joss never cried, and now she was saved from a public weeping exhibition by an old man, cadging coins or cigarettes. He pulled on her sleeve. She fished him out a full pack of Chesterfields and all her change.

"Thank you for the bum," she said to the cold air. And, "Thank you for solitude, for my cloak of invisibility," she said to no one. "Thank you for nothing much."

The preceding summer, she had met Bobby in the city. The holidays were unbearable, centuries long without him. Eternity, she came to realize at that time, could be packed into a unit as short as a mere minute.

She was early. Then, too, she had walked in the garish part of the city. Her heart had been funny. It hummed. No, it purred.

When the time came, she met him at the college kids' place, under the clock at the Astor. He was waiting. She was immobilized for the moment. She could not find a voice. "Hi," Bobby said with unusual gentleness as if he were trying to ease her into reality. She opened her lips but could only force out a little sound, like a moan. He bear-hugged her. He kissed her recklessly. The message his body sent against hers was unmistakable.

Of course, they had to observe the niceties. At the Astor, you had to have a drink. The laws in New York permitted it once you were above the age of eighteen. The bar was jammed with collegiate couples that had been unable to survive the holidays apart. She ordered a whiskey sour.

Later, when Joss stopped in the ladies' room, she faced a wall of mirrors. She saw her little self in there—quick, alive. The mirror gave her back all the glitter, the intensity of her happiness.

He took her to a sordid hotel on the west side.

It was the first time for Joss. Not that she took it lightly. Bobby had been a part of her life for as long as her life had any meaning.

That was during the last school year, her sophomore year.

Now, at the new midterm break, Joss walked and walked. She was in the city but bound up in a cocoon of herself. When she reached the hotel where she was to meet her mother, she looked first in the lobby.

Kitty was sitting there. Waiting. Always a small person, she looked so tiny sitting in a big chair there without the idea of Joe to protect her. Joss had seldom seen her mother alone without a gang of her cronies or at least some crony nearby to protect her. Her mother looked up. Joss saw how pretty she was. Kitty smiled as she recognized Joss. She beckoned. "Sit here with me, Jossie," she said. "You always seem to be prowling off somewhere. I've seen so little of you, and I need to pack my eyes full of you."

"Okay, Kitty," Joss said dully.

Kitty looked uneasy then. "You do realize we're not going to see each other for a long, long time?"

"I don't want to realize it. I want *out* of realizing anything," Joss replied.

"Jossie, I am going far away."

"Why?" Joss said so quietly she could barely hear herself. "Why?"

Her mother grimaced. "What is the matter with you, Jocelyn? You don't seem to have listened to anything I've said. All my life I have been spoken for. I have never belonged to myself. Joe is remarkable man. He always took care of everything. That is part of the problem. Joe and I have to be separate now. I thought you understood."

"But, Kitty," Joss said. "You don't need to ..."

"Oh, yes, Joss, I do need to. I need to tell all. It's part of the new me. It's just too bad but we can't always love the people who love us."

Joss sighed. As far as she was concerned, Kitty was abdicating motherhood.

"You arrived exactly six months after the ceremony. That meant you were either premature or a miracle. I went with the miracle. Otherwise it was too hard to explain you. Who ever heard of a nine-pound preemie?"

"Why do you have to tell me this?"

"You know why I do, Jocelyn."

"I think you're trying to tell me I'm the reason you married Joe. That it's my fault."

"Mother, I'm sorry."

"Sorry? Joss, I don't think you have understood a word of what I've been trying to tell you."

Well, that was for sure. She had not. As far as either of them was concerned, they might be speaking separate, incomprehensible languages. She had never been in their world. She had never understood either of them at all.

With few news bulletins, junior year proceeded apace. The girls couldn't believe it was actually here. Just study now, and the "same old same old." Of course, there were some men in Joss's life, but none of them mattered much. Frank Graham still clung to her. He never seemed to forget that she had *almost* worn his pin in times gone by. *Almost* seemed important to him still. In his peculiar way, he seemed to think she still *almost* wore it.

Frank was a senior now, looking forward to a June graduation. He and a select group of his classmates declared they would dedicate themselves to celebrating the four long years of concentration. And they did try. Frank and his cohorts were the boys with the money, all members of the Benefactors' Club. They were inclined to make perpetual whoopee their senior project. Joss knew only a few of them, yet Frank, always the faithful cavalier, dragged her along to all the parties. From March till June, he included Joss in every invitation.

Advance graduation parties flowed as freely as the hooch that powered them. Frank liked to get pickled these days. He was becoming famous for it. At the end of many a merry evening, Joss often found she had to seek alternate transportation back to Harmon House. It amused her that she made more new conquests as Frank's bereft date. As a maiden in distress, she always found boys who were willing companions, expressing gratitude to Frank for having behaved like a perpetual sot.

Even though he had never achieved his desired goal, Abbott Parish was still sniffing around, rebuffed again and again but ever hopeful. Abbott now belonged to the arty crowd. They gave parties too. Joss knew most of them from writing classes and drama club. She avoided their gatherings. Abbott would be there with his octopoidal gropings. The arty atmosphere was phony, and it spooked her though it gave her plenty to write about. One evening she watched Abbott try to board a pretty girl. As he made his usual approach, the girl, who was reciting one of her own poems, suddenly began to eat her corsage. Rose petals and protest spewed from her lips as she declared her devotion to art. Joss laughed. The gathering deemed the hungry girl was a true "artiste." Though he still ambitiously approached Joss, Abbot seemed quite taken with the petal-eater too. "Vegetable mouth but any port in a storm," he declared. Perhaps he landed. Perhaps not.

It was not long after that experience that the memorable party at the Sigma Tau House exploded and put an end to all parties at the male dorms for the rest of the academic year. The Sigmas had an old two-story frame house, part of the historical section of the old town. Perhaps it had once been a schoolroom or church because it had a platform, like a small stage within the building. The guys called it the Hell House, and it was the scene of many an uproarious night. On the night of this party, they had a cheap girl from the town performing a striptease on the stage. On such nights when they all had been drinking, Frank would drink long and hard before he began to show signs of the confusion and extreme silliness that characterized his more famous debaucheries.

Liquor was not encouraged in the boys' dorms and, of course, strictly prohibited at Harmon House. Nevertheless, there were plenty of girls at this party, and most of them were indulging. Their dates insisted on it. Joss had a few, enough to know it was time to stop even though it seemed Frank and everyone else at the party urged her to continue. She would have liked to join in. Recent opportunities had shown her that alcohol smoothed the ragged edges of too much remembering.

Abbot was at this party, and when he spotted her, he immediately set out to get near her. To no avail, she was entreating Frank to slow down his imbibing. Music, sticky gooey stuff, was playing really loud. Joss knew that Frank, who had a famously sensitive ear, would hate this stuff, and hating would only make him drink the more, but no amount of imploring could wheedle Frank out of the next drink, or the next, or the one after that. She knew him well by now.

And Abbot was approaching with his multitude of arms, eager to cage her and keep her in the magical aura of his whiskey breath.

To escape his advances, Joss turned and ran upstairs to the second story of the old house. All the dank vapors from all the smokers ascended too. It was like being in a cloud ... a stinky cloud. Out of the gray mist someone grabbed her. She saw with surprise and relief that lasted but a moment. It was not Abbot. It was Bobby.

Bobby Ochs! She had avoided him ever since the night in Cranston. Now he encircled her just as he had the first time they met on the grass at the Greensward. She was buzzed by the alcohol, shocked by the encounter.

"They dared me, so I just grabbed the prettiest girl in the place," he told her, using almost the same words he had once used to explain their first confrontation. But this was a different time. She felt a tremor of rage. Too much had happened in the interim. Again she resented his arms at first, but even as she gave mind to her rage, she was melting. Her body was. Against her own volition, her knees were buckling. Joss was not bombed but certainly still had some liquor whirling in her brain. Bobby held her too tight. The music was seductive, gooey, and saccharine sweet, "My happiness yearning for your sweet caress, evening shadows dreaming, yearning, loving, loving, loving you."

A trash bag of stupid words floated, entering her consciousness, as was the awareness of Bobby's tight and desperate grip. "I want you back, Jazz," he said. She could smell his breath, laden with the unmistakable smell of strong drink. "Oh, God, Jazz," Bobby Ocks said, and she felt his hands side down to her back where he could reel her in to feel his rising excitement. "All this time waiting, Jazz," he said and then let the sentence drop as he leaned into her. She felt his terrible urgency. She felt it all. It had an inevitable effect. These were familiar arms; she knew this body in all of its manifestations. She knew the advance of his passion, the motions of his lovemaking, which now insinuated themselves into the dance—if it was a dance—they were locked in. Their lips met but not in the kindergarten kiss they'd once shared. Joss let him enter. She could not help herself. In tasting her lips, thrusting into her, he had communicated everything. Now he was dancing her back, back against the wall. He pulled her skirt up abruptly, carelessly, not caring how he did it. Joss found herself feebly pushing him away. He grabbed her hand and brought it down to his juncture of his legs. She felt his swollen member and found herself in thrall. She could not help caressing, deeply, rhythmically.

"Jazz ... Jazz ... I need to fuck you. You want this as much as I do," she heard him growl, but she could not be sure if that was truly what he said because she heard so many things at that moment. She heard the party roaring downstairs. She heard voices not far off. She heard someone laughing. It was nasty laughter. She swiveled her eyes and saw Abbot. Lecherous Abbot Parish was leaning against the same wall taking in as much of the action as he could. So many noises but all of a sudden a different noise, a scream. An unmistakable cry, the sound of emergency. And the gray cloud of smoke thickened.

"Fire! Fire! Fire!" someone shrieked.

Fire? Good God, they were on the second floor of a woodpile.

She felt Bobby move back to cover himself. Someone else bounded up. "Joss. Joss! Get out!" a familiar voice said. It was Frank, He seemed totally sober. He led her to the rickety stairs where she could see the flames just beginning to lick the first risers of the staircase. Frank lifted her bodily over both flames and steps. He bundled her outside.

There they stood in silent stupor, and they watched the house burn down as they blinked. They couldn't believe they had been in there. How had that happened? They watched, continuing to wonder until the firemen came and made them go away.

Bobby Ochs got out somehow. Abbot Parish died in that fire.

Sleep. Sleep, becalm your little craft. Sleep too sweet to last. Ah, yawn! A yawn's a strumpet successfully retired from the Life but still parading wiles of invitation to quick relief. Oh, stretch, and damn yourself for nothing.

Codex at Night. Joss

Dangling her arm off the edge, she lay on Joss's bed holding her cigarette. First she would study it, very deliberately. Then she would puff and emit a series of perfect rings. She had the secret for this trick. You had to curl your tongue and hold it rigid in a certain way. It wasn't easy, and, in fact, Mary Ellen Rigg was the only girl in Harmon House who knew how to do it readily. Trouble was she had practiced so long to learn the trick that it now became a reflex. She couldn't remember how to smoke any other way. And the damn rings worked like a smoke signal.

"Make yourself at home, dearie," Joss said drily. Of late it made her uneasy to hang around with her old friends.

"Thanks," drawled Mary Ellen. Did she guess the sarcasm in Joss's welcome?

Mary Ellen was obviously acting, acting cool and unperturbed. A pose, Joss thought. But why?

On a recent evening, a group of the girls had gone over to the Portal. Mary Ellen saw Chooky Linkus circling around. She had been diligently avoiding him for a long, long time. The way poor Chooky was, the more she avoided him, the more fervently he pursued. So, before he could scan the room, she scrunched down, hiding below the level of everyone's heads. But of course she was smoking. Naturally the whole room was full of smoke, but her rings did seem to rise above the rest, propelled as they were by nervous energy. Chooky had only to search the air on high and then home into the spot where the nervous rings of smoke arose from the lower billows. Mary Ellen, that dope, never managed to guess how he always found her until Montrose remarked, "It's a very tribal thing, I suppose. Smoke signals."

Joss cackled out an insincere laugh. By now she was just standing there by the bed, testing the air. There was an unpleasant current of nerves astir. She stared hard at Mary Ellen. Studying her. The girl was really very pretty. Maybe the flow of nervous energy was actually emanating from her as she definitely put on this phony act of hers, Joss thought. Joss studied the languid pose. She thought she might use Mary Ellen as one of the characters in a story she was hoping to create. A beautiful girl, unaware how good she looked. Of the four of them, Mary Ellen was actually the prettiest. Long ago, during the course of endless self-studies, the four of them agreed that Mary Ellen was prettiest, deeming Montrose the most beautiful. Joss, instead, the cutest, always looked like fun, as if about to laugh. Jeannie, on the other hand, with her straight, black, pageboy hair, her bumped nose, and her crooked front tooth was agreed to be the most interesting-looking.

Now Mary Ellen had annoyingly collapsed her bones on Joss's bed. Was she testing for power? Searching for tidbits? Wanting to carry tales to make herself more important? Obvious, too deliberate. The way Mary Ellen had sauntered into their room, had taken over Joss's bed. Probably she'd come for information.

Did she know something? A cold current ran down Joss's back.

Mary Ellen, the insidious gossip, specialized in scandal. Montrose called her the town crier. She would dig for news. Perhaps she suspected something, putting Joss in a pejorative role. Joss knew Mary Ellen would never figure out her story, but whatever she did gather, Mary Ellen wouldn't hesitate to broadcast.

Cranston festered in her mind.

Joss knew now how much Cranston changed her. Of course the roommates must wonder about her. Experience had made her different. She had told no one her terrible tale. No one. She so much resented this disguised inquiry now. Mary Ellen in her familiar role as dormitory newshound was after it.

Joss was determined not to give anything away.

Now Mary Ellen was ensconced on Joss's bed, pretending nonchalance. Clearly sniffing around for a story.

Montrose was sitting at her desk. Her beautiful face was turned toward her book. Joss knew that Montrose was in eternal vigilance. What did Montrose know? Had she guessed? She must know something. She had comforted Joss that night. That miserable night when all hell seemed to be opening up. That would have been the weakest moment for inquiry. But later, Montrose seemed cognizant only of the smell of the whiskey Bobby had spilled all over her jacket. At least that was all Montrose ever mentioned. But did she know? What did she really know? Now it made Joss sick to try to recollect that awful homecoming. She could not allow herself to dwell on it. The thought was unbearable. Joss clenched her fists so tight she could feel her nails digging into her palms. If Mary Ellen could dig up some dirt, Montrose would be the first to understand it.

Suddenly Montrose swiveled her chair around. She began to file her nails, clearly also attending, awaiting any revelations.

Mary Ellen now began focusing her energy on the engagement of Nevada Gertz to Fuzzy Williams. She rambled on. "Anyhow," she announced, "before the end of the term. Nevada will get her ring. You can bet it'll be a diamond as big as the Schneider Gym. The announcement goes out in the *Times* next month. The wedding is almost sure to be early in June."

"Hmmm," Joss said by way of paying attention. So far, the tide of words was innocuous.

"Good thing, too," continued Mary Ellen. "What is Nevada equipped to *do*, I ask you, beside talk incessantly until the blue moon rises and then crack wise about it? Not that they need to *do* anything, actually. Kiddo, her father owns half of the variety stores in eastern Massachusetts. Fuzzy's just as well set too.

"No, really. I'm not just trying to be a cat. I'm *worried*. I mean, what am *I* equipped to do with *my* genteel education? Maybe I shouldn't have quit the math major. Now I know gobs of wonderful stuff about English literature. I mean, how many people do you know who have done a comparative study of John Donne and Hieronymus Bosch? But what use is it? What are *you* going to do, Joss?"

"Keep on writing and hope for enlightenment," Joss said.

"Oh, of course, the two of you were just born lucky. I mean—you both have talent going for you."

"If you say so," Joss remarked. Her mouth felt like a desert. Words stuck in there. The air around her seemed to tremble with threat and nervous irritation.

"You can just float on your talent," Mary Ellen remarked.

"More than talent," Joss interjected. "Montrose has already rented an apartment in the city."

"What!" Mary Ellen shouted. "How can she afford—"

"Mind your business!" Montrose snapped, and then added, "Writing is hard *work*! There's no floating about it." Apparently she had found it so. To Joss's surprise. in this academic year, Montrose had unexpectedly switched out of her writing classes to concentrate on a major in music. She had changed before, changed majors twice and rather abruptly.

Mary Ellen, too, had proved inconstant in her scholarly

pursuits. She had switched from a math to an English literature major. "Don't you think I know that? Didn't I work like a peon to create Donne/Bosch?"

"And that was a truly admirable work of creative fiction," Joss rasped insincerely.

"Yeah," Mary Ellen rejoined flatly, making a pseudo-serious voice. Then taking a deep breath, she returned to her investigation. "What I'm trying to say is most of us don't have the feeblest idea of where to start making a living. It's scary. Even Fuzzy. How is Fuzzy Williams ever going to support Nevada Gertz with her taste for linen bedclothes and genuine crystal goblets?"

"Are you implying that the most any of us can hope to achieve is marriage to some rich fellow?" Montrose cut in. There was an unfamiliar edge to her voice. Rarely did she exhibit such annoyance.

Joss was indifferent. "Mary Ellen, you're dripping your cigarette ashes into my shoe," she said.

Mary Ellen peered over the side of the bed and beheld Joss's loafer with a surprised stare. "Oh, sorry. Anyhow ... most of the *boys* don't know what they'll do. What's Bobby Ochs going to do, Joss?"

Joss hesitated. "Make money."

"Well, of course. I mean. I know that. But what doing?"

"I don't know," Joss answered. She stared hard at the pencil she held.

"What I mean is ... where will he start?" Mary Ellen

shot a keen look at Joss. Then she blew a perfect ring of smoke. It was a trick demanding complete governance of the tongue. "How is he going to become the big tycoon he is always telling us he is going to be, *Jazz*?"

"Don't you call her that. You scandal monger!" Montrose cried angrily. Then she balled her fists and pressed them into her temples.

"Oh." Mary Ellen blinked. "Sorry."

"It's okay, Mary Ellen," Joss soothed. "You just want to find out if I broke up with Bobby Ochs, and I have. It's over, finished, past history."

"Oh, God! Joss! You think I'm snooping!" Mary Ellen had begun to tremble. Her voice crackled in a high emergency gear.

"No, I don't, Mary Ellen. Honestly. I don't. I just think you're interested. Honest. It's okay."

The situation seemed catastrophic. Mary Ellen was in tears. Montrose may have been crying as well. She was squinched up in her bed, punching herself in the head. Mary Ellen turned bright red. Joss didn't like seeing her friends this way. She herself was almost visibly palpitating. "Really, Mary Ellen," she tried to soothe, "it's okay. Don't take on so. You're my friend. You have a right to know about me. It's my fault for not telling you about things." But Mary Ellen jumped up crying loud, lachrymose glops of tears. Tumbled out of Joss's bed to the floor hard enough to scatter the loafers lying there. Then she ran crookedly out of the room. Flopping over her own ballerina shoes. Banging through the door. Perhaps she hurt herself. Joss could hear her, still hiccoughing, with amass hysteria in the next room.

Montrose jerked her fists down from her face. Yellow fire roiled in her eyes. Joss knew by experience that she was red-hot mad. "Why must you explain?" Montrose demanded. "Now that stupid little gossipmonger can't wait. She's falling over her own feet in her hurry, running to spill out that she got the scoop," Montrose said bitterly.

"She's sure spilling something," Joss agreed. She held her palm out before her face and realized her hands were shaking hard. It had been a moment of high intensity, but why? Why? Joss wondered. Why was the air so charged, and why had a simple evening with her friends turned into such a pitch of intense drama? What was going on? Montrose looked furious. Why would Montrose be upset? Did she know something? Joss thought not, but she may have guessed more than had been admitted on that terrible night.

"Ignore it," Montrose said angrily. Her beautiful eyes gleamed with some fierce and unexplained emotion.

At this point, both girls could do nothing other than seek marked separation. They retired to their beds, mere feet apart, joined in an agony of division.

Later she opened her speckled notebook. After her hands stopped shaking, she wrote the short one act farce, "A Night in the Girls' Dormitory."

Joss courted sleep, a self-defeating exercise. If she found it, sleep could be inimical. There were dreams now to contend with. Even though she had no memory of the actual procedure in Cranston, she might dream it back into contention. She might relive that electrical smell in the darkened room where she'd lain until suddenly and savagely attacked by a power of wicked light. Occasionally a man appeared in her dreams. He never said a word, just looked at her, his eyes as disturbing as the light. Those eyes were like smudges of darkness rubbed right into his skull.

One morning she awoke in tears. Her pillow was wet. She knew she had cried. Most unusual. Joss had never been a crier. It was Kitty's fault. Kitty had appeared in a dream. She looked frantic. She was trying to say something, and her lips moved. They called attention to her mouth. Joss saw that there was lipstick on her teeth. "Sloppy," Joss thought. She wanted to help but try as she might, Joss could not make anything out of Kitty's frenzy.

Ever since Cranston, sleep was not the panacea it used to be. No one but Bobby knew about Cranston. When, in the Jitney Jalopp that night, he had attempted to revive her, his hands shook so wildly that his cheap hooch splashed all over her. That was the thing Montrose seemed to be most aware of—breaking the dorm rules—bad—and under the influence—bad. Bad and bad—two bads. Montrose had carped on it ever since. Alcohol, as was often the case, took the rap for bad behavior.

At that time, Joss had been dreading the sight of her own blood. Though she had not seen any, there *had* to have been blood, her own and more. As she understood matters, blood must be the price of such a horrible episode. Yet the only blood Joss remembered seeing was the recent spattering of rust-colored stains in the collar of Jeannie Irslinger's shirt. Was there a connection? Joss felt there must be.

It was all the more terrible to her because so inexplicable. Right after that, she had experienced some incidents of spotting. One occurrence called to the other. She wanted to talk about these awful things, but she was in a trap. No way could she consult a doctor, nor could she reveal her transgression. No one was to know. She wondered if she might have unburdened to Kitty, but Kitty had flitted through time like a bubble.

Pop! And she was gone. Not the first time Kitty had taken a powder.

Leaning the notebook against her knees, Joss scrawled in her notebook. "You kept trying to make her into a mother," she wrote. "You've got to remember who she is. She is what she always was. She's the eternal spoiled brat. That's all she can be."

Junior year was turning out to be a crucial time for Joss. Recent happenings, solutions by dissolution, unwelcome revelations, secrets rising to the level of her everyday life. Confidences given in secrecy were more than she could bear. She had not asked for any of it, she felt. Her mind was afflicted by it all.

She was lying in her bed at Harmon House reflecting on discord. Her hand hung limply on her belly, and her notebook and pen lay receptively at her side. But no great strokes of genius were forthcoming. Everything seemed hopeless. Her brain was full of all this conflict. She heaved one audible sigh. Montrose heard it from across the room. She was propped in her bed reading. "What's wrong, Joss?" she inquired.

"I can't get to sleep," Joss replied.

"Problems?" Montrose asked.

"Well, yeah. I'm having to come up with the idea for a novel, and I'm drawing blanks."

"The idea for a novel?"

"Yes, you know. Like a synopsis. A summary for the plot of a whole book. I need to enter some kind of story line for the Goldschneider & Moran Junior Novelist Recognition event."

"What's that?"

There's a publisher in New York, Goldschneider & Moran Company. Mr. Resnick told me about it. They offer a stipend for the best novel by a young author. Basically it's a contest. They dress it up by calling it a Recognition of a Junior Novelist. They give a cash stipend. Not even enough to keep you alive while you work on your project, but the great advantage is to have a publishing house interested. If they like the final result, they might just pick up the book for publication under their aegis."

"Wow! That sounds wonderful. Are you applying?" Montrose asked.

"That's what I'm trying to tell you. I haven't got an idea," Joss moaned.

"I have the utmost faith in your powers of invention, Joss. Why don't you just crib something? Shakespeare did. Or use Shakespeare himself. Romeo and Juliet are always good for a round or two," Montrose said. "Get Alan Resnick to help. He thinks the world of you as a writer." She smiled. Her serene presence and her melodious voice were always soothing when Joss was suffering from her troubled mind.

"As if I haven't already spent about half of the semester in Mr. Resnick's office. He must be sick of me."

"Oh, have no fear. Never doubt Alan. He really values your writing. He thinks you're great."

Joss fell back onto her pillow. She buried her head in her hands. "There's more," she moaned.

"More trouble?"

"More bad stuff," Joss declared. She did not intend to spill all, but now, while she was at it, why not clear some of the other questions clouding her mind?

Montrose was sitting up now, looking fixedly at Joss. "Well, tell," she insisted. "Don't just leave me here listening to the music of the spheres."

"It's about Weezy."

"Weezy? You mean Louise? Weezy Durant?"

Joss held her silence a moment while Montrose reacted visibly. Her expression grew rigid. Her eyes suddenly looked enormous. The normal milky color of her skin turned to a pallid white. "Well, speak up then, Joss! What about Weezy?"

"Just something Jeannie said. She said that during the play, you know, during the Varsity Show, Jeannie said Weezy made improper advances on her."

"What!" Montrose exclaimed as she bolted upright against her pillows. Her eyes widened, and her face took on an expression Joss had never seen before. "What the hell ..." Montrose stopped herself. She seemed profoundly shocked, shocked enough to use language stronger than was her usual custom.

"That's what Jeannie said," Joss repeated lamely.

"Jean is a hellion," Montrose declared.

"We all know that," Joss agreed.

"No, I mean the *real* hell. A minion of the one with the horns, the real spirit of evil. Horn-ed Satan." She emphasized the syllables so deliberately. Somehow it made Joss visualize him. Lucifer. The real prince of the darkness.

Joss remained still. She was frightened by as well as rather surprised at Montrose's vehemence. It was clear that Montrose was hopping mad. "Joss, you tell that idiot that she should shut her trap. She is about to let loose the kind of rumor that could ruin many of the girls in Harmon House."

"That's silly. I think you are exaggerating," Joss said.

"No, I'm not," Montrose countered. "Think about it, Jocelyn. We live in a house full of women. There are plenty of loves and hates going on right here. Daily. They change like the autumn winds. Talking mouths prevail all the way up and down this very corridor. Jeannie is a strong and often difficult character. Some may admire her for that, but lots of people don't. It's possible to pick up this fragment of an idea to discredit her. It's an idea with long legs. Anyone involved with Jeannie or Weezy, anyone connected with the play or with any of us at Harmon House can get in the focus of an idea like that.

"You are always telling everyone you love me, aren't you?" Montrose continued.

"Yes, but I don't mean ..."

"I know. I know, and I love you too. But there it is, even here among our friends, there are some who might relish the chance to get their hands on any kind of juicy scandal. Jeannie might be just such a one. There are even some boys who have been rejected and would love to find that that's the lurid reason for it."

Joss shuddered. She sat up suddenly and quietly took up her notebook. There was one last problem on her mind, one that she did not discuss even with Montrose. When just before the fire at Sigma House, she had clung to Bobby Ochs as he intoned, "You want this, Jazz." She thought now of that moment, and she knew what he had said was true.

Now Joss had to reflect long and hard to put together a synopsis for her novel. The result was something she considered superficial and far too complicated. There were aspects of it she couldn't imagine actually writing.

Alan Resnick even asked, "Can you really write this rubbish?" He frowned. "There are a lot of people mentioned here. I remember you telling me once that you found it hard to deal with too many characters on the same page."

"I could do it, but it would have to be a crummy job," Joss admitted to him.

"So why should you subject your talent to scandal, the commonest denominator of modern literature?" he asked softly. Alan Resnick had the nicest voice. Polite as he was, Joss knew he was trying to steer her a different way. Clearly he was still laughing at her blatant egotism.

In point of fact, Joss felt a little ashamed of the synopsis. The addition of characters had been simply a gimmick to fatten it up. During actual writing, those aunties might serve as elements to save the story for her. The suggestion of incest in an attempt to give it shock appeal was probably too unconventional for Joss to handle. She was, in effect, a conventional person. She needed such things as colors and composition and turbulent winds to call forth her own literary artistry. So, then, make one of the aunties be a painter.

"You really want to write about incest?" Resnick

commented. "You will have to do some psychological research. There's lots of information available on that subject, if you care to be accurate and really informed about it." He knew how Joss hated to sit still and do research.

"I want it to make me money," she explained. "I think I have to get some scandal in order to satisfy the hungry beast," she explained. "I want it to make my name for me. It would have to be a blockbuster so everyone talks about it, wants to read it. Best seller. Lots of sex. Lots of very dirty, very kinky sex. People would be reading it on the subway and bringing it into work shouting, 'Read this, Dorothy! It'll curl your hair!'

"Shockers are big right now on the best-seller lists. Very popular books about young women with older men are coming out of France. I want this book to rattle the rafters of current conventions." Of course, it would also have to have sufficient scope to allow her to "spread her wings," as Mr. Resnick liked to say. Joss took great pleasure in writing but only if she could write her own way, and her way, as some of her classmates had remarked, was a little on the "fancy pants" side.

"Baroque" was the devastating criticism started by the late Abbot Parish and seconded by several members of the group. Joss hated that adjective. She thought of herself as writing lean, spare, directed prose. Not at all baroque. As she told Mr. R, she aspired to lock in something more meaningful than narrative. She sought to shape thought into a perfect rhythm of explanatory sounds, meaningful while beautiful. If one could combine the proper combination of morphemes, they might form a chain and codify all living experience into a perfect sentence.

"Good luck with that!" remarked Mr. Resnick. He laughed. "You'd better succeed with the style you have. Otherwise you might slide from baroque to rococo to merely profane," he said.

Joss's speaking of her prose as a condensation of life into words was clearly a terribly windy description. Nevertheless, she needed that wind to float her prose. And she needed people to write about. This required much thought. When writing stories for her classes, she had learned that she couldn't really develop characters unless she knew their names. Sometimes they revealed their own names in the course of the writing, but usually she had to christen them before she could write anything about them.

Recently she had tried to envision a heroine for a short story. Her tales would always have to feature a female protagonist. She had trouble writing about men. Of course, like most of her pals, she thought most men were simpletons; they somehow came out beyond simple in her writings—just unreal. One day she picked up a baby book and studied names.

Finally she seized upon a name. Margery Bailey. There it was, a rootin'-tootin' square-shootin' American name,

Margery, sometimes called Marge. She was a mature woman. That was to be the scandal. A woman doing it with a boy. When she wrote, "Margery Bailey, a woman of mature years," she envisioned this Margery of her making as about thirty-two years old. Joss simply could not imagine a heroine any older than that. She herself was just under twenty at this time. To her, thirty-two already seemed the threshold of senility.

"I don't like her," Jeannie declared. "She sounds like an old frump. She sounds like a *lascivious* old frump. She sounds like Winky." That remark killed poor Margery on the spot.

J oss decided to disinter Emily Cappo. She scrapped the
old synopsis. It was not her habit to show her writings
to her roommates. But they had been initially amused so
she came up with a new synopsis.

Synopsis
The House of Women
A novel by Jocelyn Nye

At twenty-two years of age, Emily Cappo still
lives with her mother in an old frame house
in Bay Ridge, Brooklyn, New York. Emily
works as a clerk for a major national exter-
minating firm. The Killacoot Incorporation
is presently overwhelmed by an epidemic
of bedbugs swamping Brooklyn and most
of the nation. Emily's house is decrepit but
elaborate and clean of infestations.

Through Killacoot Inc. she has met a
man, known to her only as Schwartz. He
is dark and handsome. Professing an interest in extermination techniques, Schwartz
comes in periodically, ostensibly to make
mechanical repairs to the typewriters. For
Emily, a small flirtation ensues, not quite
a relationship. Schwartz is attractive but a
strange and evasive person.

In addition to her mother, Gloriana, there are also four aunts inhabiting an old house. Leandra, Sylvia, Aurora, Valentina, and Emily's mother were the original five Cappo girls, known to the neighborhood as inhabiting the big tumbledown structure known as the Merton House. They are all single, pious, and credulous members of the Domain of Benevolent Peace church. It is the chapter house of an obscure religion.

Each sister has a private and tragic tale of romantic misalliance. Though loath to speak of such stories, they do, indeed, speak, especially to Emily, who begs them for family secrets. Gloriana, however, has drawn a curtain over her past. She refuses to "dance backwards," as she puts it. Emily is not averse to prying. Determined to find out, she feels she needs to know. She digs. Gloriana's past is her history too. In trying to unearth the aunts' and Gloriana's stories, she hopes to discover something of her own paternity. The more firmly that remains the family's common secret, the more insistently does Emily probe. This leads to a less than tranquil relationship with her mother.

The aunts love Emily to distraction. As

a result of their adoration, Emily Cappo has developed a self-centered and unrealistic view of the world. Though they may adore Emily, on the subject of Gloriana's indiscretions they are sworn to silence. In this climate, Emily's parentage remains a mystery. She has never in her life seen evidence of a father. This is a void that she has long sought to fill both in anger and with guile.

There's also a lurid story to the Cappo house's past. The sisters are inordinately proud of that fact and keep the evidence of its history in the form of old, yellow clippings from the *Brooklyn Eagle*. Emily has struggled to learn more. She is certain knowledge about this unknown factor may help her in understanding the mystery of herself.

The house in Bay Ridge, Brooklyn, is one of those old-fashioned frame dwellings that once housed the wealthier legions of Manhattan commuters, At one time, due to a convenient ferryboat connection to Wall Street, new money built dwellings in Bay Ridge, pretending them to be mansions, villas, mountain chalets, Turkish harems, and Palladio rotundas. This architectural graveyard also attracted the mafia. No one ever objected. Their domestic presence rendered the neighborhood safe from any form of crime.

Into this female domain arrives Emlyn Olivier. He is a dapper man of about forty-five. He arrives at the door requesting permission to photograph architectural details in the old house. It is clear he is familiar with the house's terrible past. There is such a flutter among the sisters. By the power of his confidence, he easily secures permission. They seem to know the man already. Of the five, Gloriana occasionally vanishes, unfindable in the maze of locked rooms.

Emily is immediately attracted to the man. She feels he exerts a great power over her. Why? Who is this stranger? Why has Gloriana fled? Has she, like her sisters, known Emlyn Olivier before? The girl feels a strange familiarity. But who is Emlyn Olivier? Even the similarity of their names begins to titillate her. Eventually she succumbs to his sophisticated charms. Only after yielding to him physically does it occur to her that he may be her father.

The new synopsis made a hit with Mary Ellen. She exclaimed how intricate she thought it. She especially liked the old aunties.

Jeannie was less positive. Her immediate remark on the idea was, "So what?" That struck Joss to the heart. Indeed, what words could put the whole synopsis in its place more succinctly than "So what?" Jeannie got silly, made fun of the whole thing. She insisted on calling the firm Emily worked for The Bug House or The Cootie Place. Joss did not care for the mocking reception even though she had appended some names with deliberate facetiousness. She had intended to change the workplace to "Pediculex" eventually. Joss counted on how much could and would be changed in the process of writing. In the meanwhile, it was probably a good thing that Jeannie was laughing at the synopsis. Anything was better than the negativity Jeanne had been demonstrating of late.

Montrose was quite scandalized by the idea of incest.

But they were all for her. She could feel their approval. It seemed as if everybody was clapping hands, leaving Joss to put on the show.

At the culmination of four long years of study, the senior year came up as a season of extra-hard work. As a part of their successful emergence into the world of university graduates, the scholars were expected to take comps. Comps were super exams at the summit of all their studies. Especially daunting to majors in history, the sciences, political study majors, or majors in any science at all where the hard facts really mattered. When facts prevailed, memory would be challenged. Mary Ellen's major in English literature had her completely bollixed—all those eras, all those dates, all those poets.

"Can you distinguish a romantic poet from a merely pedantic one?" Joss teased. That threw poor Mary Ellen into a fresh panic.

They were exams designed to evaluate every twig and nuance of their chosen field. Every aspect and section of their major was to be tested both by written and oral examination. The proctors could ask anything. There was no way to pull up so much stuff, some of it forgotten and some of it perhaps cribbed from illicit sources. Orals were even scarier. Sitting eye to eye with an examiner could surely unmask all their past inadequacies and larcenies.

Senior year brought other radical changes as well. Frank Graham had graduated. He was now working in the city doing whatever mysterious thing he did. He still made frequent weekend trips up on the NYNH&H. Though he said he came to spend time with buddies, a call on Joss was mandatory. She was up to her ears in writing her novel, so she was less than delighted with the visits. Joss had gotten departmental permission to have the synopsis function as part of her comp requirement. But Joss need not have worried overlong about Frank's visits. The buddies he came to reunite with usually kept him busy enough for whole weekends of dissolution.

Joss was glad Bobby Ocks had disappeared. Hal Merriam told her that Bobby had gone to war.

Mr. Resnick had left them. He'd gone to the city to finish working on his doctorate.

Over the formerly merry halls of Harmon House hung the scary shadow of the comps. Every candidate for the university degree was expected to take his comprehensive examination. Now dusty texts and old notebooks, dating back as far as freshman year, were dragged out into the light. From her suffering friends there had to be some negative commentary on what Joss had arranged with the English Department. She would be permitted to use the synopsis she had made for *House of Women*. "You were going to write it, anyway," Jeannie remarked jealously.

For Montrose, the area of concentration was music. "All you have to do is stand there and sing," Jeannie commented.

"That's what you think, Jean," Montrose replied dryly. Music had been her focus, though with a minor in English expression and a skirmish with art. She had changed majors twice on the way to the music concentration. Montrose still claimed she intended to write books for children someday. That minor emphasis would not enter into her exams. It was probably true that all she had to do was stand still and emit lovely sounds. Still, she studied hard for it. She and Nevada Gertz sat with librettos in their hands and trilled random notes. "Sounds like a bunch of birds got loose in our room," Joss said.

In response to that, Montrose just sighed wearily.

Joss was luckiest. Information from previous grads told her what her comp would include. Primarily, she would be asked to submit the outline for a novel. As she saw it, there was nothing to prevent her using the synopsis she had already created for submission to the Ogden Phillips Memorial Award at Goldschneider & Moran's. The board might suggest a topical slant, usually by quoting two amorphous lines from a poem. Whatever it might be, she knew she could twist it around to fit into *House of Women*. If four years of college had taught her nothing else, she now was a summa cum laude at throwing the bull. Joss boasted that college had taught her three things: how to smoke cigarettes, how to play bridge, and how to sound as if you knew everything—in short, bull throwing. "That should be a subject for comprehensives," Joss maintained.

"Not so easy, kiddo, if you're asked for dates and textual quotes from the masters," Mary Ellen whined. She had become prettier, ever more adept with the makeup, but she had also grown mournful and whinier this year. Jeannie Irslinger's absence was not helping her improve. In the beginning of the year, there had been a scary episode with Jeannie. In spring, Jeannie had exceeded herself in misbehavior. She'd begun smoking, drinking, and even taking off with Hal Merriam for weekends that got wilder and wilder. There was something more than alcohol in it. Even her language grew coarse and rebellious. She actually let loose salvos of forbidden words. It was rumored that Jeannie had said, "I don't give a shit about the fucking school," and had delivered that opinion to Dr. Triplett, the dean of women at the college. No one was shocked at the idea, but everyone was shocked at the language—a terrible breach of all they thought sacred at Harmon House.

When faced with the Harmon House critics, Jeannie grew even more intractable. She confirmed her language and even had the temerity to add, "I had to give it to the old bag! It was liberating to fry her ears off. Isn't that what D. H. Lawrence said? 'Break the taboos and be free.'"

Joss was more surprised by the literary reference than she had been by the forbidden words. "What do you know about D. H. Lawrence?" she demanded.

"Maybe I'm smarter than you think." Jeannie laughed.

"Aren't his books banned in America?"

"For the moment," Jeannie responded, and quite sagely as it turned out. Before Jeannie's comment got very old, more shocking books from abroad were being sold in major American cities. It was the culmination of an era of repression. Joss had just borrowed an early copy of *The Naked and the Dead* in which the objectionable word had been changed to "fug." That had Joss and Mary Ellen giggling, vastly amused by the idea of tough soldiers saying evasive things like, "Don't you know there's a fugging war on, buddy?" In the earliest editions of the book, the publisher had sanitized soldier speech. Later editions reverted back to the intended copy.

One night in the early spring of their junior year, Mary Ellen had come into Joss's room in a state of turmoil. "Jeannie's missing," she announced. She was obviously upset. Joss and Montrose did not take it as seriously at first. They knew Jeannie had a history of flitting around the building, snooping, visiting, dropping in on people, invited or not, finding any reason to goof off.

On one occasion, she was forty-five minutes late for a house meeting and was reprimanded for it by Frances Danziger, the house president. "I had to go to the bathroom," Jeannie said.

"For *forty-five minutes*? That was almost the whole meeting." Frances was indignant. Even more than indignant when Jeannie responded haughtily, "Well, it was a major poop. It required serious time."

After the stuffy dorm meeting, all the girls were ready to laugh. She saw Montrose stiffen at Jeannie's unexpected revelation. Frances went red but held on stubbornly to her umbrage. "Maybe you needed to get to the infirmary," she finally decreed imperiously.

"No, Fannie," said Jeannie, using a nickname that Frances hated. "It was just a magnificent poop. The king of poops," she announced. "If everyone could have a poop like that, there would never have to be any more wars!"

Except for a scandalized few, the house meeting had dissolved in laughter.

Now Montrose, forever scarred by Jeannie's scatology, suggested, "Check the lavatories!"

But this time Jeannie was truly missing, not to be found anywhere in the house.

The sandwich man had long since uttered his last call. It was getting late, way past allowed hours, and deeper into the forbidden night. All of Harmon House was supposed to be asleep or studying for comps. "What'll we do?" Mary Ellen pleaded. "She isn't anywhere. I don't know what to do!"

"Check to see if any of her clothes are gone," Montrose suggested.

They rushed to ruffle through the clothes in the closet. "Nothing is missing," Mary Ellen reported. "Everything else is there. If she went out, she would need a coat."

"She can't have gone far without money anyhow," Joss declared. "Where does she keep her money? Does she have a bankbook? Any kind of checks? Didn't she tell us she still had lots of travelers' checks left from the summer?"

"No. All here in the top drawer of her desk." Mary Ellen whispered. She was searching but getting closer to tears.

Montrose put her arms around her. Using her most musical voice, Montrose chanted, "Pray with me, Mary Ellen, so wherever Jeannie is, God will be taking care of her."

Joss was baffled by this, but the two of them began muttering, and obviously Mary Ellen believed because she quieted at once.

It was Montrose who suggested their next action. "This is pretty important," she said. "We can't handle this by ourselves. Let's get the housemother."

"No! Don't!" Joss objected. "Emrie will just get scared and call the police. We don't want the police in on this. Call Hal!"

They reached Hal Merriam at his frat house. He was stunned and behaved like the obtuse bum they all believed him to be. "How should I know? I'm not even speaking to her anymore," he said. "All she ever did was give me a sore ass anyhow." At this juncture of their turbulent romance, he appeared truly to know nothing about Jeannie's whereabouts.

So the burden fell to Mrs. Emrie, the housemother, who was even more rattled than the girls. She had rarely needed to do anything more difficult than serve tea in the celebrated gracious-living style of the Harmon House. She huffed at the mention of Jeannie Irslinger's name. That name starred on Mrs. Emrie's list of problem people.

By this time, all of the occupants knew about Jeannie's absence. The girls were in turmoil, running around as if they were dramatic actresses in a noisy comedy-mystery. Girls were running up and down Harmon House halls doing ridiculous things, looking in laundry hampers and medicine chests, and narrating scary tales of the fate of other missing women. Some were clearly enjoying the commotion, laughing at crazy suggestions, making play of it; the roommates, however, were all huddled together on Joss's bed like a trio of scared little rabbits. All night they shared some frightened talk and a few snatches of sleep.

At about five in the morning, Jeannie Irslinger came sashaying down from the east gallery of Harmon House singing her song. She refused to tell anyone where she had been tucked away for the night, nor would she ever tell. "Ask Hortense" was all anyone heard her say about her absence.

That night was to remain forever in the collection of Harmon House secrets and mysteries.

The hullabaloo did not make her any more popular with the administration. Jeannie got suspended right away. Mrs. Irslinger flew in to collect her the next day. Throughout all, Jeannie remained recalcitrant. "It's better that I go," she declared. "I would be flunking my idiot comps anyhow. All I've done for them is goof off."

The year is late because decades have swallowed up the originality of things. What is it we wait for? Is it a little tide of luck or the oncoming change of seasons? Is it really love we wait for even while suspecting it's a trick? Yet we know, we've tested empirically; only the right kind of selfishness produces love.

—*Codex*, Joss Nye

Senior year just didn't add up to much fun for the women of the college. At the time, Joss didn't even have a reliable boyfriend to squire her. Frank Graham managed to come around, but he was always on the sidelines. Since his graduation, he had moved to the city. For a while he had a car but only with the most disastrous results. On one memorable trip toward his old haunts, he managed to park it in someone's yard. Right through the pretty wooden fence. This made a funny story that he loved to narrate on his frequent visits to the college. He still managed to come up weekends. Less fun for him these days; almost everybody he knew was seriously studying for comps. Frank's form of fun excluded study. Most of his old friends were in Joss's year. They had comps too. If he contacted them, he did them no favor. After having been grasshoppers during their four ant years, the guys had to relearn old subject matter. Frank's visits were dry, dreary, and invariably disappointed him.

In addition to the burden of her friends studying, Joss had to justify herself with a novel. It was so frustrating that she would have stopped trying had it not been for her teacher, Alan Resnick. He had dutifully led her through a welter of entrance forms for what the Goldschneider & Moran company called the Introduction to Young Writers Event. Event? Contest? Was it a contest? That was not one of the words used in the forms. If it was a contest, then shouldn't there be a prize, a stipend of some kind? She could not be sure. As far as Joss was concerned, everything was worded carefully to confuse. Even the interview was not called an interview. It came worded as an invitation. Someone at the offices of Goldschneider & Moran had sent her a note. It was just a note, unsigned, scrawled on a stiff card that bore the Goldschneider & Moran logo. The hasty script invited her to come visit the offices of G&M in the city. Who sent it? Could it be someone that mattered? Could it be some capricious clerk stricken by idle curiosity? It shouldn't matter to Joss. Someone at G&M Co. knew her name and had written asking if she would like a tour of the offices. No date or time was offered.

A tour of the offices? The whole process so far had been tedious and baffling. Mr. Resnick's encouragement had egged her on. He was gone now too, gone to the city to pursue his doctorate.

As far as she could determine, the brief card might at least indicate a real reaction to her submitted pages and plot outline. As Jeannie had advised her, she should confront. She had no solution but to go right up to the company and knock on the door.

She chose a Sunday to entrain southward on the New York, New Haven, and Hartford. The "invitation" had not specified a day. She figured she could then appear at the publishing company early on the first day of the workweek. Meet either Goldschneider or Moran. Meet whatever dignitaries she could find. Wiggle her way in. Or not. At least get a clear picture of what awaited her.

When she arrived in the city, she found herself jittery. She knew that what she most needed was a carload of brass. She needed to be brazen. She did not feel as confident as the occasion required. She lacked an iron suit, or backers, or a fearless friend, like Jeannie. Mr. Resnick occurred to her. She saw him in her mind's eye, bent and bleary-eyed, groping along. It was as if his picture flashed on in her mind. He'd encouraged her before. That's what she needed, a familiar mentor.

Mr. Resnick now lived in this city while working on studies to complete his PhD. He'd rented a room somewhere. She had a telephone number in her bag. She dialed it directly.

The call was picked up quickly, and she found herself really glad to hear a familiar voice. He sounded so nice. Of course he did. He always sounded nice. Sounding nice was his gift. He was just blessed with a handsome voice. His voice could register pleasure with a trick of the tonsils, and now he used this charm to acknowledge her with a grand measure of enthusiasm. He seemed really pleased to hear from her. Joss was surprised to find she too was genuinely pleased. Hearing him again calmed her jangled nerves.

"Joss! Where are you?" he asked.

She was in the Grand Central Station. Joss told him she had a general plan but was not too sure of how she should initiate it.

"There must be a coffee shop in the station," Resnick responded. "Wait there. I'll come meet you. I can be there in about twenty minutes. Get a coffee or something. Just wait. I'll find you."

As the twenty minutes stretched out, Joss remembered how much she really disliked waiting. Coffee shops were unpleasant places for her. This one gave her the creeps. It was none too clean. On the over-washed, dingy imitation marble of a nearby tabletop someone had left the smashed remains of a soft-boiled egg. She felt her gorge rise. She turned away. Behind her, the shiny wall reflected her small self waiting. That, too, was more than she cared to see. The reflection looked too much like Kitty McCorkle jittering nervously in a hotel lobby, waiting to deliver baffling news.

But Joss had plenty of other things to think about. She had to consider the possible meeting tomorrow. She knew an unsigned invitation was nothing, about as good as no invitation. In a way, she'd almost have to enter the scene as an interloper. Nervy. Then if she did succeed in attracting the attention of anyone important, she intended to capitalize on her youth. To her mind, youth was her selling point—a young girl writing what would be a scandalous book. The trick was to be innocent and audacious at the same time. This was expecting a lot of help from her short stature and her cookie face. She'd dressed in a blouse with a Peter Pan collar showing a face, all insouciant, poked out above her favorite yellow sweater. It was Naples yellow though Jeannie once proclaimed, "Oh, look. Here comes a little bit of yolk."

At best she was ready to pretend. It was a projected sham.

Then there was the book to think about. She knew she was a good writer, but could she handle the squadrons of complicated characters she'd invented? Or the involuted story she had projected? Truth to tell, the only part that interested her was the development of the sisters. She indulged her mind by thinking that if the project were accepted she would still have the possibility of changing things as she went along. That depended very much on G&M's belief in her basic shock appeal. The shock of it was incest, of course. But the trouble was that incest actually shocked Joss herself. It was something she had never even imagined. When pressed to ponder her relationship with her own father, she could only come up with one word: remote.

She had taken Mr. Resnick's advice and done some research on the subject, looking up numerous articles, amazed at how much information there was about it. Apparently it was quite common behavior and thoroughly documented, which should have scared her off right there. She couldn't imagine working around such a situation. She'd have to proceed with caution not to step on the psychologists' toes.

Her plan for now was to stay at some cheap hotel. Then the unwelcome memory struck her: once in this very city, she had stayed at a cheap hotel with Bobby Ochs. The combination of two things opened up in her memory: the cheap hotel, the dingy coffee shop. Juxtaposed, they reminded her of that awful night in Cranston, a terrible night that happened, happened entirely outside of her own volition.

Resnick took more than twenty minutes. Three slow cigarettes later, he arrived. She leaped up out of her chair and threw herself against him so hard that his arms folded around her. She was trembling so violently the she was ashamed. She knew that even through the sleeves of his coat he had to notice how hard she was shaking.

The next day, she regretted the episode. Initiating a hug with Mr. Resnick had embarrassed her. She was not feeling like the old Joss at all. To both her relief and regret, Resnick had come to pick her up. She was unable to speak to him with the usual camaraderie. He, on the other hand, had reacted to last night's unintended hug cheerfully. He had laughed about it, turned it into a joke. That toned down her anxiety.

After he rescued her from the coffee shop, he took her to the automat on Thirty-Fourth Street where they shared a thirty-cents sandwich. He had behaved like a perfect hero. She couldn't ask for more. He then delivered her to a room his university maintained for student emergencies. It was a small, very functional room, so plain and unadorned that it reminded her of nothing. She slept well enough, with some occasional twists and turns as she reprocessed her situation. The accidental hug puzzled her. Where should she place that in her schedule of events? Mr. Resnick seemed quite unaffected. Hopefully he'd forgotten the whole thing.

In the morning he called. He insisted on getting her some breakfast. He ordered eggs and coffee in another little café. She accepted toast. The place was cleaner than the café where she had waited in the station. At least that much gave her a measure of tranquility to face the day.

"It's was nice to have breakfast with someone for a change," he said. "I'm usually up for toast and a lousy coffee in my monastic room, Joss. The scholarly life is pretty cheerless."

"I'm scared now, Mr. Resnick," she mumbled. "I don't know what I expected to accomplish. I really don't want to go in that place."

"Be strong, Joss," he advised. "You know your own value. Remember—*you* are the author. You're doing *them* the favor of reading your work. Keep up your nerve and just keep up your usual gutsy style, Joss. If you can do that, you will surely beguile them."

With the exception of Montrose, her friends all thought Resnick was cipher, a dud. But Joss now felt that he was her pal and primary confidant. She only wished he could walk through the door of Goldschneider & Moran with her.

Nevertheless, with a lot less trepidation than she thought possible, she approached the door to the publishing offices as Mr. R. sailed off. As he sailed away, Resnick vanished for her.

She swallowed hard and recomposed herself. Here she was at last. Triumphant movie music played in her imagination. She was at the door of a big publishing company. Big door, big deal. Wherever one goes, one must enter through a door. Everywhere in the world there are doors and doors waiting for victims to enter, to be gulped down deeper into strange places they may not be able to control with such little armament as she brought to the fray—freckles, a Peter Pan collar, and a cookie face.

Joss reflected on the doors. She was impressed by the lavish entry. It was glass, and the glass was decorated with colored swirling patterns in the style of art noveau. Then she gathered up her courage and fronted right in. By the very impact of her feet, she could tell she had her intensity back. Resnick had been a restorative.

As she stood at the desk, the phone began to ring. The young receptionist made an impatient grimace and dealt with the caller very briefly before directing her attention to Joss. "Good morning and welcome to Goldschneider & Moran. Shelly LeBow speaking."

"I'm Joss."

"And who would Joss be?" Shelly LeBow said. She spoke with a nasal New York accent. Joss thought it sounded hostile.

"I'm a writer," Joss began, but even as she spoke, she recognized the message of disapproval that soured Shelly LeBow's eyes and mouth.

"Writers admitted only with scheduled appointments," said Shelly.

It was obvious that the girl did not like writers much. Joss raised her voice, "But I have an invitation," she said.

Clearly, that was unexpected. Shelly looked puzzled. "An invitation? That's a new one on me. Lemme see." Joss tried to pass over the little square of notepaper. Another phone rang, and Shelly picked it up

"I'm a writer ..." Joss said meekly.

"Oy," said the girl with a fatal shrug. "Join the club."

"... And I got an invitation," Joss said.

"Yeah. I heard you the first time. Let's see it."

"Shelly, I was invited here."

"It's Otto," Shelly proclaimed as she studied the card. That explanation meant nothing to Joss, who dumbly watched Shelly push some buttons on her desk. Shelly was still holding up the notepaper with the invitation. Joss saw the inner door with all its glass decorations swing open.

An incredibly handsome man stepped through. He was about the most handsome man Joss had ever seen—but he was dark. Darker than dark, Joss thought; he was almost the shiny color of India ink, and he seemed to emerge out of the swoops of colored glass, appearing like an act of magic.

Joss stared in disbelief. The man saw the notepaper in Shelly's hand. "You're Nye? Are you Jocelyn Nye?" he asked. She could only nod. "I expected someone older," he remarked. Then he reached for her hand and pulled her inside Goldschneider & Moran's.

"You were smart to come on over," he said.

The man had seemed to emerge right through the swoops on the glass door. Joss stared. He was an exotic thing to her, like an act of magic with the master of ceremonies appearing in an unexpected suit of skin. Black—really, really black.

In spite of its prodigious Madison Avenue address, Goldschneider & Moran's offices occupied distressing little space. To begin with, the actual area was unequal to its contents. It was stuffed with trash. What Joss saw now was an extremely cramped room. She was very disappointed. From the wide façade on Madison Avenue, she had expected spaciousness. At least her movie-going experience had promised more. She had seen publishing houses in films about authors. *Theodora Goes Wild* was one of her favorites. The setting as seen in any Hollywood interpretation was usually glamorous and wide as the prairie. One could envision a ball in the front offices of such places, but when she looked at the reality—dusty, crowded shelves and stacks of works, possibly to be read, probably to be rejected—her heart sank.

There was no talk of awarding anything. Joss just did not know what to say. She had a perilous tightrope feeling that affected her balance and made her angry with the illustrious company of Mr. Goldschneider & Mr. Moran. An unimposing little place. Sad place, a pile of sad manuscript pages, sad the eye of her objectives. A hard-cover copy of her book from such a place would smell of yellow paper. Tired pages, destined to get relegated to the old bookstores on Fourth Avenue.

"The company is very interested in young talent," Otto said. "We offer encouragement to the most skilled." Apparently the encouragement was not financial but human, a young editor, sprung on Joss to her utter astonishment. Her prize was this dark fellow who drew her aside and introduced himself as John Otto. He was, as she had first perceived, amazingly and unmistakably black. The messy offices had shocked her enough. For Joss, John Otto was a new experience. As he drew her into a dusty corner of the G&M offices she had no idea of how to talk to him.

"You're my first Negro," she blurted out, almost immediately regretting her words. She had no wish to be offensive. "Should I have said *colored person?*" Joss asked feebly.

Otto laughed. "Thanks, Miss Nye. You'd better stick with Negro. Believe it or not, 'colored person' is even more to be avoided.

"Pity—it was such a gentle evasion in its day. Negro is fine. Okay by me, anyway. I still think I'm a Negro, although my wife thinks she's black. She's always more in tune with the times.

"I'm here as a token, of course. They plucked me out of a graduate course at Columbia. I was a token there as well.

"People keep trying to prove something with my skin. Not the first time that has happened to a person of color."

Joss laughed because Otto was laughing. She was not at all sure the remarks were meant to be funny.

Otto continued, "I'm delighted to be here. It's my life's dream to be an editor. I love to read. I love books. I loved the pages you wrote for your projected novel. I would love to work with you and your book if they will actually let me."

"You really liked them?" Joss asked. "You liked my synopsis?"

He frowned. "No, I have to pause at that. The synopsis was a mess, confused and overblown. Can't say I liked your synopsis at all. But I really responded to the sample pages ..."

"You didn't get overwhelmed by my words?"

"The sweep. The sweep. That is exactly what I did like," he assured her. "Your style is so special. It's fine, complex, almost ..."

"Baroque?" Joss inquired.

It was so hellishly hot. This year, June had started with record-breaking temperatures. Even an old frame domicile like the Harmon House reflected the eternal sweltering heat. Outside, the very eaves drooped; inside, the monotonous stirring of the old ceiling fans added their rusty squeaks to the suffering rooms.

Though it was still early on their graduation day, most of the girls were awake. It was too key a day to sleep in. Their black commencement cloaks hung somberly over the doorjambs of each room. Girls dreaded donning those heavy garments in the still air. For now, the baccalaureate candidates idled, wearing the least possible, usually their underwear or briefest baby-doll pajamas. For the moment, they were all slouching in their own dens, inert and barely breathing.

Joss was draped across the bed sidewise at the head of the bed because Mary Ellen had had taken possession across the foot. Mary Ellen was such a drag now. She made the room hotter with her funeral face. She was still in mourning over the termination of Jeannie Irslinger. She had, however, come in to arrange Joss's hair for the exercises. Since her recent experimentation, she had discovered some methods to make Joss's hair quite pliable with the electric comb. Unfortunately, she always brought her sorrowful aura in with her. She felt constrained to carry it wherever she went. It was as if she was in bereavement and they all had to suffer her sorrow. Actually, they should have kicked her out, but Joss was too grateful for the hair solution, and Montrose was too nice to evict her.

"Jeannie's not dead, Mary Ellen," Joss pointed out for perhaps the fiftieth time. "You'll see her again."

"Where? She won't come back here, kiddo. And if she did, we wouldn't be here for her anyway, would we?"

"Speaking of *where*. Why won't you tell us *where* the heck she deposited herself that terrible night she pulled her disappearing act?"

"Because I don't know," Mary Ellen said sharply. "Every snoopy girl in this dumb house asks me that and then asks me again ten minutes later. Even though I think about it all the time, I *just don't know!*" Mary Ellen complained. "All I know is that she had a rip-roaring fight with Hal, and she was fit to be tied afterward," she added.

"What were they fighting about?" asked Joss.

"The dopiest thing, of course. Hal told her he wanted to go into advertising after graduation, and she blew her stack. She said Hal was a liar, a cheat, and generally an evil person, so advertising was the right field for him to practice his damnable villainy."

"Wow. All that over just his harmless advertising ambitions?"

"Yes. She was always going on about how things like little advertising songs on the radio got stuck in your head and you couldn't get them out. You know ..." and Mary Ellen sang the lyric couplet of a popular toothpaste ad.

"*You'll wonder where the yellow went …*

"See. Like that. Once it gets in there, you just about have to start singing the 'Star-Spangled Banner' or something equally powerful to get it out of your brain.

"So Jeannie asserts that's the deliberate goal of advertising—mind control. That's their job, eventually to infect everyone's thoughts. An evil thing. Hitler tried it, remember? And you know how she is, Joss. Pretty soon she was calling him every name in the book. Her vocabulary is right up to that. He was giving it right back to her. He's never far behind. They said terrible things. The air was blue all around the two of them."

"They really were made for each other, weren't they?" Joss commented.

"An extreme reaction," Montrose said. "But I'm not surprised.

"Remember how funny Jeannie was when we first came here? Everyone thought she was a comic and hung around to hear her outlandish humor. Then as time went by, her humor got sharper and sharper. She started hurting people's feelings. Not so funny anymore. I'd say that came to a head about the time of the Varsity Show."

At that moment, Anna Destri appeared at their door. Coming up from the first floor, Anna was sweaty, huffing like a grampus, and exhaling puffballs of smoke from her poisonous mentholated cigarette. "Joss, you have a caller!" she croaked.

"What? Me? A caller? Male?"

Flustered and put-upon by her trip up the stairs, Anna was less than civil. "Some kind of caller. You can't expect me to do a gender check," she snapped. "But whatever it is, he's waiting in the street! Hurry the heck up!" Anna said before scurrying back downstairs.

"Oh, shit!" Joss said. It was a new word for her mouth, a satisfying frustration word, assumed to demonstrate her increasing maturity. That Montrose did not approve of it increased its emphasis. "I don't even have any makeup on yet." Nor clothes, she might have added, as she threw a duster over her chemise and followed the puffer balls down the stairs to the front door.

A chauffeured black limo was parked at the curb in front of Harmon House. Joss knew at once who it had to be. He was small and somewhat hunched over in the big car. Though she had not seen him in more than a year, something inside her responded. She recognized the patchy blond head.

From inside the vehicle, he flung open the rear door. Reached out his hand. Joss grabbed it and clambered in.

"Hello, Joe," she said loudly. "It's my graduation day today."

"So you passed?" he replied.

"In spades," Joss said. "Nice of you to come. Did you know today was my graduation day?" Of course he didn't. She knew better.

"I'm here on business," he harrumphed. "No time for academic foofaraw." He was holding a dime store, red folder-envelope that he now pushed toward her. He explained that it contained "actions." For business reasons, the actions had been temporarily put in her name.

"Actions temporarily put in my ...? What kind of ..." Joss muttered. She was amazed, flabbergasted. "But I ..."

"Don't worry. It's all on the up and up," he said. "You don't have to worry about a thing. You will be receiving the interest quarterly as long as they're in your possession. Meanwhile you just put the whole file away in a safe place until you're notified. It's only temporary. After a while, I will be calling for them back."

Joss was confused, but she managed to spit out some syllables that didn't make any sense, not even to herself.

"Just play it close to the vest, girl. Eventually an agent will be in touch with you about the details."

"But I don't understand!" Joss argued.

Quite seriously, Joe replied, "The less you understand, the better."

"Hey, Joe! You're not talking to Kitty now, you know."

Joe laughed. He obviously caught her implication. "Kitty?" he repeated after her. "Where the hell is she anyhow? Do you know? She was supposed to be the one holding the paperwork." No more explanation was forthcoming.

Joss sat there, almost with mouth agape. She was

totally nonplussed. She tried a few times to pass the red folder back to Joe. He didn't resist. Nevertheless she found herself still holding it. She had forgotten that he had the most insidious way of getting and doing what he wanted. The folder stayed on her lap.

She looked hard at Joe Nye. This small man was still her father. He stirred feelings in her, but she would be hard put to tell anyone what they were. For the moment, she was satisfied with just cataloging him visually. He was still just a short man with scruffy hair. She tried to see him, but slumped over in the darkened car, it was hard to see anything clearly. His freckles were fading, she thought. Made him look washed out, tired, older.

"So you made it through the whole four years, huh?" he joked. He smiled. Joss was surprised how it warmed her to be smiled at by Joe Nye. "It don't surprise nobody, I guess. You always was some kind of whizz kid." She noticed that he still spoke with the thick Brooklyn accent of his childhood. He still made grammatical errors in speaking too. It made him seem tough, though he probably wanted to sound more amiable in speaking to his daughter for the first time in so long. How many years, she wondered. Surely she had not seen him for at least a year, and for some time before that too. He was not around on the rare occasions she went home for brief holidays. She wasn't sure where he went, just that she was not invited to ask.

Joe was smoking now, one cigarette after another. She noticed his fingers, stained yellow by nicotine. Except that he was short and blond, she could see little physical resemblance to herself. She'd been told many times that she practically mirrored Kitty. Undoubtedly she took something from Joe too. She wondered if he was a very smart man. Maybe that was the inheritance. Apparently he was successful, but no one ever told her what he did. He paid the bills; that's all she knew. Mary Ellen's description of Jeannie's fight was still in Joss's mind. She thought of advertising. Joe always got his way with minimum palaver. Could he be in advertising?

Joss supposed she probably took something else from him. Could it be the smarts? She noticed his gestures. The way he held and flicked his cigarette was odd. She wondered if she ever made the same motions. He had a way of squeezing the muscle in his right cheek while he talked. It made his lips pull to the side in a pseudo-smile. She thought it almost sinister.

"You were always a wise guy in school," Joe remarked. "You coulda been one of them Whiz Kids. Yeah. They had those kids on the radio ... the Whiz Kids, something like that they called them." She could hear his strong Brooklyn accent. She had forgotten that funny cast to his speech. It definitely placed him geographically. She didn't talk that way. Kitty did, as Brooklyn was where Joe had found her.

"It's quite amazing that you're here," Joss remarked.

"Well, I hadda come. Deliver the articles and all, you know."

"Will you stay for the graduation ceremonies?" Joss asked. She was deliberately prodding. She knew this question would shake his composure.

Joe looked stunned. He certainly had not expected that invitation. He hesitated a minute before replying, "Can't. Business calls. You know."

"Really, I don't know anything. I don't know anything at all," Joss declared. She paused but then added, "Hey, Joe, can you tell me this much? Am I going to be rich?"

"Rich? Not a chance." Joe laughed. "You're lucky if you get twenty bucks a month out of it, and even that's only temporary." He smiled that pseudo-smile. And Joss was handed out of the car as abruptly as she'd been pulled in.

She watched the black car make its fast departure. She looked at her bare palm and imagined a twenty-dollar bill lying face up on it. "Well, there's that much," she announced to the steaming hot street. "Pretty good for just doing nothing."

At long last, time for the ceremony arrived. Joss threw on her robe, slapped on the graduation board, then hustled to join the others. Her mind suffered as a vortex of thoughts arose: money, relationships, the future, and the past all tangling together in her brain. She raced to tell Montrose about her windfall, but Montrose had already headed for the meeting place.

Most of the girls were already at the starting location on top of Chapel Hill. At first they formed up in little clumps that quickly becoming marked by their squealed cacophony of love and farewell. Sally Petrucci and some other girls from the writing classes welled up to cluster around Joss before they all spread out to find their dearest friends among the graduates of the women's college. Each agglomeration of girls supported animated hugging and gushes of tears. Many did not expect to see one another after this day, nor for a future that extended down through mysterious channels into their forevers. Harmon House must cease to contain them and all their stories. The occasion was a happy one while yet not totally happy. Sorrows and fears were a satisfying element of it too. It was the day of their baccalaureate, a steaming hot one for all the young bodies eager to commence their lives while withering under their black robes.

In spite of the heat, many people came. Of course, parents were there. Joss saw both of the Riggs, Mama and Papa, hopping around Mary Ellen like fleas, each bearing a camera. They were funny, almost a traffic obstacle in the path of the graduates descending in a slow stream down the side of Chapel Hill toward the university chapel where the somber words of departure were to be intoned. Montrose was making her farewells with her special friends, the moneyed girls, Nevada Gertz, Dorcas Tannenberg, and Daisy Arlynn Way, all fellow members of the Benefactors' Club.

Then girls began moving down the hill at a slow, almost sepulchral pace. Her friends were near, Montrose and Mary Ellen behind her. Joss thought they looked like three penguins, a tall one, a medium-sized one, and her itty-bitty penguin self, in an instinctive march to their sea—their sea being, of course, the vast, unpredictable world before them. Inevitable.

Mary Ellen was sniveling. Perhaps she still was grieving for Jeannie Irslinger. In spite of all their encouraging, Mary Ellen still couldn't bring up a smile. Joss, instead, smiled extra hard. She smiled until her face hurt. She knew she would figure prominently in a raft of Papa Rigg's pictures. Better to see Mary Ellen surrounded by smiling friends than just to immortalize his only daughter snuffling snot into a hankie.

The girls of the women's college descended first. The men of the university would now be forming their own black file to snake down behind them. Joss wondered if Bobby would be one of them. He should be, but Hal said

Bobby had enlisted. For a long time before, he'd been hanging around trying to get her attention. Then he had quit stalking. Joss supposed Hal had told the truth when he said Bobby had gone to war.

Not for the first time, it occurred to her how wrong the scene was—the population of one small college followed by that of a major university. All the ebony figures swarming separately down the hill to collect the *same* document.

Frank had one year of college before he went into the navy. Then he served a short time before he was mustered out at the war's end. He entered the university as a sophomore. Consequently he graduated one year before Joss did. By the time Joss and her crowd got out of school, he had long since gone to settle himself in the city.

The apartment he found was very high, an airy space. There was a pleasant view of the tops of trees. Though in a cityscape, his building was up near the park. The streets neighboring the residence were all old-money territory, very dignified family quarters. Quiet. Quiet was the primary requirement for Frank: he was the genius of sound. He had graduated with a science degree with special emphasis on sonance. Joss knew he had even enrolled in some premed courses concerned with the inner structure of the ear. Sound was Frank's primary interest, and it was reflected in its absence in his noise-free apartment.

By an enviable quirk of luck, he had graduated into the era of auditory fidelity. Hi-fi was the new rage. Everyone was interested in updating sound equipment. Before joining the navy, Frank, while still a high school student, had invented a gadget that could augment the range of sound on his ham radio. This device sold and was now in production, providing Frank with a handsome income. It seemed inevitable that the same device might prove important in the growing need for medical hearing aids.

Frank was definitely on to it.

Sound was Frank's religion. Upon graduation, he set up a business in the city. Whenever she called there, she was told he was in the laboratories where he did his serious worship, bowing his head to decibels. In the lab, he allowed no telephones since he dabbled there in sonic wizardry, not to be interrupted.

Frank adored sound and its contrasts of which even an absence of sound made a facet. On an internal organ with which he had apparently been born, he constantly measured the gradients and modulations he could hear in a clink or in a common household squeak, qualities that Joss often suspected of being imaginary because she herself was largely unaware of them.

Sometimes when he drank, he would burst into tears, for it frequently occurred that the channels of his ears blurred, splashed, heard sounds that a drowning man might hear, strange sizzles and wet plops that vibrated in his mind. Then he would grasp at things—Joss's hand, if it were in the vicinity—giggling that now he was truly sloshed. He would rave about going deaf, the ultimate hell for him. "In hell you have to listen to noise. That's what hell is," he maintained.

Yet, though Frank professed to love sound and hate noise, she mistook his definitions. She couldn't drag him to a concert, for instance. On the other hand, he had some records with appalling titles that he made her listen to: *Sounds of the Ocean Deeps,* or *Sounds of the Tropical Rain*

Forest, which consisted of interminable fish whistles and simian squeals.

Jokingly, he referred to his apartment as an aerie because it was high and some kind of crazy bird lived in it. It was a lovely, large apartment, but after he'd put in a futon, a coffee table, and a few sofas, he kept the place barren. All the closet doors were speakers for his sound system to blare out the sounds of the winds, the tides, the mating cries of wild animals.

Joss suggested he might be lucky enough to catch someone's tummy rumbles. Then he could create a recording and entitle it "Borborygmus Blues." Might catch the popular imagination and ride right up to #1 on the Hit Parade.

Still faithful and true, Frank used some of his weekends to go back to his old digs at the university. He was still hung up on Joss so he visited often. Joss usually was busy writing her book, but he gave it at try. If she was too busy to spend time with him, he still knew a few fellows who could be talked into pausing to elbow bend and toss a brew or two with him.

Unfailingly generous, he kept two sofas for visitors from school. Joss and all her girlfriends were advised that he offered them sleep space anytime they came to town. They felt free to use the apartment whenever they had shopping or theater jaunts. To Frank's delight, it had been a popular stopping point for girls from the college.

Joss was invited to see John Otto's converted carriage house in Brooklyn Heights. It was a high-ceilinged, beamed room in high fashion. According to John, it had recently been the subject of an article in *Trends* magazine. He was inordinately proud of that. Joss was suitably humbled by the environment, as she had been by Otto, her "first Negro."

The living area was like an island, a space all contained on a huge Bakhtiari rug—adrift, becalmed with its jewel colors and intricate designs. This center was surrounded by a bare margin called "studio" where easels, half-scraped palettes, and canvases large and small leaned on one another. There was a permeating odor that Joss was knowledgeable enough to identify as linseed oil. Big windows framed old glass, marred with flaws that slightly distorted the view. The house was old, and even the glass panes had history. "The original glass," Otto bragged. It had a purplish cast. Through these amethyst antiques, they looked out on disciplined patches, partitioned city gardens. A canvas still on its easel reiterated the view with a geometric abstraction—squares and rectangles—held together and given unity by an arresting blending of the colors. Blocky but sound in composition, and the colors took your breath away. It was as if Davina invented new colors. So talented.

Joss was staying at Montrose's apartment while she struggled to make a book out of *House of Women*. She had written great parts of it, but now came the agony of having to put them together, turn it inside out as needed, and remake it, force it to make sense. John Otto was helping her, an immense help, but they fought like cats over passages in the book. Joss just couldn't prevent herself from balking at every suggestion. She liked the words in the sequence she had placed them. He argued for more sense in the content. It didn't matter to the alliance. They knew they liked each other.

His wife was another story. Joss had been afraid to meet her, but Davina proved to be unbelievably admirable. A special person. An artist. Hers was the painting on the easel. Art explained the luxury of their life. Davina was an artist of renown, and her paintings commanded enormous sums.

Joss thought that, in addition to the art angle, she was also an actress, one of the great actresses of the Western world. A diva. Wall-to-wall phony. You couldn't actually believe anything she said. And yet one had no choice but to be completely charmed by her. To all her histrionics there was never a trace of meanness or pettiness. She was kind. You could feel it. Warmth just flowed out of her to everyone in the room. She called Joss "honeylamb" in a drawl that vaguely suggested the sunny South, though Joss seemed to recall John saying that Davina had been born, brought up, and thoroughly educated in New Hampshire. It didn't matter. She did and said everything with a special flair. Love softened all her edges.

Very tactfully, John had said, "Bring a friend, if you like, Joss. Any friend of yours is welcome. Always." Of course he meant Frank. Both the Ottos had met Frank. Joss knew she was a subject of speculation at the Goldschneider & Moran offices, where she frequently dropped in. All the little overworked assistants like Shelly LeBow, correspondents, all the bright college girls with their useless degrees in English literature, not very different from herself, actually—all had boring office hours to speculate on everyone else's love life. They had to have something to talk about.

But she had not even mentioned Otto's invitation to Frank. She didn't even know where Frank was right now. Instead she had asked Montrose, and Montrose had dragged along her new little boy, Dorian Sivade. Dorian was Montrose's latest find. He was hired to illustrate Montrose's notes for a children's book—just notes. There was no book yet. Dorian was a seventeen-year-old boy who looked and acted like a seventeen-year-old boy. Montrose doted on him. Joss did not.

Dorian was different, to say the least. He was like an exotic plant. Maybe one of those carnivorous plants that trap bugs. His eyes slanted slightly like giant watermelon seeds. The pomes of his eyes were so big and black they left little room for the whites. He lifted his face to every stimulus, reminding Joss of something vegetable. Like a flower? A flower with a face. Turning. Responding to the sun? He and Montrose together, like two flowers responding to a tropism. Eerie. They were in some way, though not in any way easy to define, alike. Montrose's glance had the gift of bestowing intelligence on anyone held in it. By jingo, the boy needed some of that, Joss thought. He had small wit of his own.

During the evening, Montrose and Orrin sang together. His voice threaded out like spun candy, spooling into sweetness. It was a young boy's voice, or a girl's. He could not control it, but when you really listened to the song, the whole fabric of its pattern and meaning, you heard that it was deliberate, perfect, exactly right; those high reaches expressing a transport of happiness or, equally, of pain. His voice lifted over Montrose's velvet alto. Together they spiked feelings words could never express. When they stopped singing, there was a moment of hush. No one was yet ready to trust mere speech.

There was a baby too. Johnny, the baby, was eleven months old and very precocious. He already had a vocabulary. He was a spoiled, very handsome baby. His dark skin was satiny. He shone. Davina's love just oozed all around him, oiled him, even from across the broad room. His lips were puffed out like a little strawberry, pulling kisses. John called him Abe. Joss asked why, and John very casually replied, "After the great emancipator, of course," with a swift glance at Davina, who did not look pleased at all. Joss thought it must be some inscrutable private joke.

Fussing about the baby was not to Joss's taste. She

was not confident around infants. Ambivalence moved her to the far side of the room to look at the paintings. Davina noticed. She drawled, "Honeylamb, last thing in the world I want to do is be a great artist. I do not *like* to paint. Contrary to the opinion of the expert." With a great sweep of her arm, she indicated John. "I do not appreciate the odors of linseed oil and turpentine. As a matter of cold, hard fact, they nauseate me entirely. I prefer baby oil and pablum, really. Honey, all I want to do is be a mama. But no. The boss has this fixed idea that he's got to be married to a woman who *does* things. He forces me to paint. I mean it, honeylamb. Literally. Forces me. I declare I believe he'd beat me if I refused!

"I use his name. My name is Brooks, but I sign the painting Otto. That's a man's name, right? So just with those four letters I circumvent two prejudices." John pulled his lips tight to that crooked smile of his. Something about it didn't quite fit.

Was he as richly amused by Davina's declarations as he pretended to be? The carriage house interior had been converted according to her designs and under her direction. *And money, too,* Joss thought. He could not possibly earn much as a sous-editor at Goldschneider & Moran's. In that company, they were, as she was daily learning, notoriously cheap. They had so far come out with no assurances about publication, or a stipend, or even about an award for *House of Women.*

Over time, more and more of their old classmates came to the city, many to establish residence, many to hunt for jobs, and many just to visit.

In late August, Mary Ellen Rigg appeared. She brought her photo album to share the pictures her parents had taken of them at graduation. There were scads of photos. Too many caps and gowns; of much more interest to Joss were pictures that had been in the album for a longer time. There were shots taken in Harmon House going all the way back to freshman year. Joss studied a picture of herself with Frank. Probably taken when they first had known each other, as Joss appeared impressed, googling her eyes at him. He would be a sophomore. He was a grown man, after all. A service veteran. In the picture, she plucked at his sleeve for attention. Frank appeared to be listening to her intently. Very nice. Polite. Dreadfully sincere. They were sitting. She could see his patterned socks. Argyll socks. They were all the rage then. Really sharp. You couldn't buy that kind. A girl must have knit them for him. Not Joss. That wasn't her kind of thing. Joss was wearing the pale blue sweater set that Sally Dart told her was a man-catcher. Frank was there in the flower of his youth, his response seeming to confirm Sally's research on color and sex appeal. He was enchanted.

Mary Ellen had labeled the pictures with dopey comments. Here was one of Joss labeled "Joss at Haymarket Square—Boston Egg." Joss looked at her younger self, smiling prettily for the camera, flirting with the one-man band, an old man cadging pennies in the square. He had an accordion across his chest, a drum strapped over his back to be snapped into action by the motion of his shoulder blades, a harmonica dangled from his tin hat, like a tin pagoda. Joss remembered something on his legs. A tambourine that jangled with claps of his kneecaps. Every movement of his body resulted in chains of noise. Joss had felt sorry. Even in the sepia of the old snapshot you could see that his life was not an easy one. Poor old guy. But the pretty girl smiled.

The girl, who was herself, was wearing a yellow cotton print. Yes, she remembered it because it had cost such a fortune at Lord and Taylor's, something like thirty dollars—more than two months of her accumulated allowances. She remembered that girl's dress so well but not where the girl had gotten the money to buy it.

She held a flat straw hat, a little boater with a dark ribbon on it. Smiling, with her yellow hair sticking out all over the place. Two unknown young men, Charles River Sunday dandies from the look of them, observed the girl with obvious approval. Joss remembered it so well. She remembered the girl and what was inside the girl, but that girl was no longer herself.

"Mary Ellen, these pictures are ancient! Where did you get them? Here's one of Frank before any of us even knew him!"

"He gave that to you, Joss, but you didn't want it," Mary Ellen explained.

"Yeah. I was an ungrateful mooch, wasn't I?" Joss laughed. She was feeling strange and moochy and ungrateful while so internally aware of time's perfidy.

One picture glowed with the chemical yellow of old photos. A picture of Frank Graham. It had obviously been made before Joss ever met him. Taken late in the war, perhaps. He had on a naval striped middy. Maybe he was even wearing the old regulation bell-bottomed trousers, the pants with buttoned panels in the front. So young. And so handsome. He looked engraved that way, as if youth was going to remain a permanent feature of his face. Hair clipped so close, almost shaved in the style of the times. Showing a black, well-shaped cranium. He used to brag that they could shave him to the skin in the morning, but he'd have a half-inch growth by breakfast. "Five o'clock shadow all day long," he'd say, grinning. Nice teeth. Craggy face, even so young. Nice. Virile-looking. Too sincere though. Posed holding a pipe in the picture. Probably a prop. Joss had never seen him smoke one.

There was the old gang, preening and posing. Nevada Gertz holding aloft a champagne glass as if for a toast. Languid, supercilious look assumed for the camera.

Nothing in the glass, of course, just a celebration of being young and alive. Montrose aloof, ever the empress of her own mysterious kingdom.

"Montrose!" Joss called. "Come see yourself in these old snapshots."

Montrose reneged. "I don't like to dance backward," she declared. Sometimes she used that expression. Joss borrowed it for Gloriana to say in the book. It didn't mean a lot to Joss or to Mary Ellen, but it was a phrase that Montrose had used before. It always stuck in Joss's mind.

"Oh, God, Joss. Look! It's the Doe Eye Party. Remember the Doe Eye Party?" Mary Ellen chortled, pushing forward a picture of the lot of them parading their faces around. Joss amused herself trying to remember the names. In the background, she could even see little Delly Muir, Delilah de Courtland-Muir, just being herself, a little girl with a big name, delightedly taking in all the nonsense. Innocent as the day in her white nightie. "Oh, Delly was cuter than a kewpie doll, and almost as vacant," said Joss unkindly.

Montrose, standing outside the dormitory in her camel coat, the color of it just a few shades lighter than her brown eyes. She looked long and slender and graceful and smiling that smile with a little sadness to it. Wise. Foreseeing. Now refusing to dance backward. Joss felt a twinge. She suddenly understood. The old photos were upsetting her too. She pushed them aside. "I want to hear about *now*, Mary Ellen," Joss announced.

Raising her voice for emphasis, Montrose asked, "Mary Ellen, do you have any news of Jeannie Irslinger?"

But Mary Ellen could add little to what they already knew. Jeannie had dropped out of school completely and been taken home. Recently they heard she had slipped away from her home. That was all Mary Ellen knew too. "I knew they couldn't hold on to her. Her family says they don't know where she is, but I think maybe they do. I think she went off to be somewhere where no one knew her, because I truly believe she must have been pregnant."

All three were silent some few moments while this possibility was mulled over. Then Joss said, "You mean like she's gone somewhere to have a baby?"

"Either that or she's gone somewhere to get *rid* of a baby, and that would be terrible. Jeannie might just do it too, because she doesn't *know* it is a sin," Mary Ellen said.

Joss stiffened. Out of the corner of her eye, she noticed Montrose's reaction. The woman had actually crossed herself against the evil.

It took some time before they settled back into the habit of being together again. Upon her arrival, Montrose and Joss had found Mary Ellen much transformed by time and the season. Joss marveled at her hair, styled in the manner of a heroine in a gothic novel. Wisps, careless curls framed her pretty face. Joss thought it must take an hour to arrange this accidentally-on-purpose style. She looked fabulous. A kind of girlish innocence, though something—perhaps a knowing glint in her eye—contradicted innocence. She had always been the mistress of makeup. It was perfect today. Rings of smoke, another discrepancy, issued from a face that now resembled the countenance of a duchess masquerading as a little girl. Mary Ellen, always pretty in unexpected combinations, was growing beautiful now. At last she was beginning to come up to the promise of her face.

Her smile was dazzling. Her deep eyes, indeterminate in color, changed shades with her inner climate. Now that summer had scorched her cheeks, her eyes resulted green, and somewhat savagely so. She was like a wild tribal princess, invincible yet wearing a crown of Jane Eyre ringlets that pulled attention to the line of the neck, to the vulnerability of the throat. Something like innocence, without being exactly a lie, did not quite jibe, for one form of innocence had certainly been discarded the minute she began to test more intimately her chance encounters and her more serious romances as well. In short, Mary Ellen was probably not celibate anymore. Yet in the very moment of enlightenment, another form of innocence, an idiotic sort of faith in romance prevailed.

"I've been to the beach," she said, and she laughed. "I rented a share in a summer house at Bay Head, right along the New Jersey Shore. We're a bunch of girls, most of us just recent college graduates. Every weekend, we invite every single man we know, even mailroom boys and elevator operators. Hoping to meet Mr. Right. We gather them up on Saturday night for a dinner. Huge vats of spaghetti or stew are the on the menu. Lots of bread. It works. Then we mill around and get to know everyone. It's a regular party.

"You know, everyone who has been to college knows the same songs. We sing 'Let Her Sleep under the Bar' and that kind of old English stuff. 'The Foggy Dew' and 'Waily Waily.' I've had a lot of fun but met only a lot of Mr. Wrongs. Until, of course, I did meet one smooth guy at the beach. Paul Welch is his name. He's suave. He's handsome. Maybe he's the one," Mary Ellen confessed, laughing.

Mary Ellen laughed a lot. She always had done. Montrose claimed it was a defense mechanism since thwarted amour seemed always to rage in Mary Ellen's heart. Joss remembered other things about her, though. Something was blooming in Joss's memory right now. She knew Mary Ellen when. All those years ago she had pulled a gambit. Doomed and observed, it had passed for unseen. But the periphery of Joss's eye watched, registered dispassionately (after all, who cared?) and remembered. The mind's eye pretended to forget because Joss still valued Mary Ellen's flawed friendship, so she tucked it into a compartment and shelved it.

Now she suddenly remembered layers of light. Striations of sunshine. Reassembling the enigma in fractions of the past. Where was she? Shafts penetrating the breaks in clouds were recalling patches of a grandstand.

Where was that? The Field House of the college! They're watching a game. Not a very important game, a girl's game of some kind, field hockey or lacrosse. Montrose was playing. Those long, perfect legs flashing by.

In patchwork revelation, up came the memory. Mary Ellen grabs Frank's hand, tugs as if to urge him up. But Frank can't leave because Joss doesn't, so he sits in awkward stupor. And Mary Ellen keeps the captive hand. Absentmindedly, she plays with his fingers. Frank's face is dopey. Perhaps he is cued in enough to get a little scared. Patient, puzzled, and worried. Maybe wondering what she is doing. The tramp. She's working a little seduction on his hand, that's what. He's too polite to snatch his hand back. The whole episode would be funny if there weren't a taint of treachery to it. Duplicity. Betrayal.

A few years later on a summer afternoon, that same girl, desperate and scorched, savage around the eyes, sat across the table in Montrose's apartment, glowering, emitting her anger in rings of smoke. Her pellucid skin gave up shades of red, independent of her sunburn, as interior tides, angers, raged, intensified, and wavered. She was illuminated like the chimney of a candle that guards its flame from the wind.

"You don't know what it's like, Joss. You can't imagine. With seven women to every man, the city is a jungle.

"There are plenty of parties here in the city. But they are certainly not for fun anymore. They don't even *pretend* to be fun anymore. It's incredible. A roomful of people on the make. Everybody trying to put the make on someone else. Liking one another is not important. It's openly predatory. Guys actually cruise by you and say, 'Do you screw?' And they want a one-word answer. One syllable long. If it's no, they keep right on moving along, hardly breaking stride, handing out the same question to the next girl, not even bothering to rephrase it. The first few times I heard it, I got my hand cocked up to slap. But that's a waste. They're gone while you are winding up. They want a *fast* answer. Spell it y-e-s or they just scurry along.

"I was appalled," Mary Ellen continued. "Couldn't believe it. I mentioned it to Tony. Tony Bologna, he lives in my building. Oh, skip Tony Baloney. He's another zero. A whole 'nother story. Anyhow, he knew exactly what I was talking about. He said it was an established technique. It's called the buckshot approach. He says that at any party of more than six people, there is bound to be a girl there who will screw. Why not find her right away and save a lot of time?

"There's such a doggy feeling to all this. Is it because the city is so disproportionately full of females? I think back to school, and it seems to me there was more of an attempt to make friends. I mean, really try to like each other—like with Chooky. Chooky Linkus, I can't remember now why I was so down on him. He was always just trying to be a friend of mine."

"I remember Charles Linkus," Montrose said.

"He was nice," said Joss.

"Oh, Charles. Chooky Linkus. Yes he really was a nice guy," Mary Ellen said, leaning way back, letting her eyes take a different direction. Mary Ellen Rigg, who could appear like a superior being, gazing down at you from the walls of a portrait gallery—a great woman immortalized in her station as a renowned person of rank. Surrounded by dross. Nevertheless a noble.

"He was, wasn't he," Mary Ellen agreed. She leaned away, looking elsewhere, letting slide off the smutch of recent experiences.

I have my own science, my own studies. I'm a rock, maybe a little pocked. A pockmarked rock. Pumice stone riddled with the sockets of a thousand eyes, I float upon the waters buoyed by my very crevices. My senses diseased into the super-senses of a fever. Bad things can happen to good girls. Analysis yields up pebbles. It vomits up tiny multi-celled stones originating in the gut and perhaps slightly lethal so that I may spit, and, lo and behold, where I have spat no grass can ever grow."

—*Codex* by Joss

Joss was almost flat broke. She had a small bank account consisting of the academic awards she had won at the end of high school, but it was dwindling fast. Now she was staying at Montrose's apartment in the city. There was plenty of room, obviously plenty of money too. Montrose had been so generous as to have a separate phone line installed in Joss's name. The first call Joss made on it was to Alan Resnick's residence.

It was good to hear that musical voice again. "Hey, Joss. I was wondering what you've got up to since school ended. How's the book coming?"

"I'm staying at Montrose's," Joss answered in what she tried to make a flat and negative voice. Like a voice in a horror movie.

"That's wonderful! How's Montrose?"

"Not too happy. Harry transferred to California. He's in San Francisco now."

"San Francisco is the right place for him. I think he will be happy there."

"Sure, but I think Montrose misses him keenly. How are you, Resnick?"

"Ouch! I thought you'd started calling me Alan. I'd like that better, you know."

"It's hard to change a habit of the years, but I'll try, Alan," Joss said.

"So what's so bad about staying with Montrose?"

She didn't want to tell him. Even though Montrose

was housing her with the usual graciousness, life just was not going well for Joss there. In the first place, Joss had met someone, a funny man, at Brentano's bookstore. He was nothing like the college boys she had dated in the past. He was a rugged, handsome man. At the moment she first noticed him, he was grimacing, shouting, and flailing his arms. Obviously not finding what he was looking for. Incomprehensible words blazed out of his mouth at the bookstore clerk. He gestured violently as desperately trying to make himself understood. "Magyar! Magyar!" he kept shouting.

The clerk lost patience. He pretended to go off into the stockrooms. He didn't return. He just left that poor guy steaming by the dictionaries. Joss laughed aloud at the scene. Then the man stopped fuming and smiled at her. It appeared at just the right moment in Joss's lonesome life. She needed to have some fun. She needed to laugh and be alive again. A little loving wouldn't hurt either. She welcomed the attention of this wild man.

Joss had never before met anyone like him.

There followed the complications of exchanging names. It took a while, but by dint of good will and ludicrous gestures, they managed. They were both laughing throughout their introductions. Eventually she understood that he was Ferenc Gursöy, a Hungarian. He had to write that name out on a shabby little notebook he carried. The notebook was filled with rough sketches, stick figures, round puffs that, judging by the accompanying noises, she supposed must be bombs bursting. He made her understand that he had escaped from an evil regime. All this was painfully communicated. Ferenc wanted so badly to speak to her. He was making it work even though he had very few words of English. When she found him, he had been searching for a Hungarian-to-English dictionary.

She laughed. In the most amicable way, Ferenc wanted her to laugh. He was an amusing guy, even in pantomime, though his pantomime was just about as noisy as a Chinese opera. He liked her. It didn't take long to learn he could be adept at loving her too. They went from hugs to more intimate connections in the space of one afternoon.

Love, laughter, and dynamism, however, presented Joss with unusual difficulties. Ferenc was constantly ready to play. Play for Ferenc meant love and more love. He was good at it but never quiet. For Joss, who in her life had never been especially salacious, it seemed excessive. Meanwhile, Ferenc could be so tender while explosive, so imaginative in his lovemaking that Joss was willingly seduced.

He was the mad Hungarian, she the giddy American schoolgirl. Ferenc did not speak more than twenty-five words of English, but, in spite of that, he surely had plenty to say. He talked incessantly. In the manner of most language-deprived speakers, he believed that the louder one spoke, the better the message carried to listening ears. For English, all he used was a voice that could break brick. He could be heard from two blocks away. The result was bombastic. He scared people. On the one occasion when he called for Joss at the apartment, his enthusiastic greeting nearly bounced Montrose out of her skin.

Nevertheless he was an interesting person. By gestures and Magyar battle cries, he gave Joss to understand that he had recently escaped from hostilities in his beloved homeland. He had every intention of returning to fight there. This Joss deduced from dramatic gesticulations and the sounds of bursting bombs, bullets that issued from his mouth. The result was terrifying.

Unfortunately, his language of love was equally explosive.

Joss was now living at Montrose's. It was definitely Montrose's place—one degree closer to a nunnery than it needed to be. There were crucifixes in the bedrooms. Murmured sounds would have to be prayer meetings, Joss supposed. How could Joss arrange to be with this human dynamo, proclaiming his sexual inclinations at the top of his lungs? Not peachy keen at all. To her displeasure, Joss simply found that now she had to sneak around to conduct her life. Everything sub rosa.

They visited parks with some success, but they met too many crazies there. City parks were dangerous at night.

Once, with resulting strains and pains, they even tried to make out in a remote phone booth in the Pennsylvania Station, culminating in an ouchy love session with sore limbs and gales of laughter.

Joss definitely needed her own space.

And then there was this protégé, Dorian Sivade. Montrose had found him at an art school where he was just about to flunk out for truancy. His artwork was exceptional, but everything else about him was just absent. He was a nincompoop. Joss couldn't stand him. Montrose seemed oblivious to what a spoiled brat he was.

When she learned he had recently entered his eighteenth year, she decided to throw a party for him. Did he have friends? He couldn't suggest any. He had sisters, but they had already given him a birthday party. Montrose went and actually baked him a cake. It surprised Joss that Montrose would ever do such a thing. Next they had to make the requisite whoopee, just the three of them. Montrose had bought paper party hats and they blew on little rods that unfurled multicolored tongues as they tooted just like little kids.

It was incomprehensible to Joss, but she thought that just as she had needed the addition of Ferenc to her life, Montrose must need someone. After all the college years, handsome Harry Hannigan was gone. He had moved to California directly after graduation. He wasn't communicating. Montrose must be lonesome. But if loneliness was indeed the ailment, it would have been better to buy a dog than to adopt loopy Dorian, Joss thought.

The handwriting on the wall was clear. She couldn't share all her troubles with Resnick. Joss certainly had to get her own place soon, before Ferenc achieved many more clamorous consummations.

The telephone could be a real help in avoiding cabin fever except that she didn't have anyone to telephone. Ferenc had not so much as a tin can to call on. Mary Ellen did not yet have a job, apartment, telephone, not even her own pot to pee in. Joss knew Mr. Resnick was on line, but it was a shared line. Unless he answered, someone had to call him. He was so utterly bound up with his doctoral studies that she hesitated to make the call. When she did succeed in getting him, he was always genial, seemed extremely pleased to talk to her. Finally when her nerves could stand no more of self-imposed solitude, she did call him. "Alan, are you busy? Is this a bad time to talk?"

"Of course not. I just spent two hours in the archives looking up material on an obscure English poet. I'm so hung up on his name that I'm beginning to wonder if he ever existed.

"I'm really eager for a break. Go on, talk to me. Tell me everything. How's the book going?"

"Ugh! Don't ask. I write and write, but the stuff coming out is stupid."

"Most writers feel that way about their work. It's part of the solitude," Alan declared.

"No, I mean it. I've strayed miles now from whatever crap I put in the original synopsis. The characters change even as I write about them. Schwartz has become more important. Emily has a case on him, but it happens to be a borderline mental case. The whole amorous thing with the father blew up after a few paragraphs. It just didn't solidify."

"Because you didn't believe it. Well, I'm glad if you've actually gotten incest out of the plot. That would not have been pretty at all. What does your editor think of the changes?"

"Editor? You mean John Otto? He's almost useless. I go to the office and hand him sets of about twelve pages. He reads them and makes written comments and leaves the pages with Shelly LeBow until I pick them up. He thinks everything I write is beautiful, poetic, or enchanted.

"I am floundering, and John Otto is almost no help at all. As far as I am concerned, he's just someone willing to read the work. Sometimes that helps. He asks for no remuneration. Of course, I can't pay the man anything anyhow. Beside, I doubt that he has any influence at all in the company. It is as he suspected; he was hired as a token. Nobody listens to him. They keep him as a pet.

"Maybe they just needed to show a liberal stand in that dead white environment of theirs. That's what he thinks anyhow."

"Yes, right. The times are changing," said Alan.

Joss prattled right on. "He's unsteady. He's a nervous wreck. Personally I think he has marital problems too. He's disapproving of his wife's political stance. They argue about things they can't do anything about, like skin."

"You told me before about his talented wife. I thought they sounded like such a well-suited pair."

"Yes, but matters are always complicated in a marriage, aren't they?" Joss said. "In theirs, the wife is the main means of support. That doesn't sound so good, does it?"

"Joss, don't be passé," Resnick advised her. They both laughed.

"Sounds to me like she's leaving him with the baby and the damned Bakhtiari rug. It infuriates him that she wants to go rush down south to join some friends of hers in some political undertakings. He's not into that, and she's hopping mad that he isn't. There is some big argument between them."

"Tell me something, Joss. Do you ever so much as read a newspaper?"

"Not really. Why?"

"Because you never seem to be cognizant of what's going on in the real world. Otto may have very good reasons to hesitate about his wife going south right now while she, expects him to be more committed to their cause," Resnick admonished.

"Well, I'm sorry, but I'm just non-political," said Joss.

Frank took Joss to Ignatz' Place. The walls were faced with raw bricks there. Ignatz, huge and effeminate, loved prancing through—horsing around with his clientele for an audience, bantering, acting quaint. He strewed sawdust on his floor. He wore a huge apron of mattress ticking. Artificial cobwebs powdered with artificial dust trickled over dimmed lights that flickered. They said he deliberately loosened the threads on lightbulbs to get that flickering effect and augment the décor of pretended squalor.

"Hey, Ignatz! Where'd d'ya get sawdust in Manhattan?" someone cried out.

"Impawted. Of cawse. N'Jersey sawdust."

"Yeah? How about those cobwebs?"

"Also impawted, dolling. Spun glass. From Transylvania."

"You know something, Ig? You're a big fat phony."

Ignatz blew kisses to remarks like that—big, blubbery, burlesque kisses.

"Hey, Ignatz! Where'd you get the apron?"

He winked. "From the goils, dolling, where else." He grinned as he waved eastward in the direction of the Women's House of Detention. Ignatz' Place was almost standing square in its tall, skinny shadow. When people passed by, they could see the bars of cells on the upper floor; pressed behind them, vaguely seen, knobs of dark heads. Angry. In hot weather when the windows were

open, they called down specific invitations and obscenities. Sometimes they spat.

"Ignatz, I betcha your name is really Ed."

"Woise, dolling. It's Bill."

The table wobbled. Maybe Ignatz sawed off a fraction
of one leg in the interest of his sophomoric concept of
décor. Joss was not impressed. Frank was. It cracked him
up. Ignatz' Place was his find.

"I bet this place has no liquor license," Joss said. She
hoped that statement would turn Frank around and out
the door. Instead he told her that in lieu of a liquor license, the restaurant had a box policy. That meant that
diners could bring their own alcohol. Ignatz would mark
it and put it in a box for future consumption by the pa-
tron whose name was on it. He informed her that he had
earlier brought some in. "There are five bottles in there
named Frank," he said drolly.

"Five?" Joss explained. "I thought you were on the
wagon."

"Oh, I am. I am." He laughed. "It's only wine. Besides,
there no way I'm going to drink them all now." And then
he switched to a subject that might annoy her as much
as she had annoyed him with the liquor license remark.
"Heard anything from your papa, Joss?"

"Nothing. Not a blooming cent!" She sighed. "The
situation is getting desperate. I may have to get a job."

She settled back to study the stained rag of a menu

when a man at the next table leaned over to her. "Excuse me, Miss," he said. "You look just exactly like the girl on page four."

"I never read page four," she announced. But, of course, she did. Everyone did. Page four was the scandal page. Today the tabloids had run the picture of a notorious call girl. She was arriving to testify at the trial of her boyfriend, the prodigy playboy pimp. She was a pretty girl even though startled by flash bulbs. Baby faced. Demure. She looked a lot like Mary Ellen, not much like Joss. According to the papers, she specialized in "unnatural acts." Whatever those might be, they were undoubtedly sexier when performed by a round-eyed girl who looked to be on her way to choir practice.

"Get a job?" Frank wondered. "Whatever can you do?"

"I don't know. Something. Maybe something for page four," Joss joked.

One day soon she had to part with Ferenc. He was only a temporary distraction; nevertheless, the parting was emotional. To her surprise, Ferenc cried real tears. Joss was not an easy crier; she didn't really know how, but she was saddened by the departure of his powerful presence.

She went home to imprison herself in her damn room at Montrose's again. She had to produce a book before John Otto lost interest in helping her. He was her only link to G&M Inc. At least, by now, she had learned to use the typewriter. In college, at first she wrote everything in longhand. Her old notebooks were full of scrambled ink or smudged pencil patterns. She remembered how her hands would hurt after hours of writing. Eventually she had learned to type. It took less time and it was more legible, but eventually her hands still cramped up.

The hardest part of her life now was staying confined to write. That was not in her nature. It even affected the work. The writing came up too close to her face in that self-imposed prison. She couldn't encompass it. She needed to move away and stay at a distance from the page or else she thought abnormalities would arise. Things took off on their own. Characters behaved in ways she had not anticipated. Of late, when she sat down to write her own unfettered prose, she marveled at her own arrogance in explaining things she did not understand. Still, she did it so well. Words usually swelled and streamed from her in effortless rivers.

But lately her sentences grew shorter and shorter, as if she couldn't wait to put a period on them. Eventually they would cave in upon themselves and exist as a capital letter and an end mark, a period or a question mark. Truly, she could not wait to finish the damned thing. It seemed to go on forever without achieving anything.

She emerged from her struggles into the living room where she was struck by the afternoon sun. It caught her for a moment as it also caught something else, something incongruous, Dorian Sivade. He was in the parlor holding up one scarecrow arm to catch her. The room was papered with incomplete illustrations for Montrose's incomplete children's book. Incomplete seemed the order of the day with Montrose.

Paper overflowed the faces of the walls and lay scattered on counters, floors, tabletops, like junk jewelry on bargain shelves. They were garish in color. Dorian specialized in producing an undulating black line, varying its power, spinning it from fat to a thread, then allowing it to thicken like treacle dolloped off a spoon until it became a fat worm of black. Curves, bloops, excrescences like buds on yeast, held in tight areas of primary colors. They caged areas of pattern—minute paisleys, tiny florals, repeated keys, geometric and minuscular—Grecian, Aramaic, Celtic. They told no story, just competed in pure style.

Montrose thought he was a genius. She thought all the flats and broads he made must be the calligraphy of a new intelligence, perhaps of a new religion. Joss, instead, was frightened. It occurred to her that the boy was doing in painting what she was trying to do in writing. Make something out of nothing.

The art school had kept him until he was sixteen. They protected him that far because the law required it. He was on the hook for most schooldays. But beyond sixteen, the law provided permission to be illiterate. Dorian was. In addition to obstinate refusal to learn, Dorian was protected at home. He was the baby brother of six older sisters, all vying to spoil him. Francine, Olivia, Chantal, Delfia, Blaisette, and Tigra. Montrose had sung the five names to Joss as if they belonged to a litany of exotic saints. The tribe interested Joss. As long as Dorian disclosed anything about his sisters and their vagaries, Joss paid attention. She wanted to steal material for her caricatures of Emily Cappo's aunties.

Though Joss was truly astonished by his artwork, she thought any possible genius must be accidental. Dorian was a blithering idiot. She couldn't stand him. He was a creep. He loved to touch, always touching himself when he talked. He dared to do that. If he could not touch another person, he touched himself, and that was every bit as nerve-wracking. He stood in the sun and tried to interrupt her in the remainder of a scribbling madness that still occupied her mind. At least that's what she felt. He interrupted her space.

She really did not like the boy. She backed away from him. If she allowed him, he would flood her with stupidity. Commenting, describing, explaining, all in jumbled order, never apologizing for insulting English the way he did. Ferenc's physical explanations were so preferable, but they were gone now. Ferenc had gone off now to have his revolution.

Dorian stayed; that was the bad of it. Lately he came every day. He was supposed to be painting something for the children's story Montrose always threatened to write. It was a perfect job for a truant. Nothing ever got done anyway. That went for Montrose, too. The mystery of Montrose was compounded these days by her inability to get anything accomplished.

Joss's aversion to the boy made her ashamed of herself. She simply could not abide the boy. She even hated to look at him. Something was wrong with his mouth. Maybe he had no teeth. He smiled a lot but always kept his teeth hooded by his lips. She thought he might have some kind of mouth rot. The sun now stabbed at him through the big window. He didn't blink. He was so frail. His milky skin was almost translucent. In the thrust of the light, she thought she saw delicate traceries of the veins that opened up out of his heart. She expected him to scuttle out of the sunshine like a bug. His big eyes throbbed. She wished he'd get out of the light.

But at the same time, Joss was taking advantage of him, feeding off the stories of his sisters, replacing them with Emily's aunties.

Before he began to utter sounds—which was only recently as far as she was concerned—since for the first few months he had remained almost silent—she thought him almost beautiful in his strangeness. A unicorn creature. A changeling. But now as he indulged in his little rashes of words, his paroxysms of speech, a small spasm of giggles, a chill ran down her spine. It occurred to her of what he reminded her.

A fetus.

The unborn.

One day, bells rang for Joss. It was also the day that turned the corner for her. She was considering scrapping the entire project. Lately, she'd been writing such pedestrian prose. Words fell onto her pages with an almost audible thud. Dull, dull. Graceless and unimportant. Trite and corny. She had been writing for hours, hoping to ignite a spark but to no avail. She dimly remembered that once words presented themselves in happy sequences in her head. They could fly. They could dance. They streaked by, demanding attention. Writing stories had been an easy thing for her. She often felt that she was a basket full of words that had to spill. They were wonderful and lethal. If she even tried to contain them, they would cause her harm. They would choke her.

She wrote all day with meditation breaks. The floor of the room was littered with ripped paper. Joss that day, wiped out, wallowed in a sea of rejected pages. After four hours of unproductive work on her manuscript, her head was throbbing. She threw herself, spread-eagled, onto her bed hoping to conjure up a key that would enable her reenter the ramshackle *House of Women*.

Not for the first time, she considered deep-sixing the whole project. It was wrong. It must be wrong. Writing had always given her so much pleasure. This book was murdering her. But if she threw it all away, what would she have as an excuse for living? What would be her excuse? How long could she live under the aegis of Montrose's charity? Montrose, always gracious, said *forever* or *as long as needed*. That was not acceptable to Joss.

She thought—if dopey Mary Ellen had found work, surely she could too. Somehow she might wangle some kind of servile little job. She knew she'd hate it, but, to be practical, hunger was now at the door. At the very moment that Joss was thinking of hunger, the doorbell rang. The apartment had a rusty, interrupting, electronic screech of a doorbell. The sound was such an irritant that Montrose was always saying she wanted to get a gentler ring installed. Perhaps some elfin jingling or the chimes of a cathedral. But, as with so many other things Montrose said these days, nothing got done about it.

The bell squealed. A splat of rude noise.

Joss refused to stir her stumps. *It's her door*, she thought. *Let her answer it*. Montrose tended to be reluctant about domestic matters.

But Montrose must have responded because after a few minutes she knocked at Joss's door. "Joss," she said, "you've got to come out to the door." Montrose sounded just slightly vexed. Perhaps because it was *her* door and *her* doorbell, and at this moment she exerted no authority over either of them, Joss supposed. A petty thought. Matters between them had been taut lately. In a different tone, Montrose continued, "There's a courier at the door, and he won't allow me to accept his message. It's for you," she said.

Joss curled up slowly and then, just as slowly, uncoiled. Later she would remember this draggy moment and marvel at her obtuse response. She'd just been sheltering in Montrose's domain too long. Little things had begun piling up.

Eventually, she had to emerge. There actually was a courier at the door, and he really bore a long white envelope with *Jocelyn Nye* written on it. It was important. She had to sign for it.

It was a puzzle. With her brain still draggy from the bad writing. She stood and did nothing. All she could manage was to stare stupidly at the envelope and then at Montrose.

Montrose, tall in a long, elegant, embroidered peignoir, was ogling and gawking as stupidly as Joss was.

Suddenly awake, Montrose cried, "Open it! Open it. Joss!"

And only then did Joss tear into it.

She took one quick look, gasped, and stumbled to flop onto a chair.

Would she ever forget this moment? The envelope contained one slip of paper, but what a slip of paper it was—a check for two hundred dollars! Two hundred! A fortune! A king's ransom, especially for Joss under her present circumstances! "My father," Joss choked out. "Joe Nye actually came through!" Beyond that, she could say little more.

Montrose, in an excess of love and shared joy, came over to embrace both Joss and the check. "Well, I *knew* he would," she announced.

Serenity was restored. Once again they were loving friends. All the turns of this day would be remembered by Joss forever. Thrice she was summoned by bells this day. Three bells.

That doorbell counted as the first. The second was not quite so benign.

It came much later that same night. Joss was in bed. She'd been trying to recapture the good part of her day. So good. Two hundred American dollars! She couldn't stop mulling over money, not a sleep-inducing topic. The check was on the table by her bedside. She had no idea if this represented a series of payments or a one-time amount. Really, in the matter of "actions," Joe had been most unclear. He'd left her so ill advised. That was Joe, his touch. For the umpteenth time, she examined the long envelope. It bore the imprint of a legal office. She resolved to call that office in the morning. In her mind's eye, she examined the check. It was a regular bank check made out to Jocelyn Nye, who was almost asleep when the second summons came. Peremptory. Shrill. The squawky telephone.

Her eyes snapped open. She woke. She watched her field of vision define itself. She could see the radium dial of the clock tighten into existence as it clarified. Four.

Four in the morning. And the phone scolded. It was irrational. She lifted it very carefully, as if her caution could neutralize it until in the numbness of the room she could hear a definite click.

"Jazz ..."

Joss immediately recognized that rasping voice. So much time passing, and his voice still harsh, still able to overpower her.

She began shaking so hard she could not reply, so she slammed the phone down in its cradle as hard as she could.

"Joss, I thought I heard the telephone ring last night. Was there a call?" Montrose asked.

"Yes," said Joss. "And you probably heard it twice. There was a call, and then there was a re-call."

Always with studied delicacy, Montrose continued, "Forgive my asking. I know your phone is none of my business, but I've been extremely on edge lately, hoping for some kind of message from Harry."

"You haven't heard *anything* from Harry?" asked Joss.

"Only that he's sick. He claims it's only a trivial thing, but it hangs on. Oh, Jocelyn, I've been sick myself worried about him."

"No. It wasn't Harry." Joss felt genuinely sorry. She plunked down on the couch beside Montrose and laid a comforting hand on her knee. "I'm sure he'll be fine soon. He's so strong, a perfect specimen of a man."

"I'm sorry to be a nag. But, you know, he's been sick for a long time. He left with such high dreams for California. You know he has many friends there from his days in the academy, and now he's been sick almost since we left school in June."

"What's the problem?" Joss asked.

"He doesn't know. He just felt sick soon after reaching his friends in California, and it doesn't seem to go away."

"No, I'm truly sorry, Montrose. It wasn't Harry that called. It was Bobby. Bobby Ochs. Remember Bobby Ochs?"

"Oh, yes, indeed I do," Montrose replied. "I remember him as a rude and irresponsible boy. You dated him junior year, didn't you? I hope that story isn't coming up again."

"Probably not," Joss assured her. She hoped not too, yet Bobby awakened in her confusions she didn't dare face. After she hung up on him, he had called again. This time to profess undying love. "You were my first," he had declared. "A guy never gets over his first ... girl." The slight hesitation before he said "girl" made her think he really wanted to used a vulgar word, and she immediately hated him more, and herself with him.

"Get over it, Bobby. I did."

She wondered if that was true.

"Don't hate me, Joss. I only did what had to be done— for both our sakes. You know that."

"I don't. I only know I had nothing to do with the plan. I was not in it at any time. I was never consulted. My body was used but not by my will." And then, amid his protestations of love, she again hung up the phone, surprised at how much her declaration had brought to her mind the picture of a young Kitty McCorkle.

O I buy you O!
O I can buy you with a green bill, you chattel,
And donate you to a circus.
You're human just for camouflage.
It's just the easiest thing to look like,
So what does that make of me if I believed in you?"
                                        —*Codex* by Joss

Liquor did not help her sleep. She dreamed. In the dream, people kept pointing at her. Almost everyone was unnaturally kind. The word had gotten around that she was recovering from a nervous breakdown. They hovered. They laved her in beatific smiles, trying hard not to indulge in behavior that might be interpreted as threatening. They asked well-intentioned questions about her writing. When she couldn't answer, they made the questions easier, but still she flubbed the answers. She felt certain it was an examination to determine if she were really herself. And she flunked. Failed at her own identity. Couldn't even pass the Joss Nye test.

Dreaming left her so down. She went for a morning walk by the old streetcar tracks. Incomprehensible rites had become unbearable. In broad daylight, construction workers flashed lights at each other: blue was the opening remark, and green constituted the reply. Maybe it had a meaning. Or, walking purposefully along the tracks, she saw a man hold up a patch of cloth, like a red handkerchief. Though he stared straight ahead, he periodically dipped this little banner toward the ground in a deliberate gesture. But, except for Joss, not a soul seemed to be watching. There was to these actions a ritualistic seriousness that burdened her because she could not understand a bit of it.

Now the phone was her escape hatch. Unfortunately she had few friends to ring up. Mary Ellen had not set up a telephone link yet. Frank was indeed on the line, but calling him entailed the danger of encouraging a visit. Now it seemed her only remaining human resource was Alan Resnick. He was hard to get, but, with luck, he could be contacted. The phone was a shared instrument near his small studio/bedroom. There were other guys in that hall, all scholars apparently. If she got an answer at all. Alan would be called from his studies. Things could be worse. They were at least in communication. Alan Resnick did call her often. He was concerned about the book.

"Alan, I am just letting it go the way it wants to go, and, so far, it has wanted to go far afield. Far from what the synopsis promised.

"You know, Emily has got this little job with an important chemical company. They do exterminations. I did not intend to make a big deal out of its buggy aspect. That was just something I put in to make Jeannie Irslinger laugh. She had a special love for cockroach and cootie stories. Then, as things developed in the writing, it became a big part of things precisely for that reason. It had bugs. It offered the possibility for some humorous word play. This Schwartz guy that Emily is getting involved with is an entomological specialist for the company. I wanted to keep the bedbugs around for the opportunity it gave me to insert some humor. It's really needed in such a dopey book. Schwartz is kind of a weird bug himself actually."

Joss rattled on. "Then there are the aunties. Their tales have become mostly comical too. I've been basing them a lot on what Montrose's protégé, Dorian, told us about his sisters. But I can't use him as a resource anymore. He's gone."

"Dorian Sivade's gone?" asked Alan.

"Gone, gone, gone," Joss gloated. "But about the book, Alan. It sounds so dull to me. I'm so used to having the words fly right out of me. I love when they do that. It's so cathartic."

"Orgasmic," he added.

That shut her up for the moment. Orgasmic was not something she wanted to consider. It was not an avenue she cared to walk down with Mr. Resnick. She wanted to talk to him but not about the book because she believed the book was trying to stop.

Stuck. In vain, she'd ponder it through the night. She felt mocked by all the blank paper, alone in her struggle. So little. Just a little egg. Trying to hatch.

Lighting sequences of cigarettes in the night. Snapping matches. Listening to the sounds in the apartment. Sometimes she could hear Montrose stirring. So quiet. So damn still. Probably eating something.

The distant hum of electricity. She thought she could hear Montrose breathing, all the way off in the kitchen.

Opening the refrigerator door. The woman was always hungry. Joss thought she could hear items being drawn out of the fridge. Trying to remember whatever was in there. Cold cuts, melon slices, wilted celery stalks. Did this count for some lunatic form of meditation? She needed help. So alone. What if she could not write? She'd based her whole life so far on the assumption that she could.

If it was night and dark, she resorted to the bottle Frank had given her. She had stashed away in the closet. Occasionally a little alcohol oiled her mind and produced a squeak. She told Frank that. He was worried, but he knew what she meant. Sometimes the liquor inspired some incredible scribbling. Done in pencil. They were temporary scrawls. In the morning, they might even make a kind of sense.

"Joss?" Resnick's voice interrupted her.

That brought her back.

"What?" she demanded.

"You went away for a minute there," he complained.

Darned tooting, I did, she thought. The man was not helping her even though she was such a small person. So much in need of help. Like a little egg trying to hatch.

She said nothing.

"Joss! Hey, Joss, don't go away again. Talk to me."

"The fault is the damn synopsis, Resnick."

"Alan," he corrected.

"Yeah, Alan. The fault is with the damn synopsis. It's a girdle! Damn it, it's a stinking straitjacket.

"I don't want the restraint, Alan."

"You need the discipline, Joss."

"Sure. I know.

"Alan, today I found myself making sentences sorter and shorter. It was as if I wanted to bring the periods closer and closer to the initial letters. When I looked at the shrunken bundle of sticks they made, I thought they looked like the bones of a corpse long dead. It was a pretty clear sign that I should end the book."

"That's right!" he exclaimed. "End the damn book. Finish it!"

"No. I meant, just stop. Throw it away and go look for a job."

"No, Jocelyn, don't kid around. You've got to write. So just do it," he replied. "Now come off the dramatics and talk to me. What happened with Dorian? Did he leave for greener pastures?"

"No, Alan. He got canned. And I was glad. He was a real sleazy character to have lurking around the corners all the time. Montrose treated him as if he were the heir apparent. But he was uncouth and trashy. I knew he was picking up articles the whole time he was in the apartment. As far as Montrose was concerned, he could have gotten away with that forever. Just alabaster ashtrays and porcelain figurines. Pretty things. She hardly notices such trifles."

"So what got him booted?"

Joss resumed, "His mouth. He really did not know how to speak decent English. Montrose put up with as much as she could until he graduated to really offensive, smutty language. You know, just as verbal punctuation marks. One particular taboo word began escaping from his lips frequently."

"Don't tell me. I bet it was the f word in all its ancient glory. I know the word," Alan said. "It's a practical Anglo-Saxon verb. Somehow, I'm hearing it used out of context more right here in the twentieth century."

"The real climax came at the opera. There was a Stravinsky opera in town. *The Rake's Progress* I think it was. I found an excuse not to go because I had already been lambasted with the *Rite of Spring* when we were studying for our comps. Montrose had a recording she played over and over. I got Stravinskied to death. The discord was more than I could bear. She decided to take Dorian.

"Alan, you know Montrose can be really weird sometimes. Imagine taking Dorian Sivade to the opera! A complete travesty. I guess he sat for it for about thirty minutes. He does have some musical taste, you know. But not for Stravinsky. He couldn't resist opening his mouth and bleating out his opinion. He caused quite a disturbance, His opinion was fierce and ferociously expressed. Right there, in the world-famous opera house, using a voice audible for six rows forward and six back, using a quantity of gutter words, he advised the great composer to go befuddle himself. Montrose was aghast," Joss narrated. "On the spot she gave that slimy little worm his walking papers."

Alan was laughing. "Joss, this is wonderful! History repeats itself. He gave Stravinsky the same treatment the man got for the first performance of the *Rite*. Dorian did no worse than Stravinsky's first audience did years ago. The night the *Rite of Spring* had its debut in Paris, the audience was so unruly, they had to call the fire department to control the angry mob."

Nevada Gertz and Fuzzy Williams lost no time in getting hitched. They were joined by solemn nuptials on the very night of the graduation ceremonies, and at the very same university chapel. It was all part of the groom's family tradition. The happy couple then embarked on a two-week honeymoon, fully underwritten by Frederick Williams Senior. After two weeks of connubial bliss, they joined in the general exodus to the city, where Frederick Senior had provided a palatial apartment and a peachy job as a trader for Fuzzy.

Montrose heard that Dorcas Tannenberg, Nevada's a bosom pal, was now in the city too, visiting from her home in Maine. Since both Nevada and Dorcas had been in Montrose's special groups—the Benefactors' Club, and (Nevada) in music classes—Montrose thought she should entertain them with a tea party. She was pleased with the idea. She busied herself planning the event, soliciting Joss away from her typewriter to ask for social advice.

"I'm going to get little cakes from Schermerhorn's," Montrose announced. "They make wonderful little cakes."

"So I've heard. They're supposed to be the best," Joss agreed.

"Won't it be wonderful to see the girls again?"

"I suppose so," said Joss. "I never truly knew either of them well." She didn't want to say it, but neither of them had ever seemed to care for her very much either. They were both consistently distant. They, by the very nature of their assumed social position, didn't much care for anyone. As far as the population of Harmon House was concerned, they were both appalling snobs.

One day, after the apartment had been thoroughly put to order, after Schermerhorn's had delivered delectable little pastries and ribbon-wrapped little cakes, after the hired maid had prepared the tea things in the kitchen, the bell rang to announce the arrival of the two classmates.

The maid scurried to answer the door. As, side-by-side, the two alumnae sauntered into the room, Joss was overtaken by a fit of coughing. The sight of the two of them so pompously parading in had tickled her funny bone. In spite of uncommonly warm weather, both were wearing fur stoles. Coughing covered Joss's inevitable laughter. Montrose stood horror-stricken, preparing to be mortified. She had feared just this. She knew exactly why Joss was laughing. Now she hoped and prayed that the two newcomers would not catch the gist of it.

She knew what Joss would be thinking and that Joss couldn't help her laughter. The sight of them was too much. There was Nevada, skinny as a string with her small knob of a head offering the world a tiny face, arm in arm with Dorcas, who had a gigantic face and a neck thick enough to hold up a bull's head. They were a funny-looking duo, fabulously furred and outfitted by Saks Fifth Avenue. Fortunately, masking her laughter as bronchial distress, Joss succeeded in seeing the two women in. Montrose drew a long, grateful breath, and the party was on.

First they had to tour the apartment. Joss could see that Nevada had her eyes peeled in comparative attention. It seemed she had to make sure that this apartment was somewhat less splendid than the one bestowed on her and Fuzzy by his magnanimous daddy. Fortunately it was less spacious, so Nevada appeared to be appeased. Joss reckoned she could be quite nasty when disappointed, as Fuzzy must be finding out by now.

Next they all settled in Montrose's parlor. It was furnished with overstuffed, comfortable sofas into which all of them sank luxuriously, except for Nevada. Nevada was electric. She was practically jumping. She had so recently been a star performer, now inaugurated into the new dimension of wedlock. As a bride, she had gone through it all—the admiration, applause, and endless flattering baloney. She was still under the spell of herself. She had a physical need to talk about it.

"I'm married!" she exclaimed dramatically. She flounced around the room making a balloon of her floaty dress of figured red and white.

It hit Joss at once. Recognition flashed through her mind. She knew this person! So familiar. So funny. Joss was immediately overwhelmed by a paroxysm of coughing.

"Joss, that's a terrible cough you have," scolded Dorcas.

She was a known health nut. Her reproach issued forth majestically from her preternaturally large face.

"I'm married!" Nevada repeated. Somehow the focus of attention had slipped away from her, and, with this declaration of achievement, she wanted it back.

Joss coughed. Montrose, who could read Joss's mind, glared at her.

"Have you seen a doctor?" Dorcas demanded.

"It's nothing," Joss explained. "Something's caught in my throat."

"I hope it's nothing," Dorcas said. "If there is even *one* germ in this room, I am bound to catch it. It comes straight to *me*. And if I catch it, it develops into something of epidemic proportions."

Nevada Gertz looked a little frazzled. She had never been an especially pretty girl. At Harmon House, she had been famous for her frequent noisy attempts to increase her bra size. As if noise and effort could help do the trick, she had a little cadre of flat-chested acolytes that would join her in the hallway to do their exercises, all chanting as they flexed, "I must. I must. I must increase my bust." Her sad petition unanswered, she remained perpetually as skinny as a string. With her black hair pulled back into a tight bun held screwed on to the back of her small head, and now, flouncing in a loose dress of red and white, a flash of recognition struck Joss. Immediately, she identified who this was! Nevada was Olive Oyl!

Joss Nye had now to choke back another bout of coughing.

"God, Joss, that sounds dreadful!" Dorcas exclaimed. "Holy Hortense, it sounds like a really serious contagion. I'm sorry. I have to say this, but I don't like sitting in this room with you, Joss. Cover your face at once. I think you should see to it fast. Montrose, you're stuck with her. You should pack her off to a specialist!"

Joss bristled at what she thought was a cutting remark. She didn't like to think Montrose was stuck with her, especially since the snotty remark was true.

Montrose jumped in, handing Joss one of the napkins from the tea table. "So you're all married-up now, Neva. How was the wedding? Tell us about your honeymoon. Where did you go? How's Fuzzy? What did you—?"

"Excuse me," Joss interrupted. She weaseled out of the room to finish her false coughing out of earshot, because, now that Montrose had introduced Fuzzy to the conversation, she was nearly hysterical. In her mind's eye, she could see Fuzzy. He was like a big dumpling. Over the four years of his college education, he had grown more and more dumpling-like. In other words, he must by now present a perfect picture of Wimpy! She laughed herself silly over the idea. They would both fit neatly into a Popeye comic strip. One most important individual was lacking, however, and that would be Swee'Pea. He was undoubtedly expected soon.

She returned to the gathering just in time to find that her thought had been prophetic. Swee'Pea was on his way! Nevada was to be his vessel. She was happily explaining to the others the complex efforts that had been made to get him planted. Frederick Williams Senior was, it seems, in a mortal hurry to get a Frederick Williams the Third. That was a requisite of their marriage.

While Joss was gone, Nevada had treated them to dramatic tales of the wedding night. Now she was wound up. She wanted to divulge more particulars of her most intimate event.

Joss looked over at Montrose. Montrose would be shocked at hearing such revelations, of course. She had paled to a white so deathlike that Joss feared for her. Joss knew it was up to her to save the day. She did so by immediately initiating another devastating salvo of frenzied coughing.

Joss had shut herself in a small room, going gung ho on writing the book. She realized such hasty writing must need some kind of editing. In the past, she had used her college writing classes as her gauge. Just reading it aloud to classmates often revealed weaknesses or trouble spots. But reading it to Montrose was no help at all. She didn't want to listen and satisfied all critique obligations by simply saying everything was wonderful, delightful, and really keen. Joss, angry, accused Montrose of total deprivation of any critical sense.

In class, people like Abbot Parish and Maddy Traywick, Joss's archenemies and both aspiring authors, had been quick to jump on any misplaced modifiers or spavined semicolons. And, of course, outshining them all was Mr. Resnick. He not only knew what he was talking about, but he, Joss thought, had her best interests in mind.

Now Alan Resnick was far off in his ivory tower. For the present, Joss had no one. No one but John Otto, who was still willing to edit. Otto envisioned himself as conducting some major author to glory. He determined to "find" her and conduct her to fame. For the present, she could pay him nothing. Prizes were big but only at the end of the road. Pulitzer prizes, perhaps even Nobel. John thought of himself as being on the fringe of the literary world. He hoped some day to be a literary agent. Joss was his first client. He was satisfied to accept payment upon the publication of her first book. Meanwhile they just had words between them—words and promises. He really wasn't that much use to Joss, but she liked him.

She'd leave a thick envelope of writings at the front desk of the G&M Company. Shelly LeBow was still at the desk being rude and sarcastic to all comers. She was still predicting her immanent firing, though it never did happen. "Maybe the boss likes me," she said to Joss. "I think he just wants to get into my pants." When Joss was shocked by this remark, Shelly called her a baby, a dope, or an innocent. According to Shelly, the removal of people's pants was the inevitable goal of all social interactions.

Joss never even saw Mr. Moran, if there was one. Goldschneider usually was absent. For now, Joss thought it better this way. She could slip into the offices of Goldschneider & Moran, leave her writings, and sneak away unseen by the management. Goldschneider was unaware. Joss thought the Moran probably didn't even exist.

After a short time, John Otto would return her manuscripts to her, either by mail or by inviting her to come to his house on the weekend. She preferred the latter. It was an easy subway ride to the Otto's dwelling in Brooklyn Heights. Joss liked to go. She got out of the apartment so rarely. She liked the artistic atmosphere at Otto's. The short subway ride from Montrose's apartment gave her a chance to do her people watching, a popular underground game. Everyone she knew did it but only through furtive eyes. Sneaking a peek.

Joss thought it gave her story fodder. She watched veteran straphangers who lurched and compensated, as if with little suction cups attached to the soles of their shoes. All with the same blank looks on their faces. Ideas she could use later or even right away.

Descriptions ran through her mind. Obliquely, she'd watch some stolid commuter mash his chewing gum. She could almost clock the steady pulsations of his mandibles while she mentally pondered the intricacies of Emily Cappo's world. People chewed there too. Who would it be ... Francine or Blaisette? Not Chantal who Joss had already identified as the family farter. Joss had written Chantal as the problem sister. She runs the carpet sweeper. That's her only job. She runs it hard and frequently, much more than is necessary. She was born lacking things. She was born without a septum in her nose. When she speaks, which is, fortunately, infrequent, it is almost impossible to understand the sounds she makes. To the uninitiated, her words sound like gusts of wind. She's very large. She stumbles. She's dim in her mind as well. Somehow she never menstruated. She is without those particular female complications; nevertheless, she often falls in love with men she has spied in the neighborhood. It amounts to a problem for the rest of the family.

Joss thought of the subway as a great resource.

The best part of John's house was Davina. To Joss, it was a very special place because the whole idea of being friends with Negroes was exotic to her. Alan Resnick objected to this. He accused Joss of being prejudiced. "I am not! I love them!" she declared.

"That's just it," Alan remonstrated. "They're not your pets. You don't seem to be aware that they're people, just like any other people."

Joss thought the carriage house was wonderful. She marveled that she could feel the vibrations of the Otto's new hi-fi system through her very feet, right through the precious Bakhtiari rug, while she stood admiring the scarlet throats of Davina's prize gloxinias. She wondered if one of Frank's auditory gadgets had anything to do with the wonderful sound in the air.

John enjoyed acquaintance with some literary types, hopeful writers and editors, and Davina knew young artists from the city. In Joss's eyes, it was as close to an artistic American salon as she would ever get. Some of the guests were young men. Joss found herself appraising them with interest. In spite of her proclaimed aversion to romance, she was getting restless. Ferenc had awakened something within her. The inescapable truth was Joss was languishing for love.

Friends and ex-Harmon Housers in droves were showing up in the city now. Nevada was living in town. Mary Ellen was too, but in another dimension, settled into an apartment a world away from Nevada's and just as far from Montrose's.

Mary Ellen's abode was a dump. It was awful. Her room barely had bed space. You could just squeeze around the single bed. Good thing Mary Ellen was skinny. If she gained a pound, Joss remarked, she would skrootch up into the sheets when she tried to tuck up the bedclothes. A tiny bathroom adjoined this so-called bedroom. It had an ancient, rust-stained commode and a little tub. The tub was half-length, but it was enough. "I wash my dishes and my face in that same tub," Mary Ellen boasted. There was no sink, no kitchen, the barest excuse for a parlor.

The place was far uptown in an area that had been ritzy but was now cutting up residences into ratty rooms, transforming itself into a slum. She lived above a rather hot market where all kinds of pungent goods were exchanged. All the way up her stairwell one could smell strange trade. As Mary Ellen's informer, Tony Baloney, told her, "Better not to ask what."

But the job, at least, was starting well. Mary Ellen was teaching English at a very hoity-toity private school in the upper seventies. The kids were affluent. Mary Ellen, on the contrary, was paid a pittance. She had classes of teenaged girls who rather than polish their grammar wished to emulate glamorous models. Mary Ellen was very pretty now, adept with the makeup. The little girls idolized her.

Joss was pleased to learn that Sally Petrucci was now in the city as well. Sally was a special friend from writing classes at the university. In fact, Sally had procured herself a job editing for a small magazine with offices in the Bronx. She was living up there somewhere with her family, quite a journey away. Because Joss had a lousy sense of direction, she knew she would soon get lost up in that wilderness to the north. So Joss had not been able to see her since she arrived in the city.

In the early fall, both Mary Ellen Rigg and Sally Petrucci came for a visit. It was a far jollier occasion than the recent tea party for Nevada and Dorcas. These were two people Joss felt comfortable with. Whatever Montrose felt, Joss could not guess. Montrose was a perpetual mystery, ever more mysterious as time passed.

In any case, they all had shared in the experience of enduring Harmon House.

"Strange for the three of us to be together without Jeannie," Joss commented.

"Oh, right," said Sally. "That Jeannie Irslinger was a fourth of your gang, the Fabulous Four." Sally wore huge horn-rimmed glasses. Her black hair hung on either side of her serious face. She told people she was a member of the Communist Party now, and she looked it.

"The Fabulous Four? Is that what we were called?" Montrose asked.

"That was the *nice* label," laughed Sally. "There were some more descriptive words for the four of you."

"What?" demanded Mary Ellen.

"Supercilious Circle was another," Sally answered. "I heard Snob Hill, too."

They were shocked to find themselves accused of snobbery. But Joss noticed a funny thing. Both she and Mary Ellen had passed swift glances at Montrose when Sally accused them of arrogance. Supercilious Circle seemed so wrong for their amicable group. Now they thought Montrose's habitual reserve might accidentally strike outsiders as insufferable hauteur.

"Seems strange to be together now without the fourth snob," Joss laughed.

"Oh, the Irslinger," Sally recalled. "I remember her well. She was a fourteen-karat brat. Crazy too. Remember the night she disappeared? Whatever happened to her?"

Mary Ellen replied as she sent some smoke circles soaring. "We don't know. I'm sure Jeannie is alive somewhere. She and I have been friends since third grade. But the family isn't very forthcoming with news about Jeannie. That may be because her relationship with her mother was always just turbulent. They were never exactly friends."

"She can join the club," Sally said dully.

"I want to hear about your job, Sally," Joss demanded. "I hear you got something to do with writing."

"I wish," Sally remarked. "Not really as close to writing as I'd like. I have a job as editor for a small magazine. And I'm not kidding when I say small. It's called *Little*—in giant letters—and it's about little things. I mean just about anything small and insignificant. *You* might be featured there, Joss," Sally said, oblivious to how much Joss hated being "minimized."

"They print articles about dollhouse furniture, mostly written by the readers and fans of little stuff. Even occasional articles about miniature paintings but mostly letters from the aficionados. That's what I get to edit mostly. Let me tell you, and it is disheartening. Most of the American public seems to be illiterate when it comes to letters to magazines, but they don't mind writing long letters, so full of grammatical errors that they hardly make sense. I get to fix them. You know, just enough to leave the matter recognizable, massage the grammar for public consumption. The pay is like the magazine—little. But it's a job. I am so grateful to that course I took in Exposition. Mr. Resnick made us keep to the track. You were in that class, weren't you, Joss?"

"I hated that class," Joss responded. "I thought it was totally restrictive. But I loved Mr. Resnick."

"Well, for your kind of writing, I suppose it was

restrictive. You liked those baroque flights of multisyllabic words circling in the sky."

"Oh, for Pete's sake, I want to know what's going on!" Mary Ellen demanded.

"If I read you right, Mary Ellen, you mean what's going on with everyone's love life," said Joss.

"Yeah! Yeah! Yeah!" chortled Mary Ellen.

"Gimme a cig, will ya!" Joss demanded. She was economizing. Both Mary Ellen and Sally hastened to offer first. Then all but Montrose settled back to puff away. She had quit smoking recently.

"Oh, nuts to love life," Sally muttered. "I'm still seeing Danny Flax, from school. It's pretty static though. I don't expect it's going anywhere fast. He is living and working in Boston now. Meanwhile I'm having trouble finding a guy. Any guy. I'm getting older and more particular while Danny Flax is getting farther and farther away."

"Zilch for me," said Joss. Sensing Montrose's discomfort with the subject, Joss answered for her. "Handsome Harry Hannigan is in California now, so we are both unattached, like two rats circling around in the same cage. Mary Ellen though, has been pretty active, I think. Tell us, Mary Ellen," Joss commanded.

Mary Ellen was more than happy to contribute her information. "I'm still going to the Jersey Shore on weekends. I got in with a bunch of girls, and they rented a big house together. They are all recent college grads and all single, so what we do is each weekend we cook something. Something big. We invite to Saturday night dinner every single guy we meet. Mail clerks, elevator operators, any guys. It's very safe and a lot of fun." Mary Ellen took a long draft of her cigarette, enough for several more seconds of smoke rings.

"Oh, Mary Ellen, didn't you get together with that Paul fellow you told us about?"

"Paul Welch. Nertz. Forget him. I thought he was so smooth and continental. He turned out to be just another jerk." Mary Ellen took another long puff and continued her harangue. "But I sometimes get to parties in the city where the action is faster. The trouble is every guy you meet in the city either wants to roll you back on your presumed round heels, and with a minimum of interference from words—a simple yes is all the conversation they can handle—or else they present you with some kink that makes you sick. Like this one guy I met in a bar on Fire Island. He looked like a football player. You know, big and muscular. Very male. He drew me out of the crowd for what I thought was a friendly chat. He worked up a sweat trying to be charming.

"Finally he made his pitch. It all led up to the request that I *do it* with his boy friend! I tell you I was baffled. His boy friend was this tiny, squinchy guy with a huge head and a scrawny, almost humpbacked body, who scuttled around the bar frantically while never taking his eyes off me during this exchange of words with his buddy. He seemed to be anxiously, breathlessly awaiting my reaction.

"In the time-honored tradition of Priscilla Alden, I said, 'Speak for yourself, John.' And that big lout blissfully replied, 'Oh, I just want to watch.' Can you believe it, kids? He just *wanted to watch!*"

Suddenly Montrose jumped up. "I'm so sorry, girls," she said. "I am going to have to excuse myself. I almost forgot, I promised to go to Sodality Meeting this morning." Without another word, Montrose bustled out of the room.

They sat silent about a moment before Sally loudly remarked, "What the hell is a Sodality Meeting?"

"It's just some Catholic Church thing," Mary Ellen explained.

"I see the mother superior hasn't changed much," Sally announced. "What a stick! For Christ's sake, Joss, you have to get out of here. She'll suffocate you. You need to get a place of your own."

Undaunted, Mary Ellen prattled right on. "And the funny part of all this is I just felt sorry for the two of them. I mean can you imagine what a drag it must be to go around explaining such a thing over and over? Thank God we had no such garbage in the days of Chooky Linkus."

Sally turned and smiled at Mary Ellen. "Chooky

Linkus? Did you know him?" she said. "He was Danny's best friend in college. Danny talked about him all the time."

Mary Ellen's face turned very red, and in the moment Joss realized that, for Mary Ellen at least, there was some unfathomable importance to the memory of Chooky Linkus.

Montrose sidled quietly into Joss's room. This was unusual behavior, requiring some attention. Her room was Joss's sanctuary. Here one might expect to find Joss either sitting at her desk, staring at the typewriter, or crumpled up on her bed trying to concoct a string of words that would mean something deep and worthwhile. Montrose had always respected that.

Joss looked up. She was not displeased; rather she was puzzled by the visit. Even more baffled when Montrose said, "I've come to make a confession."

Joss responded glibly. "Sorry. Wrong church."

"Joss, I lied. There was no Sodality Meeting," Montrose whispered.

"What?"

"There was no Sodality Meeting. I just couldn't stand staying in that room a minute more with the old Harmon House gang gabbing about their amorous adventures. Not for a minute longer, Joss. I just had to concoct a reason to get away. So I lied."

"You could have done worse," laughed Joss. "You could have conjured up a fake attack of bronchitis and coughed us all off to the hospital.

"But why? Didn't you care for our old gang?"

"I didn't dislike them. I just can't stand the way they talk now. Things have changed. I could tell they were going to start spilling their love stories, unleashing intimate details. Just like Nevada did about her gloppy, disgusting,

wet wedding night. Because from all that I was bless-
edly removed, they excluded me like a pariah at Harmon
House. I was not like them, nor am I now. I'm sure my
leaving the room left no void in the conversation."

"You're right about that," Joss said. "Mary Ellen kept
right on talking. She has become much more bawdy since
college. And much more verbal about it, too."

"I don't care. It has nothing to do with me. That's exactly what I mean. What I felt awful about at school was
how they made me feel. In the world of dating, I was like
a giant lemon," Montrose said.

"Montrose, you are so beautiful. I'm sure you were
sought after."

"Oh, yes. I went out a few times in the beginning. But
the boys I met were so desperate. They couldn't hide it. It
superseded good manners and everything. I could sense
their cruel anxiety to fulfill on my person some destiny
that I could not begin to understand. It wasn't civilized. I
felt unarmed while under attack, and if I pretended participation, as I knew some other girls did, I felt embarrassed
as if I had assumed a disguise. Then if I shirked from their
insistence, I was mocked. I was called the ice queen. It
spread to the girls. They called me the mother superior,
or the BVM, unaware of the blasphemy of that.

"Joss, do you remember a conversation you and I once
had about love? You stressed your belief that since one had
to 'fall' to be in love. You didn't want to fall."

"Oh, I was such a baby then," Joss replied. "I do remember that though."

"But you did fall," Montrose continued. "And it was awful. You were transformed. Not for the better."

"Yes," Joss agreed. "I was like a crazy person. I guess when I fell I must have cracked my skull a little bit."

"That boy was really typical of the lot of them. Did you actually love him?"

"I don't know. I thought so, but in retrospect I think not. But I still loved *you*, Montrose."

"And I you. But that's a different kind of love. It doesn't require any kind of falling."

"Amicable love. Didn't you feel that kind of amicable love for our roommates?"

"I did for a long time, especially in the early days. But Mary Ellen could not stop bemoaning how she failed at finding the other kind of love—passionate love. It was difficult to have a conversation with her about anything else. And Jeannie ... Oh, Jeannie was such a troubled girl. It was hard to understand her. She seemed to be deteriorating with the times. Descending. Going along with the deteriorating preferences of the era. Manners. Language. Music. Everything sinking."

Deciding to turn the subject another way, Joss asked, "What about handsome Harry Hannigan?"

"Harry was as downgraded as I was. He was my rescuer. He understood. He was always kind and considerate.

He made no demands. He was pleased to be my escort and friend. Harry was wonderful. I think I should go to him now."

"Do you love him?"

"As I love you. He was truly my friend, Joss. And now he's sick, and I cannot help him. That's what I came in to tell you. I think I need to go out to California to see if I can give some comfort to my very dear friend Harry Hannigan."

"Then go, Montrose. Go. You make and change your mind too often. Go to Harry. Don't vacillate."

Mary Ellen, toting a sheaf of newspaper ads, came over the following Saturday. She was all het up to help get Joss an apartment. "Where's Montrose?" she asked. "Should she know that we're doing this?"

"Why not?" Joss replied. "If I find an apartment, she would certainly have to be told about it. Wouldn't she? Anyhow, she's planning to go away herself. She's talking about getting back with Harry in California. Right now she's out, gone with Frank to buy groceries."

"What? With Frank?"

"Sure. She and Frank are old friends. He's available. Still hung up on me. And he's like a flea. He keeps hopping over here to see me.

"But he always makes me lose precious writing time. So Montrose helps by rustling him out on some errand. Buying groceries is a wonderful way to do it, because

Frank understands that. He likes to eat, so he knows enough to buy real food. He's better at it than Montrose. She eats like a horse, but she has crazy appetites. If left to her own devices, Montrose would have nothing in the house but some cartons of ice cream and some little cans of oysters. She'll buy hors d'oeuvres. At least Frank knows enough to load in some cans of beans. I hope."

Mary Ellen had brought an armload of newspapers rescued from the trash bin nearest her subway stop. That was to be the last resort of her searching method.

"We go to newsstands and candy stores first," she declared. "Every neighborhood has candy stores. They're only dinky places. People go in to buy smokes, chewing gum, newspapers, and little things.

"You can get phone calls there, if you time it just right. There's a constant stream of people going in and out. They buy newspapers and discuss the news, both world and local.

"They talk. They know things in there. Sometimes people even post ads, but that is nothing compared to what they know. So we ask. We go into candy stores and just ask around."

"There are no candy stores in this neighborhood," Joss said.

Mary Ellen let loose a sneering laugh. "Do you *want* to live in *this* neighbor?" she asked. "This is for people like Montrose and members of her Benefactors' Club. Are your finances up to it?"

"Truly, I don't know what they're up to, Mary Ellen. I'm getting these strange amounts from the 'actions,' whatever they are. They are getting larger each time, and they seem to be coming in more and more often.

"As things stand now, I can certainly afford a modest rental. But I don't where the money actually comes from or when it will stop. My daddy is very devious that way. He always has been."

"Your daddy's a real brick, kiddo. You should be half the man he is. Live dangerously! Come on. Let's go look for candy stores."

"I'm ready," Joss agreed.

"You're coming like that? You could do better. Pull yourself together. Put on a little makeup, kid. Try to look like someone you'd like to rent to. For Pete's sake, Joss. Stick your hair down. You look like a scraggy-headed little hobo."

Joss was abashed though she recognized the remark as justified. She'd been holed up with her writing for far too long. She spent long hours in trancelike conditions. Sometimes she wrote things down. Later she could not remember writing anything. She worried about her mind.

She applied a little makeup, hoping to subdue her freckles. They would be horribly evident on such a sunny day. She even painted on doe eyes, which she seldom used. Then she plopped on a little blue pot-hat that she had affected of late. It completely covered her blonde squiggles.

"Do I pass?" she asked. Mary Ellen winked and nodded. Both were in a pleasantly happy mood. They knew each other so well. They sailed out to search in tandem, armed with laughter and high hopes.

The neighborhood was residential. They had far to travel before reaching the kind of street that might present news vendors of any kind. They walked until they reached a busier street.

In Mary Ellen's company, out on the street, Joss felt elated. The feeling was mutual. Rather than walk, they were skipping and hopping. Occasionally they held hands. They were dressed as they had in college, styled by the fashions of midcentury America. Both wore plaid skirts to the fashionable point over the knee, cardigans matched with sweaters in muted shades of blue (Joss) and green (Mary Ellen). Both girls wore well-shined loafers with no pennies. They looked so young, and they felt it.

Joss had worked too hard for too many days. She had underestimated the amount of time it took to produce a novel. So she had come up short. It needed more before she dared present something tangible to back up the promises she had made to John Otto and, presumably, to the G&M publishing company.

Recently, she had worked far into the nights. Often she was not sure whether she was producing sense or gibberish. When she awoke in the mornings, she'd often find a confusion of illegible words on her pad.

Frank sympathized. In kindness and generosity, he gave her a large bottle of cognac. "It's magic writing juice," he explained. And it worked. Sometimes it worked. It released something. "Use with caution," she told herself. Made sense. It was just for an impetus.

Of late, she had begun availing herself of Frank's remedy. It helped. In the morning, she sorted the sense from the nonsense. A little sense was left for her to wrap around her aching head.

Now, flouncing down a morning street with Mary Ellen Rigg, Joss felt liberated. They passed a small park where children were playing. Mary Ellen began singing in a high, silly voice. Passersby heard her. Some smiled. They had almost forgotten the purpose of their mission when they came upon a news store. There were few customers. The proprietor greeted them pleasantly. He knew of no apartments available locally, but he did have a board up for ads. The ads seemed discreetly to offer ladies giving personal services. "What do you suppose the personal services are?" wondered Mary Ellen.

"Oh, I don't know. They could write up your little ads to post in candy stores. Or maybe they could teach you to tat," Joss replied. "Or tit," she laughed, "which goes with tat."

Both began giggling. In young girls, giggling, once begun, becomes contagious and epidemical, almost impossible to extinguish. They each had bought sticks of gum and continued walking, chomping away and being extravagantly silly. Joss joined heartily in the nonsense. She didn't get much silliness living with Montrose, and she missed it. But sweater sets are really too much for a sunny autumn day. After visiting a multitude of shops, they were tired. The shops frequently had notice boards with notices very similar to the first one they'd seen. Shopkeepers did not like them lingering overlong. Many recommended that they consult the classified section of the papers.

"Jeez Louise," Mary Ellen huffed. "I'm hot and so hungry." They were in front of a small café. Alexander's Nosh said the sign. "Have you got any money?"

Joss dug into the pocket of her skirt and jingled something. She came up with change. Mary Ellen threw a few coins into the mix. "Maybe we can get something in here for that much," she said.

The money bought them a packet of cheese crackers and two bottles of Coke. "Leave the rest for a tip," Joss suggested lavishly. They settled into a small table and spread out the few newspaper pages that Mary Ellen had carried along in her tote bag. Under the blue hat, Joss's scruffy blonde head almost conked Mary Ellen's smooth, auburn coiffure as they leaned in to study the housing ads.

"Something's funny," Joss suddenly whispered. The shop was ominously quiet. They were the only customers. Both had noticed the extreme handsomeness of the counter man when they entered. "I hate coffee shops. Look, that guy's staring at us," Joss remarked. She wheeled around to meet his stare. He averted his eyes at once.

"Beautiful blue eyes," commented Mary Ellen. "But they're shifty. Why don't you talk to him, kiddo?" Mary Ellen suggested.

Joss turned toward the man and gave him her most fetching smile. "Do you mind if we do our little research project here?" she said.

The good-looking man grunted something neutral— neither yes nor no.

"Were looking for an apartment. Do you know of anything in this area?" Joss asked. The cute guy shook his head and continued to look away. He busied himself with the cash register.

The girls persisted in their study for a while. The lowest monthly rental rates they could find in the paper were in the thirty-five to forty-dollar range. Discouraged, Joss wasn't sure if she could handle that much on a long-term basis. "That's just crazy, kiddo. The irony of it is that in Bay Head, the town I stayed in this summer, since it's off-season now, you could probably rent a whole big mansion for half of the rents shown here."

They couldn't help but notice the distant behavior of that shop clerk. They were both girls and young, used to more of a visual response from men, but this guy continued to fuss with his register. He kept dinging something up, but it did not look real. Deliberate ding-ding-ding. Maybe he was fixing it. After a few minutes, a really tall person sauntered in, a very striking-looking older man. He sighted Joss and Mary Ellen and immediately looked away for the clerk. Then he went up to him. The arriving man leaned in toward the cashier, and they exchanged some whispered words before the tall one made a graceful turn and exited. He had given Joss and Mary Ellen hardly a glance.

They studied the newspaper a while longer, becoming ever more discouraged about their quest.

Then they just settled back, smoked, and chewed their gum until it got tasteless in their mouths. While they chomped pensively, they saw that a parade of men, most of them remarkably well dressed, most of them good-looking, came in to indulge in the same obsequy with the counter man—in quick, whisper, turn, ding-ding-ding from the register, and be gone. That dinging of the cash register added to the mystery because the girls could see no money had been exchanged.

By this time, Joss and Mary Ellen were silently cutting strange faces at one another. They rolled their eyes. They raised their eyebrows. Mary Ellen let fly a sequence of tense smoke rings.

"Something's funny," Mary Ellen murmured. They were silent now, smoking as silently and intently as if their whole purpose in coming in had been to smoke. As they finished their cigs, several more men came in to exchange whispered words with the bar guy.

Mary Ellen arose and gathered up her newspapers. She headed toward the door, and Joss followed. Both marched toward the larger street. As they rounded the corner, they fell into each other's arms. Mary Ellen began laughing hysterically. "They were all so good-looking. But what the hell was going on?" Joss demanded.

"Didn't you get it, kiddo? We just wandered into a gay bar!"

"What? They have their own places now?"

"They have their own everything!" said Mary Ellen.

"What a waste of manpower!" Joss exclaimed sadly.

Quite by accident, it was Frank who solved Joss's apartment problem. He didn't mean to; later he told Montrose he regretted it. As long as Joss stayed at Montrose's, Frank knew he'd get a welcome there. But if Montrose was out and Joss was writing, no one even answered the door. In her own place, Joss would probably turn into a recluse, he predicted.

During a visit to Montrose, Frank began complaining about his "boys." His boys were actually two smart young men who were employed in Frank's laboratory. They were both special fellows, probably geniuses as they partook of Frank's scientific obsessions. Frank liked them a lot. He talked about them so much that Joss felt she knew them personally. They were Henry Reed and Domenic Montagna. Joss wondered if drinking with Frank was part of their job, though Frank never bragged about any binges with them. Frank loved his binges, but he loved his work more. Chances were he wouldn't risk drinking with the employees in his precious lab.

When Hank and Domenic were happy, Frank was happy. Today Domenic was not happy, and Frank was sad about it. "I can't always be solving this kind of problem for the guys," Frank moaned.

"What kind of problem?" Montrose wondered.

"Dom," he replied. "He's in love."

"That's nice. Why is it a problem?" asked Joss.

"Sharon, his girl, is Jewish. Dom's an Italian Catholic, and Sharon's family refuses to accept him."

"That is serious," Montrose agreed.

"Not necessarily," Frank said. "Sharon has her own place. I told him he should skip the ceremonies. He should just move right in with the girl. Her family would come to terms with it any way they can. Or not."

"Oh, Frank!" Montrose cried. "They can't *do* that. They would be living in sin."

"Who cares about that?" Frank said.

"I do. People do. It's terrible." Montrose's face reflected her disapproval. She was quite thoroughly shocked.

"Well, more and more people are doing it," Frank said casually.

"I know, and the more's the shame on them. Nobody seems to care about propriety anymore. And that's reprehensible. It ignores the whole concept of family. Frank, I'm surprised at you."

"Domenic doesn't want a family," said Frank. "Sharon is trying to be a model. I'm sure she doesn't want to be bothered with kids or pregnancies."

Before Montrose had a chance to express more disapproval, Joss cried out, "Frank! Wait a minute. Does Domenic have an apartment?"

Domenic did, and after suffering more of the romantic tale, Domenic and Sharon made the scandalous decision to merge without benefit of clergy. Then after the lovers had made all the necessary decisions and came to terms with any deviations from their old conventions, Joss claimed Domenic's little place on Hardesty Street.

It was a sweet little place on a street that was almost impossible to find. The two rooms were on the top floor of a very decrepit building that looked ready to be condemned yet sat square shouldered in dilapidated pride. Joss liked it. It was a palace compared to Mary Ellen's rat hole. There were two small but respectable rooms. It had kitchen facilities against the wall of one of the rooms, where the piping went through for the small bathroom on the other side. In short, it would do very well. Domenic left fast. He must have been in a blooming hurry to start sinning with Sharon. Joss was grateful.

The guy didn't leave things a mess. His few sticks of furniture would stand her in good stead. She had only a futon that Montrose gave her from her own stored goods. Joss felt that things were moving along well for her now.

Frank, Mary Ellen, and even Montrose had been making too many demands on her. She didn't think moving into her new little apartment on Hardesty Street would discourage them enough. Her determination to finish the novel was strong, but, unfortunately, she had not given enough consideration to the weather, and it was changing. Beguiled by the clement November weather, Joss had foolishly taken two weeks' rental on a small house by the ocean. Almost overnight after she took up residence in the little place on the shore, docile November was transmuting itself into a fierce December.

She had made a foolish mistake.

At Bay Head Junction, there were howling winds in the morning—the sky, the sea, both boiling with rage. Joss appreciated the mood of the day. It matched her anger at her own wordlessness. Her "sonorous words filled with all of time's vastness" were failing her. Where had they gone? Rushed to copulate and to beget litters of bastards and cheats. Damn. Damn. Damn. Words did not matter except to define the truth. She knew that.

Joss was out of sorts. She hated what she was doing. She was suffering from a severe writer's block. Worse. A constipation of words, she called it.

Usually walking helped, so she walked the entire town, street by street, parallel blocks to the sea, working landward. She walked for more than three hours in that blast. Sometimes the wind shoved at her so wickedly that she had to shelter against the walls of unoccupied houses. The town, essentially a summer town, was empty, but the houses were still friendly; they offered her walls to hug for a windbreak. Then she'd push against the bulwark for the impetus to surge back into her passage through the hostile air.

In the early afternoon swirls of snow, patches only, flurries but frenetic ones sizzled around her head. Where they landed they fizzled out. Nothing much happening at the shoreline. In fact, the turbulence seemed to abate as the snow started. Inland, though, it could become a killer. A real blizzard.

She kept walking, arguing with her own thoughts. She walked against the wind. Gusts made occasional attacks. She was pushed and buffeted. The Atlantic was in a towering frenzy. It gnashed at what was left of the beach. Ragged slats of an old fence held each other's hands in panic as they were pulled into the ocean's maw. Not a living thing to be seen except for Joss.

Where do they go? she wondered. *Where do the sea birds go?*

By about four o'clock, she reached the little railroad station. It was shut tight. The caretaker at the junction had not even bothered to come by and switch on the one lightbulb. Perhaps the current was off. Well, of course, with the storm, these tinker-toy trains down the summer route would be the first things to stop. Perhaps they'd be halted for the whole weekend. Too bad. She had thought she might go back to the city for the weekend, but this storm killed every chance of that. Beside, words were now beginning to collect in her head. Ideas and names.

She thought of Schwartz by name, a character she had created. His name had been misty to her before. Now he sprang up. It was Barthold.

Bart Schwartz was a problem. She had to try to make herself like him. Emily Cappo did. Emily even believed she loved him. So Joss tried to see him in a more agreeable light.

He was a tall man. Dark of complexion. Very strong. He had to have charms to seduce the dopey heroine. Schwartz must exude a sort of power, sexual attraction. All the clerks and secretaries at the company adored and spoiled him. They made him even more full of himself. He reminded Joss of no one. She only knew she really didn't like him.

Deep in her thoughts, Joss eventually reached the little summer cottage that she had rented for this off-season. The request for a winter rental surprised the owner. Pleased, he kept the price low, just in the range of the possible for her meager budget. Anyway, she had heard from Joe, her father. He had found her and reappropriated the mysterious actions. With this dangerous deprivation came the promise to have his office send her a regular allowance until she "found herself." She was pleased.

Enough anyhow to keep this summer shack, pieced together of clapboard as it was. It was unheated, but Joss had brought an electric heating grate. There was a fireplace that, even when burning full force, gave little heat and much danger of conflagration. The worst inconvenience of the place was the lack of sufficient hot water for bathing. It had no stove. Joss could heat just enough water for washing up on the electric grate she had brought in. That was a real hardship, but she intended to stay there and finish her book. Though the place was old and ramshackle, it would have to do.

She had brought along a supply of soup cans and crackers. They held her away from famine. Joss didn't eat very much anyway.

By dint of time and caprice, the original synopsis had changed. Early in her writing she had scrapped the idea of incest.

"Emlyn Olivier has shrunk. The new guy now takes up importance. They call him Schwartz. Schwartz is German for black. That's enough name as far the office gals are concerned. He is tall, has black hair that he combs back into a ducktail. In his way, he's dynamic. Emily is stupid enough to love him. She's a grown-up woman of twenty-three. He's twenty-nine."

Joss mulled over the work. She didn't even know if she had been awarded the fellowship, even less had she been made aware of any stipend. They played with her at G&S.

Keeping her on a string until they saw if they liked the novel or not. Right now she was being sustained by an allowance from her mystifying father. No. Why should she conform to a synopsis that wasn't right for her? She would write from her spirit. She would write what she liked.

All of a sudden, new stream of narrative occurred to her.

Schwartz, a student of Brooklyn history, knows something that has escaped the women. He wants to get near Emily in order to get near the house itself. So does Emlyn. The women are only an excuse. The men want the house.

Joss raced to the table. An idea had occurred to her. It brought on an onslaught like a mental tidal wave. She could hardly keep a rein on her thoughts. She began shredding pages. At the same time scrawling notes on an open notebook. "House of Women" was printed large right on the cover of the notebook.

House. House. House. Was the story about Emily Cappo or was it about a house?

And now words began branching into ever more complex tributaries of a different book that was fighting hard to surface. Her cramped hand gripped a pencil, and immediately words began to pour out over the little tendon that connected her thumb and forefingers to the pencil. Words were filling the loose page. She was speedwriting on a downhill course.

It was about the house. Emlyn had originally come

seeking permission to photograph the structure of the house. What was he looking for? He photographed the corners of the floors and of the ceiling. He must be looking for a discrepancy.

Schwartz, a student of history, also knew something more. The women were proud of their story. It was known to all that in the past some unscrupulous, murderous thieves had inhabited the old house. But there was more.

Joss remembered a strange fact of historical lore that she had once read in a book of oddities. In the early 1800s, people did not know what to do with their insane or dangerously ill family members. There were no facilities. The afflicted continued to live, sometimes for years, contributing nothing. They depleted family resources as they disrupted life in the home. There was no good solution to the problem. The family had to keep them. Throwing them out onto the streets was a solution that would disrupt the neighborhood and was, quite possibly, against local laws. According to the oddity book, a devious solution that some came to was simply to wall them up. Yes, just close them up into a small closet-like space that must remain inviolable. If the family was less than cruel, they might have a panel in the wall where food could be passed through. That could only delay matters. Encapsulated in a cell of his own stink, the madman would soon die. So a few old houses had spaces *behind the walls*. The House of Women was such a house.

Both Emlyn and Schwartz had knowledge of the people who had owned the house before the Cappos, a group of crooks that knapped stolen gold. Both were after the gold that was said to remain on the premises.

Perhaps half an hour passed writing this new twist to her story. She wrote franticly. Writer's block dissolved, going at a great pace, when the latch flew up. The door banged open. And there he stood.

Frank.

Joss just stared at him.

Snow clung to his eyebrows.

She was annoyed. But Frank was so ridiculously proud of himself that it was impossible to ignore the fact of his arrival. It was an unnecessary feat of heroic proportions.

"Did you drink your way down here?" she asked.

"Cold sober," he said. "Maybe just a little to prevent frostbite," he then added. He told her that he had gotten as far as Elizabeth on the previous evening. There everything had stopped. The storm was serious. Parts of New Jersey were to get eighteen inches. To the north, New England was already paralyzed. The snow had started around Elizabeth on Thursday evening. It continued all day Friday. Frank had slept in the train station until early morning. Then, before dawn, he had walked and hitchhiked to the Garden State where he continued walking and hitching. There was nothing to hitch on except for snowplows and a rare, slow delivery truck. So that was what he mooched on to, happily making friends with Parkway crews and garrulous truck drivers along the way. Somehow he managed to make it all the way, carrying his precious sacks with cartons of cigarettes, two lovely bottles of hooch, and not so especially needed cans of exotic foods.

He grinned from ear to ear, so pleased with himself. Expanding. He just knew he had rescued her, saved her from a dire fate of some kind. She had to listen to his tale. She could not let herself be so cruel as to ignore him. But she sat there like a lump, with her chin resting on her knuckles, partly listening but mostly waiting for him to finish as her eyes kept straying to the work started and waiting quietly on the table.

Then, smug and humming, he busied himself. He muscled around. He stoked the fire, worked on the door latch, cooked up something foul and spooky from one of those ghastly cans. What did he bring this time? Two bottles of strong spirits. A can of cream of cucumber soup. Fried grasshoppers. Frank had quixotic tastes. At least she was released to write. But there was no way she could work up the same fever of inspiration. At the edge of her consciousness burrowed the little thread of guilt Frank always brought her.

He was narrating a picture into her mind: Frank suffering. An expedition of about nineteen hours duration, sustained by the thought of her. Herself—Joss. Mentally calling her name. Oh, it was just too sticky. During the same nineteen hours, she had thought of him only once, during her pause at the train station when she had stopped to be glad that he would not be able to make it to the shore.

Fortunately he was exhausted. He conked out early. Joss worked on the manuscript until three, and then, forgetting he was there, she crawled onto the futon. He opened his long arms, and she slipped right in. He pulled her over himself like a blanket. He moaned, and his body jerked. He moved to spoon her. She pushed him brusquely away.

Frank moaned and moved to stroke her scraggy hair.

"Quit it," she barked.

"I love you, Joss."

"Go fly a kite," she croaked.

"For God's sake, Joss," he muttered. "I'd get more affection if I went to a prostitute."

"You're probably right, Frank. Why don't you try that thing? See what you can pick up out there in the snow."

It was bad enough that he kept trying to make her an elaborate present of something she did not want. She was certainly not about to start putting on dramatic performances in lieu of the truth.

Nevertheless, she found herself stroking the stubble on his cheek. It felt comforting to know someone was there. Anyone. Her sex life was like that now, like a soporific, inducing sleep.

Frank had passed out.

Joss slept.

The flesh is dead serious even when we aren't.
Life forces are absolutely in earnest, impelling
one toward various dooms. Stasis would be safe
enough were it not that lack of participation
might push one into one of the various evasions
more horrible than life itself.

From the Codex by J. Nye

In the morning, she heard Frank stumble around. He was humming some tune. He seemed inordinately merry. He left to go back to the city. Perhaps he'd find another commuter or a truck.

Joss slept on.

She didn't awaken until past ten. She stared out the window sullenly, smoking nervously. What would last night's episode cost her? Frank always read a whole lot into things. It was still blustery out but not in such a determined way as yesterday. Little wind spouts carried charges of the dry snow. Her thoughts aimed painfully into the previous night's abyss.

Last night Joss had to force Emily into being attracted to Schwartz. She didn't have to urge him at all. He was always ready. And that was all wrong. Schwartz was a sneak. He lied so easily. He was bound to be a cheater someday. He just understood money. That's what he talked about. He understood money in all its ramifications. And there came the revelation of the day. Schwartz was something like Bobby, so writing the sex part came easily. She needed to describe Bobby's chest, the muscles of his thighs as she began to finger his penis, first very softy, then harder to direct his entry into the void, that hungry nether gullet. Her heart beat in synch with his.

Now she rustled through all the papers on the table. It was the denouement of her novel that she had needed to work on. She had to get rid of the two men, Emlyn and Schwartz. Even though it was trash, the writing had excited her. She worked it out by replicating it.

The farce with Frank Graham ... How did that happen? She wanted to deny all responsibility even though she knew she would have to pay for her error.

She had pretended to forget her episode in Cranston, but this stupid blooper she could not. Cranston had tucked itself into the back of her mind from whence it clearly could leap into recognition at any moment. She told herself that she had nothing to do with it. She'd known nothing about how it had started. Arrangements had been made outside her intentions. Now she understood only too painfully Kitty's "moment of inattention."

Cranston was the cover-up, originating with Bobby Ocks. Not her fault. Except in dreams, she allowed herself to think that whole drama had happened to someone else.

Montrose once told her that she cried in her sleep.

"Not me. I never cry," Joss averred. She thought she never cried, but when she did dream, she often awoke to find the pillow wet with tears.

Now she had made a blunder. This time with Frank. This one was on her too, on her very own, on her list of transgressions. She had initiated it all. She had wakened him by almost plumping down on him and the narrow mattress. He thought the obvious, that an act of intimacy had ensued. Joss could not shirk the blame of it.

Stupid! Stupid! Stupid!

These were still the days when girls believed that casual sex was a moral error. Nasty sex could only be forgiven by love. Sex, Joss thought, was the most intimate of acts, to her mind immoral without the benefit of sentiment. Frank probably thought the same thing. He'd been so happy that morning at the cabin. The dope went whistling a birdcall. He was so happy she wanted to kick him in the pants. He was practically singing when he left. God only knew what he thought. Maybe he thought they were engaged. He had long hoped for just that. Joss would have to overcome the irrational idea, would have to convince him of the reality of the situation without hurting his delicate feelings.

After so many washless days, Joss needed to soak. She also needed to pick up on the tapestry of her life. It had been cast aside ever since she went to Bay Head to finish the novel.

In order to pick up the threads where she had left them, she went first to Montrose's apartment. There she intended to wallow like a buffalo. She lolled in the hot water for a long time. She soaked until her fingertips were pruning up. She let herself luxuriate in the perfumed waters while in her mind movie music played. She imagined she was the Lady of the Lake.

Her body tried to float. The feeling was delicious. She began to mull over recent events. It was so nice to do nothing and feel the comfort of hot water. The tub was an enormous thing. If she stretched full length to admire the twinkle of her occasionally surfacing toes, she thought she might drown. The tub was like something out of *Gulliver's Travels*, king-sized, of course. It was Montrose Arbejean's tub.

Everything in the apartment was too big—chairs too big, cupboards too high, rooms too deep. It was sort of written into the script that the whole place would be elevated and out of Joss's reach. Montrose spouted loving old-fashioned endearments like, "Joss, my dear, I hope you will stay on. Just let that little apartment go. Think about it. You have more than everything you need right here. I set apart this room with views of the park for you, but if you need something else, I'm sure we can supply it." As always, Montrose's voice, smooth and musical yet imperative in the way it had always been in their long history of days, crooned. A mood change swept the air. Joss was displeased. She felt that offensive giantism surrounded her. "Stay here, Joss," Montrose moaned. "I don't want you to go."

Joss sat up straight, making a tide in the perfumed waters. "I have to go to Hardesty Street tomorrow, Montrose. I'm getting a phone installed. What the heck do you care, anyway? You're going to California, aren't you?"

"Maybe. I'm not sure. I haven't got the ticket yet. Harry doesn't answer my questions."

"There are times when you turn up to be the most indecisive person I know. You vacillate. You did that with your majors in college. Never could decide. Is this more of that same thing?" said Joss.

As if never interrupted, Montrose continued speaking. "This building is old," she said. "It has space and views of even more space. I believe it once was owned by dreadful rich people who could afford to pay for whole parks to compensate for their commercial pollution of the air. They needed to mooch on the souls of the parks. Now it belongs to itself, but it still breathes money. In huge gulps. Don't worry, kiddo. I still have those annuities. They'll cover it all."

"Montrose, you're nuts." Joss came dripping out of

the monstrous tub. Montrose stood ready to engulf her in a towel as big as the Bronx. It trailed on the floor. She tripped over to sit on the edge of the tub. "I could suffocate and die in here," she remarked. "No one would find me wrapped in this ten-foot shroud." As Joss spoke, she was incubating her discomfort about things. Maybe it was more than the towel engulfing her that strangled her thought. She knew she still loved Montrose. Montrose still led the way in her sure and classy way, but Joss felt different now. She did not want to be led. Clearly she didn't fit the plan. She was very troubled about the conversation she'd had with Montrose just moments before.

Of course they'd had catching up to do after Joss's three-week writing binge. "Are you glad to be back?"

"Back in civilization? Wow, yes! But they were valuable days. I finished the blooming book," Joss assured her.

"Great! And I'm so happy to have you here. And I'm not the only one. You might be surprised at how many people have been looking for you."

"Looking for little old me? Who?" As she spoke, Joss was engaged in the old and often-attempted exercise of reading Montrose's face.

"Frank has made a real pest of himself. Hanging around here wondering when you would return."

"What a drag!" Joss muttered. "He was down every weekend. He knew exactly what I was doing."

"Joss, I would like you to stay. Please stay."

"Uh-uh. Now I'm really eager to get to my new abode. I'm having a phone installed tomorrow."

In the long history of their friendship, Joss had early learned how to study Montrose's beautiful face, and she was studying it intently now. Montrose's face was tense, an indication of trouble. "And Ocks, that Bobby person. He came."

"Bobby was here? What the heck did he want?" Joss said.

"You," Montrose declared. Then she thought a minute and added, "I think he just wanted you to see him in his soldier suit."

Joss stiffened. Even the mention of Bobby's name was anathema to her. Negative thoughts flooded her mind, mixed with the thoughts of what she had recently been writing. Upon request by Otto, she had written a scarlet story. She had recently, in vivid terms, disinterred it to describe a sexual encounter between Emily Cappo, her protagonist, and a very agile Barthold Schwartz. It was unlike anything Joss had ever written before. Pulling up her insides to relive her relationship with Bobby Ocks. Using memory as writing material, Joss had made a very specific, very graphic description of a hot sexual encounter between Cappo and Schwartz. She was proud of this chapter while at the same time shamed by it. She blamed the writing of it for her subsequent skirmish with Frank Graham.

Written in Joss's elaborate style of writing, the same style that her old classmates had liked to call "baroque," the material sounded even dirtier. Joss thought her careful words sounded awful, almost pornographic. She made the mistake of showing Montrose this passage.

Montrose read a little and then exploded. "This is disgusting!" she exclaimed. And, rudely, she threw the manuscript down on the floor. "How can you write such foul garbage, Joss?"

Joss stood conflicted. She hadn't liked writing it, but her characters were human beings after all. She had to write something about their erotic lives. Sexual expression was something as innate for human characters as it was for birds, bees, and turnips. "You know those two characters are going to die, don't you?" she half-whispered.

Montrose nodded.

"Well, I just thought I'd let them have one colossal fuck before I bumped them off!" Joss shouted into Montrose's face, which was now contorted in disgust.

"Oh, shut up. You sanctimonious, old fogey!" Joss shouted at Montrose, but Montrose had already stalked righteously out of the room.

On Tuesday morning, two linesmen came from the Bell Telephone Company. Joss was so happy to get the telephone installed. She even flirted a little with the men as she fussed and made them take special care with the ringer. It came to her mind that Montrose's squealing phone had interrupted many a peaceful Sunday morning. The men cheerfully gave her a nice ring tone. This was all so wonderful to her, her own apartment and her own telephone. Her very own dulcet ringer. At last she felt like a real person. An adult to be reckoned with. No more little egg.

The apartment was sunny. It was on the top floor, and a big section of glass ceiling allowed in a stream of golden sunshine. Joss was pleased, happier than she had been for a long time. She fondled the new phone. It was a shining black miracle of modern technology. She dialed Alan Resnick's residence. Before she got him, she spoke with a series of grad students. The silliness that had affected her with the telephone men prevailed.

"Hiya, handsome," she said as she greeted some unknown scholar. "I have a brand-new telephone," she told the answering scholar. "How come I'm having such trouble getting Alan Resnick?" she finally asked.

"Oh, he's just a grind," came the answer. "You can't pry that guy out of his books. Try again in about half hour. He usually stops in here to sharpen his pencils before lunch. Miss, you sound pretty. Let me leave him your number. If he has any sense, he will call you back as soon as he sees the note."

She was so pleased to have a number to give. She was so full of herself that she even assumed the boy she'd just spoken to would call her.

Now she busied herself around her new digs. Not much to do. Still very sparse but just furnished enough. And Domenic had either been a very neat tenant or had spent little time in the apartment. Every thing was copacetic. She had brought in a mop and broom when she first came up to the apartment, but she made no attempt to mop anything now.

Finally the phone rang. She let it go ten rings just to enjoy the sound of it . It was Alan back from lunch. "I'm done," he said. "I've taken all the orals, and I've handed in my dissertation. Now all I need do is wait for confirmation of my work. I'll be a doctor by the weekend."

"Doctor! That's great. Alan.

"I took the book in to G&M. I actually showed it to the elusive Mr. Moran. He was a total grizzly bear."

"What about Otto, your so-called agent?" Alan asked.

"Gone," said Joss. She had always suspected that Resnick was jealous of John Otto. "He followed his wife down to the southland. He doesn't work for G&M anymore.

"My book's in limbo, Alan. Moran didn't like it. He said I had obvious talent, but the book's too literary.

That's what he *said*, Alan. 'Too literary.' He certainly did not read a word of what I wrote. I asked what too literary meant. He said, 'Style. It's all style and no bang. Not for the list at Goldschneider & Moran. We don't do that kind of thing,' he said. He told me I should look for a publisher—I assume he meant I should look *elsewhere* for a publisher."

"And then I guess he wished you good luck and said good-bye," Alan added.

"Exactly," Joss responded.

"I know, I used to work for that firm," Alan said. "That's how they do it—give the axe with just a few softening words."

Then Alan interrupted himself to say, "Joss, aren't you going to say anything more about my triumph? Aren't you even going to congratulate me? I've been working on this project for a year."

Joss took a deep breath. She felt censured. Of course he deserved some complimenting for his success. "Certainly, Dr. Resnick. That's the reason I called," she fibbed. "In fact, I was planning a big celebratory bash for you in my new apartment on Hardesty Street.

"Please say you can come. Eight o'clock, Friday night—Seventeen Hardesty Street. Top floor."

"I suppose you're terribly busy right now," he said. His diction was perfect. His mouth held a discipline that she assumed was the result of some alcohol. The effort not to slur words made a more audible comment on his condition than actual slurring would. His pronunciation was so tense, words pressed out through painfully controlled lips. Such total care gave it all away. He was in some state of inebriation. She knew the signs. He was high and probably aiming to get higher. It was just four thirty in the afternoon.

"I have time to talk to you for a while, if that's what you mean," she said with a patience so thick he could probably hear it, if he could hear anything, that is. "A little time, just a little. I have dinner guests coming at seven."

"Oh, that's okay! It's not important. I'm home, anyway. It's okay, Joss. I'm in the apartment. Nothing important. Sorry to trouble. Sorry." And then he hung up so abruptly it almost echoed. At least it echoed in her ear, hurt like the ghost of a box on the ear. She fought back her irritation. Frank usually had good manners. Joss thought she had felt a touch of hostility there She attributed his rudeness to drink.

Twenty minutes later—Mary Ellen had arrived by then—Frank telephoned again. "Joss, did you say you were busy tonight?"

"I have dinner guests tonight, Frank."

"Oh, gosh! That's right. You told me that before, didn't you? I'm sorry."

"Would you like to come over?"

"Who? Me? Oh, no. No. I wouldn't think of it. No. Hey, I'm okay. I'm just home in the apartment. Not going anywhere. Just a quiet evening at home." He chuckled unevenly.

"Come on over," Joss insisted. "You know everyone. It's just Mary Ellen Rigg and Steve Robbins, her current boyfriend. Sally Petrucci and Danny Flax. You remember Danny? Oh, and Mr. Resnick."

"Who?"

"Alan Resnick, my old writing teacher. You know Alan. He played with you in *Carousel*. They're almost all people you know, Frank."

"Montrose?"

"She's in California with handsome Hal."

"Bobby Ochs?"

She winced. Her jaw tightened. Was he trying to be spiteful or was he simply soused into insensitivity? "No, Frank," she said quietly. "Bobby Ochs is not in town. He's gone to make his fortune on the West Coast. Don't you remember?"

"Bobby Ochs—not there?"

"Gone," she sighed impatiently. "Gone, gone, gone."

"Stoo bad," he said. All the discipline was slipping. His

speech began to swirl like liquid stirred in two directions at once. "I wanted to tell him something."

"Well, too late now."

"Huh?"

Fate should dole her out more forbearance with drunks, but Joss's patience was dwindling. "Frank, you know where I live. Why don't you just grab a cab and come here to Hardesty Street? Mary Ellen is cooking. She's a gourmet cook. I know you'd like that."

"Uh-uh. Better not. Better stay in tonight. I'm home. I'm in the apartment. Jus' home. Cozy. On Seventy-Second Street, isn't it? In case you need me." Again that ragged, unconvincing laugh. "Not going anywhere. I think."

Disturbed, Joss returned to the kitchen. Mary Ellen had come over early to teach her some new culinary wizardry with strips of meat. She trussed it up, juices running pink, shaped like little game birds and dimpled, wrapped it in leaves and aromas—laurel and marjoram, or rosemary, thyme. The room was sweet with wonderful smells. The counterfeit squabs could never taste as fine as their palates did right now, caressed by delicious aromas.

"Mary Ellen, it's like paradise in here. Just like heaven must smell. But are you sure you know what you're doing?"

"Hand me a bay leaf. Just hush up and trust me, kiddo."

"I guess I have to. What's a bay leaf?"

Mary Ellen giggled.

"I hope this doesn't turn out to be just another atmosphere party," said Joss.

"What a memory you have, Joss. Must be kind of a curse."

"I think you're right," Joss agreed while sniffing concoctions. Mary Ellen was in complete charge, doing the dinner. She was better at it than anyone. Joss was so bad at it, and Mary Ellen was born to the silver ladle. Her little ratty apartment did not offer the right atmosphere, so she often came to Joss's place to practice her cookery.

"I need to find myself an apartment soon," said Mary Ellen.

"If you're ready, I'll go with you. We had such fun last time," Joss remarked.

Mary Ellen said, "Who was on the phone?"

"Frank."

"Sorry. I don't mean to pry," said Mary Ellen, "but I thought it might be Steve calling in his regrets. Things are about at that point with us. Not too wildly excited about sitting at the same table with me."

"That's too bad, Mary Ellen. I really thought this guy was the one. I only invited him to please you."

"Easy come, easy go, kiddo. Don't worry. Doesn't matter whatever the feelings. Hell's bells, you can never be sure what the feelings are anyway. But I am here to tell you—whatever they are, they're mutual as far as I'm concerned. I mean I've made up my mind to put my life—everything, every time—into balance. If the man is crazy about me, I'll just put everything I have into being crazy about him. But if he cools—well damn it to hell, Joss, I'll cool too. I will. No matter how I felt ten minutes before. I'll cool if it kills me. I'll be damned if I am going to keep on investing and investing in someone who doesn't want me. If you do that too much, you get bankrupt. You turn into a beggar."

"I certainly enjoy your financial comparisons, but it sounds to me as if your new doctrine will just be 'playing the game' all over again. You have to be a consummate actress. If I take your meaning, I guess you have a very wise but completely untenable philosophy going there," Joss remarked.

Mary Ellen shrugged. "What about Frank?" she asked.

"Not mutual. Continual overinvestment. Marginal bankruptcy. Some begging."

Mary Ellen looked up sharply and blinked. She looked embarrassed. "I just meant—is he coming to dinner tonight?"

"Unfortunately, I didn't think to invite him until just now. And I don't suppose he's coming. Not so much because he's offended, though he may be that, but because he sounded like he's already three sheets to the wind. I think he's simply too smashed to move."

"But at five o'clock in the afternoon?"

"Afraid so. It's just the dawning of his drinking day."

"Jeez! Getting to be a problem?"

"Long ago. Past tense. But tonight ... I don't know. Something's peculiar. Fishy. I don't like it. He's gotten under my skin. Something is *off*, Mary Ellen." They both lit cigarettes and puffed. Mary Ellen threw some major smoke rings at the ceiling. "He called me a few minutes before you walked in. Told me over and over again that he was home tonight. He kept saying that, like a broken record. I don't like it," Joss repeated. She wrinkled her nose.

"Delphic Oracle say: Dionysus still trickiest god of all."

"Watch it, Mary Ellen." Joss laughed. "In a minute you'll be putting Confucius into the Parthenon again."

They laughed. Everyone came. Steve came and paid flattering attention to Mary Ellen's cooking of the ersatz squab. Otto brought just the right wine. When Alan Resnick appeared, they all cheered him. He had just completed his work for the PhD.

"What's next, Alan?" Mary Ellen asked.

"I'm going back to the university. My old job will still be available—only better. As a doctor of letters, I'll have more power in the English Department now. I'm really looking forward to the university scene, backbiting as it may be.

"Now you girls should get back into it. Not much you can do with a bachelor's degree. Just come back to school to get your master's, and I can guarantee you jobs correcting papers."

"Nuh-uh," Mary Ellen responded.

"Tell us about the book, Joss," Sally requested.

"Well, nobody wants it. My so-called agent has skipped off to the south to sing about his rights. So far no one wants the book." Joss then decided to tell them about the last-minute idea she had had concerning hidden chambers in old houses where the infected or maniacal had been detained. "Pockets in space," she called them, but as she described it, she saw Mary Ellen getting more and more excited. She was almost jumping out of her skin when she shouted out, "Yikes! That's Harmon House!"

"I don't think so," Joss said.

"Yes! There must have been a pocket like that, and Jeannie knew about it."

"That's impossible," Joss insisted.

"Well, the house was old enough. And the Harmons were known to have been a particularly mean family. Don't you remember, Jeannie was always going around measuring things? I bet that's where Jeannie hid that terrible night."

"We can never go back to see," Joss interrupted. "Harmon House was scheduled to be demolished the week after we graduated."

It was a pleasant evening. Frank called twice more to assure her that he was home. Everyone left, and, finally, Frank quit calling.

Drunken imposition that the phoning had been,

silence was even worse. It was ominous. It crashed down upon her head, a leaden yoke of senseless guilt.

Well, there, he had done it again. He always knew exactly how to get to her. Repeatedly he won these petty, unarticulated victories. They made a current that passed only between the two of them because everyone else thought that she was clearly the victor. She looked to be a winner. She looked as if she was in possession of the moment, owned the situation, owned herself—certainly appeared to be in charge of Frank. No one could ever see how, in the silence that crashed in upon her when all the guests were gone, she lost over and over again.

Of course she knew about the drinking. He'd been soaking it up for quite some time now. Years ago, he had indulged openly and more sporadically. He bragged about "getting swozzled." Then it descended, slipped deep inside him where he could be quiet about nurturing it. Private, nevertheless, it was just another secret that he slipped to her. Stealthily, confusing innocence and guile, he contaminated her with his weakness so that she could be totally alone to reproach herself when all her guests left. As the last trailing of the last voice sank down the stairwell, she could feel in back of her eyes the source, the lode from which he mined the motivation for his collapse, herself.

He didn't answer his damn phone. She listened to it ring. Her imagination followed the vibration through dull spaces, searching through his apartment just as the ringing phone probed for him and received no answer. But he was there. She sensed him. Perhaps he was propped up in the shadow of a corner, still as stone as he listened, extravagantly ignoring the summons of the telephone but smiling ever so slightly because he knew he had won. He had won one of those petty, negative victories that meant so much to him. Or perhaps he was out, passed out of all responsibility while the phone's vibrations made meaningless eddies in the tides of oblivion in which he floated. Her breath came short, betraying her anger. It was another measure of his power that she worried.

She had an appointment for hair dressing in the morning. She'd found the one woman in the city who could dress her ornery hair. Then she'd ordered photographs, new portraits for publicity for the *House of Women* in case the manuscript ever got picked up. She should sleep now. Sleep, deep and dreamless, was indicated so that she might look crisp and intelligent for the camera's scrutiny tomorrow, but he had cleverly forestalled that, inflicting her with stupid worries. She pictured him lying motionless, a wedge clipped out of his forehead by a corner of the marble coffee table. She so hated that slab of white table. It reminded her of something dreadful. In the silence that had so subtly insinuated itself into the space that her guests had recently vacated, she shivered.

Her teeth grated. As her anger mounted, so did her conviction that he was wounded. The monotonously ringing phone, an extension of herself, was not adequate to rouse him. At last, she hung up.

She puffed, then coughed. Gasped, hyperventilating on her cigarette. She felt herself sicken with her own exaggerated response. She pulverized the cigarette in the big brass ashtray with which Bobby Ochs had once threatened to brain her. She shrugged. She turned on the radio. Some cretinous females, pretending to be high school sophomores, were singing "Mr. Sandman" with studied syncopation. She followed a few strophes, taping her foot mindlessly. Then she heard her own voice declare, "Well, something's got to be done. He's a friend of mind, after all. The fool." And, enclosing herself in her floppy coat, bat-winged while gray as a dove, she slammed out into the night, astonished both at the concessions she was making and at the rising fury she felt accompanying them as she flung herself into a taxi that seemed almost to be waiting for her on the corner of West Fourth.

The lights. Everything was blazing. She noticed that from the street, and she did not like it one bit. The lights were indiscreetly screaming an impolite message out of all the windows of his apartment. He was obviously out of control and sloppy, without volition, spilling things, leaking out his secrets, this time to the night, which seemed to pay no attention at all.

When she opened the door with his gift to her, a rarely used key of base metal on a circlet of purest eighteen-karat gold from Cartier's, the silence lashed her like a whip. His flat, though dull to the eye, was sumptuously equipped to overindulge the ear. All the doors were actually giant speakers. Now all those mouths gaped dumbly. No sound emerged. Just silence. That super amplifier that had the capacity to animate circuses of performing noises was lighted. But no record played. He was musical, and he was a genius of sound; even so, nothing woofed or squealed or fluctuated from supersonic yelp to groveling growls. Silence. The light alone screamed.

There was a half-filled glass of whiskey on the low table. Amber fluid accumulated, puddled around the base of the glass where it stood on that repellant slab of white marble. His taste. Coffee table of mortuary solemnity. She had never liked it.

There was a faint smell like the odor of overheated electrical wiring. Every goddamn possible light in the place burning.

Maybe he had stepped out.

Maybe he went downstairs for cigarettes, a newspaper. Something. Maybe he needed to walk, clear the clots of whiskey from his brain, air the circuits of his mind, or simply cruise the night streets. No.

No.

He was there. He was there all right. She knew he'd gone nowhere. Her eyes swept the room suspiciously. She knew he'd gone nowhere. Nowhere at all.

Slowly, but rapidly too, she searched while her breath accelerated. Quick, sharp little breaths gulped. A bellows. Anger. Angrily she searched while with care—slow and hurry in paradox—she found him in the bathroom. So banal. She forced herself to the obvious understandings while gasping, muttering after the fact. "Don't you dare, Frank. Don't you dare do this to me." Her own voice was a revelation to her. It sounded alien and so rational. It said, "Don't you dare," so dispassionately. So unemotional. She held herself apart for a moment to admire her voice.

But the room. The funny bathroom. It elongated before her cool eyes. The room elongated itself into a shape. A tunnel. A long vista of catastrophe, continuing even though she could not quite believe it, thought it an idiot's catastrophe. The room felt like a platform on the old Third Avenue El but white and suspended in some nebulous eternity. Yes. Now. This minute, as if eternal. She felt her breath beating like the wings of a trapped bird because she was so furious.

At the far end of that long platform that, though white, was as eternal as the moment, he lay trashed by his own doing. Junked. Like an old gum wrapper. The crumpled innards, guts of finished packages. A peeling, discarded by himself. Her breath caught. She gagged. Her gulping style of breath flailed at her lungs as she fixed him with her stare and saw him stare back out of his own deep pit. Conscious. He was really there in spite of lunacy. His eyes flickered cruelly within the blankness of his face, which was dead white while shaded blue with incipient beard. He held his ground. He glared back at her. On the floor, near his outflung hand lay a little razor smudged with blood. With ever mounting fury, she observed the ultimate indignity. On the tiles he'd scrawled a red hook. She saw the letter J.

Once again.

Once again he'd succeeded in failing.

Like an eagle, she soared into Schermerhorn's. Stark in contrast to the pretty teapots and the sea of pleasant matrons sipping their afternoon beverages out of little porcelain cups. She looked over the ladies with an eagle's penetrating eye, not to be fooled, unmoved by pleasantries. And she was right, of course. This was serious. Though full of goofy blunders, this was not even remotely a joke.

At the moment, that woman's child was lying abed in a very exclusive clinic room, which temporarily sheltered his confusion. Sober, dazed, he was beginning to see the ramifications of his failure. He had that prospect to study as he lay there. Everything was out in the open now. Another aspect of the situation was now revealing itself to Joss, increasing her discomfort. In addition, there was this feeling of respiratory distress lately.

Since Friday night, Joss had felt she was unable to catch her breath. She was so overwhelmed by Frank's performance. The situation had only been guessed at previously. Now everything was laid open to public discussion. Rude. As impolite as a death notice. Frank had been like a corpse awaiting autopsy. And Joss was in his story. She knew, little Joss, as innocent as an egg, was part of his raison d'être. She was part of this mess. How or why, she did not really comprehend. Neither summoned nor welcomed, it was something that had just happened to her. All privacy snatched off. Stolen away like an irreplaceable artifact of only sentimental value. Your pride, Mister. Your integrity now as insignificant as some great grandma's thimble.

Shaken by it, and shaken again by the present moment, Joss realized she was frightened, frightened by Frank's action and frightened again by this day's obligation, represented by a giant woman wheeling through the genteel tea room at Schermerhorn's. Such a contrast to the nice ladies in their little hats, nibbling dainty cakes. She soared over all, this giant woman, angling her great joints, which should connect to wings and fledge out white pinfeathers sharpening into absolute black, ending in a hard, steel shade of gray, like her hair. Joss knew who it had to be but found she could say nothing, not even raise her hand in greeting. The predatory eyes, liquid black and as precise as a metal BBs, spiraled their focus inward, a device of entrapment until centering upon a tidbit, a frightened and gasping little mammal.

"Miss Nye? Jocelyn?"

"Mrs. Graham?"

"I am Margaret Graham," the woman agreed as she tried to settle into the quaint iron chair across from Joss. This struggle to work her long body into the unlikely space reminded Joss of something funny from long ago. The tearoom chairs were works of the ironmonger's art; they were of tortured metal, wrought into intricate curlicues and pretzel knots, far too small for the likes of Mrs. Graham.

"We two should have met years ago. Heaven knows I've been hearing about you for years," the woman said while still making battle with the ridiculous chair. It could be comical. Her knees jutted up awkwardly under her black greatcoat.

Joss tried to look intelligent, or at least rational, even though she felt herself helpless, somewhat mesmerized. Mrs. Graham extended long fingers. They were cold but quick, making short work of a handclasp. "I do feel I know you rather well, however. In addition to hearing so much about you, I've read your work."

"That's flattering," Joss replied weakly, realizing it had not been a flattering remark at all. She was reluctant to ask Mrs. Graham if she had enjoyed it. After all, the section she read might have been that trashy one that Frank had photocopied, the "love" scene from *House of Women*. That was the only one he had. He liked the sexy aspect of that piece. As usual, she was embarrassed to be ashamed. Her prudery was a relic of Harman House. She cringed that she might be judged on that piece of sexual raving.

"Very clever, too," said Margaret Graham. "Somewhat too wordy for my taste. Still, it represents a remarkable achievement for such a young woman. I believe I heard that you have a new novel about to be published."

Joss shook her head, not in response but to agitate her own brains. It was hard to believe that they were sitting in Schermerhorn's having this conversation. "Publication is not assured, but there is a new novel," Joss replied. "It's untitled as yet. Tentatively, I think of the title *Wherever the Sun Goes.*

"You know, the sun goes everywhere," Joss added.

"It's primarily a codex. I wanted to get it to a representative or a publisher by the end of the month. That is, I wanted it to be ready to take advantage of possible Christmas sales." She smiled wanly, apologetically, and without feeling. Gray. Like iron. Like the woman sitting across from her.

"I see. Of course. Every business has its exigencies, as I well know." She smiled, but it was only a response to Joss's anemic smile, a vacant one. "Do you know the flight took exactly five hundred minutes?" The woman spoke on. She said, "Five hundred minutes, exactly as advertised. Five hundred minutes. Add to that the hour and a half it took to get from my office to the airport at St. Louis. And the almost two hours to get into town through incredible traffic from LaGuardia Field. That makes almost eight hours just in travel time—the better part of a workday gone on so-called speedy travel. Gone, of course. Lost. Lost time that cannot possibly benefit anyone."

Mrs. Graham snapped open a silver case. It was shaped like a large bullet. She offered Joss something that looked like a pencil-thin cigar. In the reflecting lid, Joss saw an image as of a rapacious avian giant. "I suppose I can anticipate a similar time loss on tomorrow's return voyage. It is beyond question the most unfortunate moment, as you said. Just before the Christmas season. I am now getting the new subsidiary shop launched. It is the worst possible moment for me to be away. But, of course, that's part of it," she complained. Her long fingers curled around a slender cigarillo.

She seemed to cast a spell. Joss felt locked into reality, an impossible blocked position. "You are opening a shop?" Joss asked. Her voice was tinny. She was not in the least bit interested in the answer, and she thought her voice gave that away.

Mrs. Graham bared her teeth, a sort of smile. "Would you be more comfortable if I were to talk about Frank?" she asked abruptly.

Joss puffed audibly. "Have you seen him?"

"Not yet," said Mrs. Graham with an unwavering look at Joss, as if meeting any possible reproach with the crux of her dead-centering eyes. "I came here first. When you telephoned, I thought it best to see you, meet you first, Jocelyn. I thought you might enlighten me about the situation."

"Well, he is all right. Physically, that is. He is quite unharmed, Mrs. Graham. But the serious—"

"Please. I'd like you to call me Margaret."

Joss felt her face tingle. The idea of calling this woman by her Christian name was offensive to her. "Oh, yes. If you like," she said, even while she rejected the very thought of it. "Anyway, he fumbled it so completely—scared himself. I think that he didn't even do enough damage to leave a permanent scar. But the serious part, of course, is the psychological—that is, that he underwent such a destructive mental phase that he entertained the idea of ..."

"Are you describing his inebriation as a mental phase?"

"Excuse me?" Joss said.

"This whole clumsy farce of his was undertaken in an extreme of alcoholic indulgence, was it not?" Mr. Graham said rather matter-of-factly as she lit her little cigar.

"Yes," Joss admitted reluctantly. Why did she need to feel like a little girl trying to help her little boy friend cover up his naughtiness from his mother? She was beginning to feel more than a little bit frightened. The conversation seemed not only unreal but also inimical. Nor did proximity to Frank's mother help put the woman into proportion. Rather, she seemed to be growing larger by the minute.

"It is incomprehensible to me. Though I personally have never opposed drinking; alcohol has always been repugnant to me. And my husband, as is well known in our part of the country, has openly fought its availability as both a social and political obligation. But Frank has always gone to great lengths to find forms of personal expression that would not only run counter to our convictions but would embarrass us as well.

"Oh, I know. I know," she raved on and waved her skinny little cigar in dismissal of some words that Joss had not spoken. "It's our failure in some way. It is said to be our failure, though I personally find the logic of that to be somewhat absurd. It's what he does to himself in a most deliberate fashion and which, very obviously, is also destructive to himself—

"That it is *our* fault is disproportionate in view of the facts. I'm sorry, Jocelyn, I am not about to sit here and make excuses for myself. Frank is not only a grown man, but he is a remarkably intelligent one. Don't you doubt that. He is a veritable genius in his field. Copyrights he registered on his sonic refinements in '46, long before he had even gone to the university, would in themselves be enough to ensure him a substantial income for many years. With the patents on just those two gadgets, he has already out-earned both his father, with an illustrious thirty-year career in jurisprudence, and my own considerable enterprise in merchandising. He is a success on his own merits. But in addition to those very same merits, all his own, he has become a very poor excuse for a human being. His prevailing social motivation is spite. Just that. Spite, I am sorry to say. I have told him this on more than one occasion, almost as tragic-comic as the present one.

"Yet, he loves me dearly. He adores me without bounds. You needn't take my word for it. Ask him. I know with every confidence he'll verify my words. But you don't need to ask him, do you, Jocelyn? He loves you too, and immeasurably. Is that not the case? So, perhaps, you are beginning to get an inkling of just what that means. This little performance of the other night was a love present. Retribution. That's his style of love. He can't love any other way. He can't assume it. He thinks himself to be unworthy of love." She laughed now, mirthlessly but completely in control. "Watch him. He'll be wanting to possess your soul, take away from you whatever power he thinks you have in your own right. And his attempts to do this will become progressively more ludicrous. He doesn't really want to own you. After all, what would he do with you? He only wants to keep wanting. You are a focus for his self-disgust. He will—"

"Frank tried to kill himself on Friday night!" Joss exploded. "It's very serious though you—"

"If it's very serious, how come he's alive? Alive and unmarked?" Mrs. Graham demanded. "If you think it is so serious, why do you need to keep on saying so?" She glared at Joss, held her fast with those sharp eyes, then relaxed her glare and let Joss escape. "No, my dear. He did exactly what he tried to do. But all this is beside the point, Jocelyn. Or, perhaps I am trying to excuse myself after all." She sighed. "An unnecessary luxury. Can't do a bit of good anymore. What I need to know before I see him is which one of us is he blaming, you or me?"

"Mrs. Graham ..."

"Margaret."

"Oh," Joss moaned. It was so terrible, a terrible trap. Her face was hot. "I don't know. I don't know that he's blaming anyone."

"Well, I think you do know. Of course you must. If you intend to remain a friend of his, young woman, you had better remain scrupulously honest with yourself. Don't try to make evasions do the work of truth as Frank does, or he will certainly succeed in destroying you. It's Frank's way, and we are his beloved ones, just the ill-matched two of us sitting here at this ridiculous little table."

Schermerhorn's, the elegant meeting place for elegant matrons, expanded. It swelled beyond the little round table until it met its confines in a wall of leaves, huge variegated leaves of the giant dieffenbachias for which the place was famous.

"I think you hate him," Joss said quietly.

"I don't. But I think I've made you hate me, and for that I am truly sorry, Jocelyn. We two should have been friends. I think we needed to be. We could have weathered Frank's love better. It is a wretched trick of fate that you shall walk away from this meeting hating me, because all I've done is tell you the truth."

Frank tried to get married once. He tried, but he put his losing touch on it, his touch of the farcical. He had been entertaining a dry season for a while, managing to hold off the wall of crisis, putting one foot in front of the other and walking upright on his hind legs, doing a reasonable imitation of a man. Then there was silence. He seemed to have dropped out of the world entirely.

At first it made little difference to Joss. Then an uneasy feeling, something that transformed guilt into worry, crept up to nag her. She called his office. As usual, he was the absentee genius.

After long trying, she finally connected with his apartment only to hear a woman's voice, which threw her for a loop. It surprised her so much that she was brusque, almost rude. "Where's Frank?" she demanded. She realized at once that she had been imperious. The woman put him on.

He sounded silly. She thought she could see an embarrassed grin on his face, a rictus, utterly insincere smile. "Oh, Joss," he said. "What an amazing coincidence. I was just talking about you. I was telling my fiancée about your book."

"Your *fiancée*?"

"Yes. Would you believe she has never read a single word of your writing?" his voice steadied, gaining control. Joss could hear the woman in the background cry out an objection, but he continued. "As a matter of fact, Joss, she never even heard of *you.*" He laughed. It rang real. The rat might even be deriving some perverse pleasure from this.

"Very few have," she said. And then she added, "Are you quite sober, Frank?"

"Quite. Absolutely. Certainly. For months. For years. Forever. It is one great big beautiful world, Joss, you know that? And it is going to stay a beautiful world; at least for me it is, because I have finally found the right person to share it with. Someone to give meaning to everything ..." He was overdoing now, poor boy, going overboard, gushing.

"Frank, that's wonderful!" Joss exclaimed. "I am so happy for you. Best news I've heard in ages. When did all this happen?"

"What?"

"Well ... when did you get engaged?"

"Oh. It isn't formal or anything yet. No ring yet. It wasn't like a party or announced or anything like that. We sort of have been hanging around together. You know, a movie now and then. A late cup of coffee. Listening to records. Then, just this afternoon, I sort of thought, wouldn't it be nice if this could go on—indefinitely, you know. So I asked her. And she said yes."

"Who?"

"Pardon?"

"Frank, what's her name? You haven't told me her name."

"Oh, gosh, yeah. Of course. Excuse me. It's Dorris. Dorris Asgard. I'm sorry, I just ..."

"You're going to let me meet her, aren't you, Frank?"

"Meet her? Well ..."

"You aren't going to shelve me, are you, Frank?" Joss said jovially. "You can if you want to, of course. But I'd hate for you to put away a friendship as old as ours is. I hope you are going to give me a chance for all three of us to be friends."

"Sure. Of course, Joss. She says she wants to meet you too."

"When?"

"Now. She just now said it."

"No, Frank. I mean when can we meet?"

"Whenever you like. I mean, when would be convenient?"

"Right now."

"Right now, Oh, yoicks. No. I mean, no. I tell you what, Joss. Are you free tomorrow? Tomorrow evening, I mean?"

"You bet."

"Okay, then. We'll pick you up at seven. Is that okay? I'm going to take you girls to a fantastic new restaurant. It's called the Ultimate Artichoke. Have you been there?"

"Can't say that I have. It sounds awful."

"Never mind. You're going to love it. I hear it's fantastic."

But it turned out to be Ignatz' Place done over in newer plastics. Vegetable shades, illuminated by a glow that did not flicker. She was astonished to find herself there again. "Don't you remember this, Frank? Not so long ago, this used to be Ignatz' Place. Poor old Ig. I heard he died of stomach cancer."

"Oh, no, Joss. Ignatz' Place was on Macdougall Street."

"No, Frank. Right here. Don't you remember the long, skinny room with a jog in it like an exhaust pipe?"

"Oh, yeah! Yes! You're right, Joss. Well, I'll be! Ignatz' Place! We used to come here all the time when Joss first came to town."

Dorris smiled. She had a pretty, round, valentine face. Sweet. A little plump. Joss liked the look of her. She was likeable, pleasant. She didn't intrude. A little on the country side. Her sweater and tweed skirt would have gone better in the old Ignatz though. The Artichoke was too new, too bright with artifice. Joss was wearing a wonderful white coat that fell like a capital A. And her white plastic boots glistened as they conformed to the exact dimensions of her calves. Joss fit here or in Carnaby Street. Effortlessly.

"But it was different then, Dorris. There was fake dirt, fake cobwebs all over the place. Remember that time chunks of junk kept falling on our table, Joss?"

Joss smiled. "And Ignatz yelled out, 'Don't eat it, dollings! Don't eat! Dirt you can eat. Dirt's healthy, but spun glass can kill you.'"

Frank laughed. "He was a real character, that Ignatz. I wonder what ever happened to him."

"I just told you."

"Oh, yeah."

They had a nice table. Nothing at all wobbled. The menu was written in parvenu restaurantese—a sort of debauched French. Joss knew the language reasonably well. Every pushy eatery in town used it.

"What are we going to eat, Joss?"

"Gratinee. Supremes de volaille artichaud, haricots vert au maitre. Mousse later. How does that sound?"

"Beautiful," Frank said. "Okay, Dorris?"

"Okay," Dorris said. She smiled.

"Vin rouge?" Frank asked Joss.

"Never! Vin blanc," Joss declared, but then she reconsidered. "Wait a minute, Frank. Is wine a good idea?"

"Oh, hell, Joss. I've got to live in the world, you know. This is a celebration. Besides, you don't need to worry. The past is dead. Finished. I'm a happy man now."

Her smile welled up. She was so glad. She really wanted him to be happy. She was fond of Frank. She hoped for him to be whole and as happy he had seemed to be when first she knew him, long ago.

"What work do you do, Dorris?"

"I've only been in town a few months. I work in an office, in the stenographic pool. But I want to work up to a private secretary, if I can."

"Of course you can," Frank said heartily. He grinned and smelled the vin blanc. "Good wine, Joss. You had to bring your own to Ignatz' in the old days, Dorris. He didn't have a license, so he used to number all the bottles that the patrons brought in. Remember that, Joss? I used to have him keep a couple of cases for me. I don't think you knew that. Ignatz didn't like doing it. It was against the law. Every time I would bring wine in, he made me stand there while he numbered the bottles. He was a real stickler, all right, old Ignatz."

"Or old Ed," Joss said archly.

"Or old Bill," rejoined Frank.

They both laughed.

Dorris smiled.

They ended up at Frank's place. He wanted them to hear some recordings. "As long as it's not the mating calls of frustrated fish," Joss demanded.

"Joss can't stand my Nature Sounds collection, Dorris. But I will tell you something, Jocelyn; they just happen to be the best indicators of dimensional quality and vibrancy for my sound system. The range is enormous—particularly that deep sea one. They always help me pinpoint any malfunctions."

"Or any indigestion on the part of the fish," Joss said and yawned elaborately. "Of course, if the lucky little fish haven't just bolted a plate of haricots vert cooked in baking soda. Perfectly bilious."

"Okay. Okay. But just let me play you this short disc, Joss. One of the young engineers taped this on the Atlantic beach in November. I had to transpose it to a record at a very slow speed. This little one spins at 10 rpms." They listened a few moments to distant roars and splashes, something creaking. It could have been anything. Someone jumping up and down in a trash barrel.

Frank kept looking at Joss expectantly. "What do you think, Joss?"

"I really like music better, Frank."

"I mean ... does it remind you of something?"

"The mating cry of a lovelorn hurricane?" Joss joked.

"Come on, Joss," Frank urged. "Listen. That shack down on the Jersey coast? Halfway to nowhere?" he coaxed. "You see, Dorris, Joss was writing her first novel when she was only twenty years old. And it was a damn good book too, all about the conflict between human nature and society."

"Frank, sometimes you amaze me," she said and only half-sarcastically.

"Anyhow, I loved it," Frank insisted.

"Well, some of my friends were kind," Joss admitted with a wry grimace. "But it certainly bombed as far as Goldschneider & Moran were concerned. I made no kind of money on it. Good thing I had a rich daddy." She suddenly became animated, amused. She wanted to tell them how the critic Mr. A. Abokair, of the now defunct *Contemporary Directions* magazine, had once said of her work that it "was a pity a few respectable ideas had been subjected to such an inflation of words," thereby, in the largeness of her own mind, establishing himself as her very favorite critic forevermore. If only she knew who he was or where. But Frank wouldn't let her say anything.

"Joss rented this shanty down on the beach, Dorris. And there she sat in that freezing place writing her story. The *inside* temperature must have run an average of forty."

Dorris winced.

"All she ever had in the godforsaken place was crackers and envelopes of dry soup that she didn't actually have the sense to boil water for—"

"Now, Frank," Joss interrupted.

"Every once in a while, I had to hop a train down there just to see if she was still alive."

Joss rolled her eyes. "If it hadn't been for you, Frank, there's them what doubts I ever would have made it."

Ignoring her sarcasm, Frank was grinning broadly, sparkling, happy. He winked at he as he walked into the kitchen.

"Weren't you afraid, Joss?" Dorris asked.

"Nothing to fear except frostbite, or maybe chilblains, whatever they are. Beside I was too young ... too dumb to be afraid of anything."

"I think you were awfully brave. Really. I'd be afraid to live down near the Village like you do."

"Afraid of what?" said Joss.

"Oh, well, I hear it's very rough down there. You know, a very rough kind of neighborhood."

"We thought it was stylish. Bohemian. We still used that word for the grubby way we had to live when we first got out of college," Joss claimed.

"Well, I think you were brave to go it alone. I hate living alone."

"I was never alone in those days. My best friend was living not too far away. We could run over to each other at need. Help, support, and tender, loving care were all available at a moment's notice." Frank reentered and made a face at Joss. "Where's the coffee, Frank? I thought you were getting us coffee."

"Hmmm. Yes. I had forgotten to light the burner," he said sheepishly. "Anyway, Dorris, as I was telling you, one night there was this terrific snowstorm ..."

"Here we go again," chanted Joss.

"Really bad, you know," he continued. "I got worried that she was probably buried in a snow drift, so I started out. But I only got as far as Elizabeth, and all rail traffic was stopped on the line. I had to grab some sleep on a bench in the train station."

"Frank, I don't think Dorris wants to hear this."

"Sure she does. Wait a minute, though. I better check

the burner to make sure it's on high. I think there may be something wrong with that burner." He ducked out.

"What do you think of Frank's Natural Sounds collection?"

Dorris smiled. "Well, I prefer music, too, but I do think they are very interesting." After all, she had gone and said yes to him. She deserved credit for trying to reconcile herself to his outré tastes.

"I understand the company is preparing a new one that reproduces the sounds created naturally within the large intestine of an Indian elephant," Joss said. She meant to be amusing, but she saw right away that she had carried too far in her flippancy. Dorris just blinked.

Frank bustled in, rubbing his hands together. "Okay. Everything hunky-dory. Anyhow, girls, you never saw anything like that train station. It had facing swinging doors that never stayed shut all night. The wind just banged free. I kept waking up to pull snow out of my hair. It was flying all around as if it was falling right in there, right inside that station waiting room. Nothing for me to do but start hoofing it. The storm had sort of started dying down by then, but it was bitter cold and, I am here to tell you, dark. Darker than the heart of a witch. Even with the white snow underfoot, it was pitch dark, because it was the kind of night when snow had nothing to reflect.

"Anyway, I finally got a ride on a milk cart. One of those old-fashioned milk carts drawn by a miserable horse! But that old trap jogged along and got me down to where a bunch of snowplows were getting ready to start working their way toward the highway. The old milkman yelled out, 'Hey, you guys! This here young feller is tryin' to rescue his girl who's snowed in somewhere south of Asbury.' The drivers were all laughing at me, telling me I was crazy, but one of them took me on."

"Frank, I don't really think ..." Joss began.

"Good thing, too. When I finally got there, she was half-dead. No fire lit. She said she forgot! Hadn't eaten. Half out of her mind. All she could do was stare at me. I think she was scared to death. Okay. Okay, Joss. I know you'll never admit it. But you kept shaking. Dorris, she kept shaking even after I got the fire going. And there were cigarette butts all the hell over. Miracle she didn't burn the place down that night." Joss shot him a cautionary look. "Well, I can't help it. It's true," he declared. Then he disappeared into the kitchen again.

"Frank never forgets a story. Especially if it's long." Joss sighed. "Now, look, Dorris, we've got to do something because next he's going to dig up this interminable tale of how he found me with a ruptured appendix and too dumb to know it, so had to rush me to the hospital in a gallant race against sure peritonitis, and then afterward nursed me back to pink and radiant health again."

"Really? Did that really happen?"

"No. But just wait. He'll cook up some story. But don't say you weren't warned."

Frank came in on pretend tiptoes. "What is she telling on me, now, Dorris?" He laughed. "Joss, are you telling my girl nasty things about me?"

Joss swung around toward him with sudden insight. "Where's that coffee, Frank?" she demanded with an edged voice.

"Oh, yeah. Yes. That's what I came in here for. To ask you. What does it mean when coffee goes like this zzZZt! zzZZt! In the language of the coffee pot, what does that mean?" He laughed. "Whatta ya think of my imitation of coffee, Dorris? Pretty good, huh? Did Joss happen to tell you how good I am at imitating coffee?"

"All of a bloody sudden, Frank," Joss rasped angrily, "all of a sudden you are terribly funny."

Dorris started to smile but decided against it.

"You're never funny unless ..." Joss said.

"I always thought it was supposed to go buRRup! BuRRup!" He flapped is arms. "Like that!" He slipped back toward the kitchen again.

"I can see it from here," Joss said dully. "I'll go tend to the coffee, Frank."

"No. Don't," he said. "I'll take care of it."

"I'll go."

"Better not, Joss," he laughed. "You're liable to see

something you won't like in there." He started back into the kitchen.

"I can see it from here, Frank," Joss repeated dully. "Well, might as well bring it in here. Now that it's in the public domain anyway, you might as well share."

Dorris got up and smoothed out her skirt. "I'm going to leave now, Joss." She took her coat and started for the door.

"Don't, Dorris. Please. Stay until Frank ..."

"Oh, it won't make any difference to him," Dorris said.

"How rotten!" Joss exclaimed. "How could he slip back and be so rotten?"

Dorris's pretty, unreadable face looked straight at Joss. "I don't know. I really don't feel able to say exactly who is rotten," she said. "But I will certainly always remember meeting *you*, Miss Nye."

Joss kept staring at the door long after it had closed behind the girl.

Frank came in with the decanter and handed Joss a glass. "I'm way ahead of you," he declared with a crafty wink. He didn't seem to notice Dorris's absence. He didn't even mention her right away. For a long time, they sat and drank in parallel silences. Then he said, "What did you think of my girl?"

Joss took a long sip. "I think we both behaved abominably to her all night long. I'm ashamed. And I don't think you will ever see her again."

"I don't think she even liked me," Frank said petulantly. "She was just looking for a meal ticket."

Joss drank deep.

"I couldn't make it with her anyway," he added.

She made an irritated sound. "Oh, shut up. I don't want to hear any of that crap anyhow."

"I never could make it with anyone but you."

"Shut up. Please."

Again silence intervened and blurred the boundaries of the room. "You actually told that whole old story," she mused. "That must have been the supreme moment of your life."

"You were always special," he said dreamily.

"And you were happy then. You didn't need to fade yourself out with this poison, did you?"

"When?"

"When I was sick or captured in a place that I couldn't get away from and you could have me all to yourself. That was the only time you were ever really happy."

"Sure. Sure. For a while. Sooner or later, she would have to come and take over. She would come swinging in and say, 'This is *my* little girl, Franky. Take a powder.'" He threw some whiskey at the back of his throat. He licked his lips. "High and mighty, always high and mighty. Kiss her ass. The old bitch," he muttered.

"She didn't have to slam out that way. I wanted her to

like me. I didn't expect she'd be so ... inarticulate. I tried to be nice. It's not my fault if she hated me," Joss reflected.

"What made her think she had to protect you from *me*? I ..." Frank wondered.

"She was *illiterate*, Frank. I'm sorry," Joss interrupted. "I'm sorry but it's the truth. She was scared. She said so. Scared of silly things. All she wanted was to find somebody to ride her into security so she wouldn't need to be afraid anymore."

"She always knew just how to work it too," said Frank. "No matter what, she always made sure to make me look like a fool," Frank said loudly.

"Who?" Joss exclaimed. "Who in hell are you talking about?"

"Montrose. That bitch," Frank muttered.

Joss was silent, shocked, exposed to a truth that had never occurred to her.

A long time passed before anyone spoke. They lit cigarettes first and watched the smoke furl sensuously toward the heat of the lightbulb. Frank had collapsed completely on the futon. His head was lolling off the edge. Joss nursed her whiskey until she felt tired of the scene. Then she approached Frank's heaped body to settle his head on the cushion. She pulled him up by his dark black hair. Through painful slits, his coal-black pupils moved to behold her. "She wasn't you, Joss," he rasped.

She lifted his head. It had rolled over to the side. When

she plopped it back down on the cushion, she saw that she was standing directly above his right ear. She studied his ear for a while.

It was a beautiful thing. Like an intricate, pink porcelain cup. Black hairs had begun to invade. There were canals that must have led into still stranger channels that opened into his special sensitivities. It waited there now to collect all the vibrations swirling in the room, and right now, Joss could feel them too. Vibrations trembled dangerously around her. She stared at the convoluted cup of his ear. Frank had the most special ears in the world. And there lay one, his tender curve of being, his raison d'être, lying piteously naked n her sight.

When she heard her own voice again, it sounded as though it had been startled out of a huge glass jar somewhere on the far side of the room. "Montrose?" it sounded. "Montrose is gone."

Someone was screaming, screaming for her attention in a high emergency voice that Joss did not recognize. It seemed to be a woman's voice. Uncomfortably pitched. Not Montrose's. Someone else. Who would call her? Deep in her consciousness, she knew she was totally alone. Montrose had taken herself off somewhere else.

She was alone in this new place. It was her place. Slowly she began to sort things out. But her head seemed to echo and didn't want to help her.

Oh, Hardesty Street. This was her place on Hardesty Street. Hardesty Street was almost a secret. It did not appear on any city map. That was all right, but her head hurt. The streaming light stabbed at her eyes. A pain that of late was almost becoming familiar. She tried to piece together the previous night. It was coming back—so painfully—Frank, the girl, the lapse, both Frank's and hers, and the rest of it. She had tried to join Frank. Helping him destroy himself when all she ever really wanted do was tell him the truth.

So now someone was screaming for attention. Joss didn't think it could be that girl or Frank. It dawned on her that the dulcet tone of her telephone had gone electronic. She had to answer. In a clogged voice, she greeted, "Hello."

"You don't sound right," he said. It was Alan Resnick.

"I just woke up." She tried to open her eyes. They hurt enough, but when she opened them, things got worse. The sun rushed in cruelly. She gave a squeal of pain.

"Joss, listen. I'm in Grand Central Station. And you know what I'm thinking? I'm thinking that last time I was here, you hugged me."

For a very long moment, Joss said nothing.

"Do you remember that?" Alan asked her.

He was answered by another long moment of silence. She could hear Hardesty Street gurgling in its mysterious walls. Someone in the building must be running water through the ancient pipes. There were always things behind walls, in walls. Sometimes pockets. Cells for crazy girls.

After a considerable wait, Joss replied, "Yes, I remember, Alan. I do. And it felt so right."

"Exactly!" Alan confirmed happily. "It did. Joss, it felt so right." After another long silence, he added, "I like you too much, Joss. How can I go? I can't leave you or your stubborn pride or your crazy prose."

The conversation was stopping and starting, full of interminable waits. Finally Joss said, "Alan, meet the New York, New Haven, and Hartford train when it pulls into Providence Station tomorrow afternoon. I'll be on it.

"And I'm bringing my notes for a new novel. We're going to start all over again."

"*We* are?"

"You heard me, Resnick," she said.

From the *Codex* by Jocelyn Nye:

"Consider broad streets in the town. High fountains. Ancient domiciles enduring from more gracious times. Long rooms strung along corridors like beads; rooms so vast furniture fits as free as the remnants of other stories. Great chairs like thrones and walls of sweating stone in which you think your forebears brooded. It makes one covet massive artifacts, big tubs of soapstone, pirates' chests, wine glasses that freight your arm even while empty. Floors of majolica tiles bearing burdens that are bound to collapse the flimsy timbers of the old places.

"On an afternoon smelling of strange weather, gulls swept across a sky both incandescent and gray. It suggested snow, but it did nothing. People strolled through it. Massive buildings had belched some walkers.

"There's the mystique of exteriors to consider. Shall Martina Hughes become an advocate?

"There are smells of great importance too, signaling mortality. Cold rooms where hearts used to beat. Interiors but with implications. The corner of the room protects a cobweb. A slime of dirty gossamer. There is a paper on the table—mystique!

"Mystique!

"It may reveal the formula that transmutes life into something significant.

"Yes, It does. It is the check. Pay it and go forth, Martina thinks.

Made in the USA
Middletown, DE
18 October 2016